Arlis lay entwined in Jar nor spoke. Each felt the daughter endured at the hand of blame passed between them, just a sense of deep sorrow. Finally, Jamie spoke.

"Darlin, you're going to have to help me; help me to let go of the hate. God forgive me. I have so much hate in me, I'm choking on it. Now I know what ye felt all those years ago with Minnie. I'm so sorry, darlin. I didn't understand your pain or your hate then. But I do now, God knows, and along with all the hate I feel, I'm filled with so much pride in ye. Ye let it all go. Ye took all that hate and pain, and ye turned it into love.

"I see what letting go has done. Because ye refused to let the hate eat at ye, ye raised a fine woman in our Claire. Ye taught her right, and because of what she saw in ye, I know she'll survive this."

Arlis's heart swelled with love. Long ago, she'd chosen love over hate, life over death. Together, she and Jamie would make the same choice.

She brushed his thick black hair off his brow and looked into his eyes, catching a glimpse of his soul burning bright with love and hope. She pressed her lips to his, and in that kiss, she offered him love, forgiveness, and salvation.

The Music
of My Heart

by

Jayne M. Simon

The Music of My Heart

Contact Information: info@thewildrosepress.com

Cover Art by *Jennifer Greeff*

The Wild Rose Press, Inc.
PO Box 708
Adams Basin, NY 14410-0708
Visit us at www.thewildrosepress.com

Publishing History
First Edition, 2021
Trade Paperback ISBN 978-1-5092-3480-6
Digital ISBN 978-1-5092-3481-3

Published in the United States of America

Dedication

This book is dedicated to all the Minnies of the world.
Your stories will be told.
Your voices will be heard.

Acknowledgements

A wise man once said that you should always remember to look in the rearview mirror whenever you achieve something. There you will see the people who were responsible for your accomplishment.

I am very fortunate to look behind me and see so many family members and friends who continue to support my writing endeavors: my husband, Steve, whose love and patience go far beyond the norm; then, of course, there are my children and grandsons, the light of my life.

Where would I be without my faithful sisters and dear friend? Elaine, Kathy, and Liz—my test readers—I couldn't do it without their love and support.

Once again, I must thank my writing group members for their reviews and critiques of my work. Their talent inspires me.

Special thanks to Melanie Billings and the staff at The Wild Rose Press.

One final acknowledgement—to composer Paul Cardall. Thank you for your beautiful music, which was indeed the inspiration for *The Music of My Heart*.

Chapter One

Teaghlach, Ireland, June 1966

Claire O'Brien ran from the building, sucking in the fresh night air. Her breathing was ragged and shallow, her throat raw from screaming. She leaned against the cold brick wall and slid to the ground, sobbing. White-hot pain seared through her body. Angry bruises slowly appeared on her arms and legs. *How did this happen?* One minute she was stacking pots in the restaurant storeroom, and the next, he emerged from the kitchen and dragged her to the floor. The violence of the attack continued to terrorize her as she struggled for control.

Her tears finally subsided. She wiped her face and looked down at her torn blouse and rumpled skirt. *Sweet Jesus! What am I to do? I can't tell Mum. What will she say? What will she do? Oh God, Da can't ever know.* The fear of her father finding out surpassed the terror she just experienced. *No, no, I can't tell anyone— ever!* Claire forced herself to clear her head and figure out a plan to get into her house without being seen. *I have to clean myself up. I have to pretend nothing happened. I have to…I have to.*

She stood on shaky legs and walked back into the restaurant, locking the door behind her before heading to the loo. She vomited into the toilet as she recalled his parting words: *"Just remember, girlie. Ye tell, I tell. And my telling will be so much better than yours—I promise ye that. Think of the shame to your family. And your da being a copper."*

His evil laugh continued to echo in her mind long after he was gone. She emptied the towel roll and began to wash her face. Screams erupted from deep within her as she wadded the towel and pressed it hard against her mouth, trying to quell her hysteria. She made a feeble attempt to fix her knotted hair, but her hands continued their violent shaking. Taking a dirty apron from the laundry bin, she attempted to cover her torn blouse; a hairnet hid her tangled hair. If her mother did see her before she made it to her bedroom, she would tell her that she'd been too busy to remove the hairnet and take off the apron.

Her mother would accept the story because there was no reason not to. Claire had never lied to her mother in her whole life. Arlis wouldn't suspect her daughter was lying now. She re-entered the bathroom and took a final look in the mirror. That's when she noticed the bruises appearing on her mouth. There was nothing she could do about the shadows tonight, but she would be sure to apply some of her mother's makeup in the morning before she went down for breakfast. As she gazed at her reflection in the mirror, tears welled in her eyes. She shook her head, raised her chin, and headed out of the restaurant. It was over. No one ever need know her shame.

****

Arlis sat in her usual spot, watching the tellie. Minnie, her younger sister, sat next to her, tenderly holding a doll close to her tiny bosom. She laughed when Arlis laughed. Minnie didn't follow the television show. Just sitting next to her sister, her protector, made Minnie happy. When she was alone, Minnie would sit and stare into space, holding her ever-present doll close as she whispered its name...Brian. Minnie was there in body, but her mind—her spirit—had departed long ago.

Claire fumbled with her keys as she entered the house. She hoped her mother and Aunt Minnie would be in bed, but they sat watching her aunt's favorite TV show, waiting for Claire to come home from work. Taking a deep breath, Claire peeked her head around the corner of the doorway, careful to stay in the shadows. She knew her words were coming out in a rush, but she couldn't control her speech. "Hi, Mum. I'm home. It was a madhouse tonight, super busy, so I'm right off to bed. Love ye. Night. Love ye, Auntie."

****

Her mother frowned as she caught the unmistakable panic in her daughter's voice. "Claire? Darlin, what's wrong? Come in here for a proper good night kiss. Auntie's been waiting for ye." Arlis heard Claire shuffling in the hall and then slowly enter the parlor, her head bowed. Claire's reluctance to look up was obvious. "Darlin, what is it?" It was then she noticed the hairnet and the dirty apron. Her eyes traveled up the soiled pinafore as she spied the torn shoulder of Claire's blouse as well as the bruises on her neck. As Arlis was taking in her daughter's appearance, her husband entered the kitchen from the back door, humming as he removed his shoes and hung his jacket on the clothes hook by the door.

Claire raised her head sharply and made eye contact with her mother. Comprehension burst in

Arlis's mind, and she quickly gestured toward the front stairs. Claire's head jerked in understanding, and she ran from the room, quickly tiptoeing up the stairs and into the relative safety of her room.

Minnie was silently watching the scene unfold before her. At the sound of her brother-in-law's arrival, she drew herself into a tiny ball, hugging her doll to her chest. Jamie entered the parlor as silent tears traced their way down her cheeks.

Jamie stopped abruptly and stared at his sister-in-law, his handsome face expressing his concern. "Min, what's this? Why are ye crying, me girl? Is this any way to greet a fella when he gets home from work?" He looked questioningly at his wife. "What's going on? Sweet Jesus, is she having another spell?"

Arlis walked to her husband and gave him a light peck on the cheek. She forced a smile as she turned toward her sister. "Oh, we were just watching tellie, and something set her off. She'll be fine. Just a bit tired." She drew her sister up from the divan. "Come on, Minnie. Time for bed." Avoiding her husband's eyes, she put an arm around Minnie and guided her from the room, trying to control the panic in her voice. "I won't be but a minute, Jamie. The water's hot, so make yourself a cuppa. I'll be down as soon as I settle her." Jamie slowly shook his head as he headed back to the kitchen. "Daft women. Never know what's going to set 'em off."

Arlis guided Minnie to her room and tucked her into bed. Her heart ached for her sister as she noted the agony in her eyes. Torn between settling Minnie and taking care of her daughter, Arlis knew that Claire would understand if she tended to Minnie first.

She wasn't surprised at Minnie's reaction to Claire's disheveled appearance. Instinctively, she knew it wasn't so much Claire's appearance that upset Minnie; it was Jamie's arrival that unsettled her sister. Did she remember their father all those years ago?

Arlis sat on the edge of Minnie's bed, stroking her head to soothe her. Her sister now lay on her side, legs drawn up to her chest as she clung to her doll. Tears continued to flow from her tightly shut eyes. She kept repeating her mantra, *"Brian, Brian."* Arlis's heart tightened as she noted Minnie's hands clutching the tattered doll; hands that were gnarled and scarred from scalding water, bleach, and lye. Swollen, arthritic fingers crooked and claw-like from numerous breaks. Anyone looking at Minnie's ravaged face and disfigured hands would never believe she was only thirty-five years old. The physical suffering she endured was evident, but it was the emotional abuse—and the spiritual betrayal—that had destroyed her fragile mind.

When Minnie appeared to be sleeping, Arlis rose from the bed and tiptoed across the room. As she reached for the doorknob, she heard a small voice call her name. She turned back to the pathetic form lying curled in a ball. Minnie's eyes were open and staring somewhere far away. Into the future? Into the past?

"Arlis?" Minnie whispered. "Don't let him take her to that place. Don't let Jamie take her to them. Protect her. Promise me."

Deep sorrow—and fear—enveloped Arlis. She answered in a raspy whisper. "I promise ye, luv."

"No, Arlis, say the words."

Arlis choked back a sob as she spoke the words Minnie wanted—no, needed—to hear. "I swear to ye,

Minnie. I swear to ye before God Almighty. I'll protect her; I'll keep her safe." She closed the door behind her, Minnie's plea echoing in her mind.

She entered Claire's room and saw her daughter lying in the same position as Minnie—knees pulled up to her chest with her arms wrapped around her legs as if trying to make herself so small, she would disappear. Like Minnie, silent tears seeped from Claire's closed eyes. Arlis's stomach lurched as she saw the pile of clothing tossed on the closet floor. She noted the torn blouse and—was that blood on her skirt? *Holy Mother of God, give me strength.* She crossed the room and sat on the bed, gathering her daughter into her arms.

In the warmth and safety of her mother's embrace, Claire's muted weeping changed rapidly to uncontrolled sobbing. She felt Arlis bury her face in her hair and heard her mother's heart-rending sobs as they blended with her own. Neither spoke, each lost in their own thoughts, their own emotions.

Arlis held her daughter until the tears subsided. She raised her head and cupped Claire's chin, gently forcing the girl to make eye contact with her. Her breath caught in her throat as she noted the dark bruises on her cheeks and the purple blister-like swelling on her lower lip.

Continuing to look steadily into her daughter's swollen, bloodshot eyes, she slid her hands from the young girl's shoulders, down her arms to her hands where she stopped and clasped the girl's hands in hers. She would not prod her; she knew Claire would tell her when she was ready. As she waited for her daughter to speak, her mind traveled back twenty-one years to the day her sister's life was taken away.

Chapter Two

Teaghlach, Ireland, May 1946

The young girl knelt by the brook as she wretched what remained in her stomach. She gagged at the foul taste in her mouth, a combination of stale tobacco and whiskey. She hugged her knees to her chest and rocked back and forth, keening in agony.

The man emerged from the bushes, hitching his belt as he finished relieving himself. She shuddered as he loomed over her. "Stop that yammering, girl. It wasn't so bad now, was it? I'll say this—you're not the worst I've had. You're not the best, mind ye, but you're not the worst neither. First-timers can go either way. I'd rate ye somewhere in the middle. And don't speak of this to anyone, do ye hear me? If ye do, I'll tell them how ye flaunted those pretty little plums in my face, and I couldn't resist ye. Now, who do ye think they're going to believe? A respectable married businessman or a young tart? And what will your da say? Why the shame will kill him. And your mum, her being a respectable church lady and all? No, little girl, ye keep your mouth shut." He yanked her ponytail as a final goodbye. His ugly laugh drifted back to her as he walked toward the road.

She waited until his car's tail lights faded out of sight. Minerva O'Shea lay down in the wet grass and looked up into the now star-studded sky. The rain had stopped; the night was still. She felt so dirty, so ugly. She trusted him; she even thanked him for offering to drive her home after work so she wouldn't get caught in the storm. He didn't have to threaten her into keeping silent. She would never tell another living soul what he'd done to her. And he was right; her da would die of shame—right after he killed her.

Minerva rolled over and stood up, her knees threatening to buckle under her. With pain shooting through her body, she collapsed back to the ground. Her breathing slowed as she waited for the pain to subside. Minerva O'Shea raised her eyes to the sky again and then squeezed them shut, uttering a desperate prayer.

****

Gwen O'Shea heard the back door creak. She noted the time and shook her head, tsking her displeasure as she continued her knitting. *That girl will be the death of me.* Rather than lift her bulky frame from the comfort of her rocker, she raised her voice to her daughter. "Minnie? Where have ye been, girl? You're lucky your da isn't home yet. Ye better not have been with Mickey Doolin again. If this keeps up, I'm going to have ye speak with Father O'Toole. He'll give ye what for. Minnie? Do ye hear me, girl?" She waited for a response, but her daughter remained mute. "Minnie? Get washed up and to bed now." Gwen felt a twinge in the pit of her stomach as the silence continued. She rose from her chair and walked into the kitchen.

Minnie stood at the kitchen sink, her back to her mother. Gwen could see her daughter's rigid stance even in the dim light of the small table lamp. She felt her heart constrict as she crossed the room and took in the girl's disheveled state—her skirt and blouse were damp and wrinkled, her usually tidy ponytail was loose and hung crookedly to the right. She grasped her daughter's shoulders and slowly turned her around. "Min, what is it?"

Her daughter kept her head down, avoiding her mother's eyes. Gwen put her finger under Minnie's chin and raised her head. "Minnie, look at me. What's all this?" Her breath caught in her throat as she noted the girl's swollen lips and flushed cheeks. "Holy saints, preserve us," Gwen cried, her fear quickly turning to anger. She grabbed Minnie's thin shoulders and shook her, all tenderness gone from her touch. "What have ye been doing? No, never mind. It's obvious what you've been playing at. Get up to your room right now, before your da gets home. That Mickey Doolin is in for it, I can promise ye that."

At Gwen's accusation, Minnie came out of her trance. She sobbed as she covered her face in shame. "No, Mum. You're wrong. It weren't Mickey. It weren't."

Gwen's anger was raging. "You're just protecting him," she screamed. "Well, let me tell ye something, girl. Your da will fix his wagon, that's for sure. Holy Mother of God, you're only fifteen. What were ye thinking?"

Minnie stood before her mother, her sobs becoming deep gasps as her whole body shook. Gwen's mind raced. *What if she's pregnant? What will everyone say? Oh, the shame, the shame.* She fought for control, but anger won the battle. She couldn't help herself as she began slapping Minnie all over. The girl fell to the floor, her arms folded over her head in protection, screaming and sobbing as Gwen continued her assault. She raised her hand above her head, aiming for one final slap when she felt her arm stop in midair; Paddy O'Shea stood near his wife, his large hand wrapped around her beefy arm.

"What, in the name of all that's holy, is going on?"

****

Minnie slumped on the hard kitchen chair, her head bowed in total defeat. Her auburn hair—now loosed from its usual tie—hung on either side of her face shielding her, somewhat, from the hard stare of Father O'Toole. His small black eyes never wavered from her face. On the other hand, her parents hadn't looked at her since last night when all hell broke loose in the O'Shea household.

The priest sat alone on the company settee while Minnie's chair was positioned directly in front of him, her parents stood behind the priest—the accused before the judge and the jury.

"Minerva, your parents have told me what transpired last night. To say I am shocked is an understatement. Ye come from a good Catholic home with good Catholic parents. I dare say your older sister has always behaved in a good and decent manner. And now this? Your seeming bad behavior has brought shame to the entire family. I am a fair man, child. I don't judge ye 'til I've heard the whole story. Did Mickey Doolin force himself on ye?" The priest's words hung heavy in the air. The only sounds were the ticking mantel clock and Gwen O'Shea's stifled sobs. Minnie remained silent.

"Child, know this. Your silence is damning ye. Nothing will be gained by protecting this lad. And if it wasn't Mickey Doolin with whom ye were whorin, ye must tell me who it was. I adjure ye now to confess your sin before me, before your parents and, most importantly, before God." The black-robed clergyman reached for the book that lay beside him. Holding it in his hands, he rose and stood before the quivering young girl. "Minerva O'Shea, stand and place your hand on this Holy Bible and confess your sin."

Minnie's mind swirled with thoughts. *Whorin*? Dare she tell them the truth? Would they believe her? He said he would make sure everyone thought that she tempted him. Her da would surely die of shame. She couldn't; she wouldn't do that to him. Father O'Toole wanted her to place her hand on the Bible and tell him who it was. Should she say it was Mickey? No! Why should he get into trouble? And besides, she couldn't lie with her hand on a Bible.

She sighed and slowly raised her right hand and placed it on the sacred book, her whole body shaking in fear. She raised her head and looked steadily into the priest's ferret-like eyes. "I swear. It weren't Mickey Doolin."

Swearing softly, Paddy O'Shea shook his head as Gwen brought her damp handkerchief to her mouth, gasping in shock. The clock continued to tick as Paddy covered his face in shame, and Gwen, sobbing, collapsed in a chair. Minnie remained standing, arms hanging loosely at her sides, weeping silently.

Father O'Toole returned to the settee and glared at her. "I see that we have all misjudged ye, girl. Ye are a whore, and as a whore, ye must repent. I will immediately make arrangements for ye to enter the convent of the Guardians of the Penitents where ye will remain until you are cleansed of your sins. And may God have mercy on your soul."

Chapter Three

The phone was ringing as Arlis entered the house after her trip to the grocery. She kicked off her shoes and crossed the room. As she picked up the receiver, she heard her mother sobbing and babbling incoherently—something about Minnie and Father O'Toole and her father. "Mum, wait...wait. Stop, Mum. I can't understand what you're telling me. What did Minnie do? What did Father O'Toole call her?" She blanched as her mind started to sort through her mother's scattered rants. "I'm on my way, Mum. I'm on my way." She grabbed her purse and hurried from the house. *Ah, Minnie! What have ye done, girl? What have ye done?*

She walked to her parents' house, and as she rounded the corner, she noticed her father pacing up and down in the backyard, away from neighbors' prying eyes. His head was down; his hands clasped behind his back as he muttered to himself. She trudged up the walk to the rear of the house. "Da?"

Paddy O'Shea jerked his head up to glare at his daughter. "By Jesus, I'll kill her. I'll kill them both when I find out who it was. Do ye know who the bastard was?" He took a step toward Arlis and grabbed her arm, his face contorted with rage.

Frightened by his intensity and knowing that whiskey fueled his wrath, Arlis wrenched her arm free and took a step back. "Da, I don't know what you're talking about. I don't." She quickly skirted around him and fled into the house, leaving him to his angry mutterings.

The nightmare continued inside the house. She found her mother sitting in her favorite chair, her head buried in a pillow as muffled screams escaped in tiny spurts. Arlis was surprised to see the usually bright room darkened by drawn curtains. She crossed the room and knelt before her mother. "Mum, tell me what's happened. Where's Minnie?"

"Minnie? Minnie? The whore is locked in her bedroom. Oh, sweet Mother of God, the shame, the shame."

Arlis rose, shaking her head in futility. It was clear she wouldn't be getting any answers from her mother, so she headed for the stairs. *No wonder Da is furious; Minnie locked herself in her room?* She waited a moment outside of her sister's door, inhaling deeply to steady her breathing after climbing the stairs. Standing in the hallway, she noted the heavy silence surrounding her. She rapped softly. "Min, it's Arlis. Let me in…please?" The silence deepened. It was then that she noticed the key dangling from the door lock. *Why did they lock her in her room?* Confusion and fear niggled Arlis's thoughts as she turned the key. Twisting the doorknob, she entered the room.

As it was downstairs, the room was in shadow. Through the gloom, Arlis could barely make out the petite figure of her sister lying in her bed. She immediately called to mind a picture she'd seen recently—a fetus tucked snugly within the safety of its mother's womb—just like the child she now carried. As if her baby shared her thoughts, it stirred within her. Her nervousness heightened. She tiptoed across the room and sat on the edge of the bed. There was no acknowledgment of her presence; Minnie just lay there, staring into space. Arlis reached out and stroked her sister's thick auburn hair. Images of Minnie as a baby flashed through her mind.

When Minnie was born, Arlis immediately assumed the role of little mother to the infant, tending to her needs while her mother was coping with her father. Although there were six years between them, they were as close as two sisters could be.

"Min? Talk to me, darlin. What has Da and Mum so riled? It can't be so bad ye can't tell me."

She waited for a response, but the silence continued. Arlis's vision adjusted to the darkness of the room, and she took in her sister's appearance—eyes swollen from crying, tears staining her cheeks. Her lips looked puffy and bruised. Arlis lifted her hand and gently pulled back the neck of Minnie's blouse, revealing the shadowed bite marks marring her milky white skin. Tears choked her as she reached for her sister and gathered her in her arms.

The touch of her sister's embrace broke through Minnie's emotional hypnosis as she wrapped her arms around Arlis and wept bitterly. Arlis held her close. She wanted to whisper words of comfort, but no words came to her. So she continued to hold Minnie as she rocked to and fro, hoping that her touch, her tears, were enough to soothe her.

The minutes ticked by when, finally, Minnie slowly pulled away from her sister. She kept her head bowed as she began to speak, her voice raspy from crying. "I'm not a whore, Arlis. He raped me. I trusted him, and he raped me."

The ugly word hung in the air. Rape! Mickey Doolin raped her? Anger surged through her. *Da's right. If he doesn't kill him, I will.* Minnie's next words broke through her dark thoughts.

"It weren't Mickey, if that's what you're thinking. I haven't even seen Mickey. Da wanted me to say it were Mickey, but it weren't. Now, they all think I'm a whore. And Father O'Toole is sending me away." The words caught in her throat as she began to cry again.

Arlis struggled to control her anger. *Someone viciously attacked Minnie, and a priest was sending her away? And Da was allowing it?* She had to stop it. She put her finger under Minnie's bowed chin and lifted her head so she could look into her eyes. Fighting to keep the panic from her voice, she began to speak. "Tell me, Min. Tell me who did this to ye. Ye must tell me what happened."

****

Between her violent sobs, Minnie recounted the attack. She carefully omitted the identity of her rapist, his parting words emblazoned in her memory. *"Ye don't speak of this to anyone, do ye hear me? If ye do, I'll be sure to tell them how ye flaunted those pretty little plums in my face, and I couldn't resist ye. Now who do ye think they're going to believe? A respectable married businessman or a young tart? And what will your pa say? Why, the shame will kill him!"*

"I just got off work, and I was walking home. It started to rain. A car came by, and he offered me a ride. It was raining pretty hard, so I got in. He was real nice. We were talking when he said he had to stop at

Kilkenny Brook to pick up his fishing gear. He got out of the car, and I just waited. Then all of a sudden, he opened the car door and dragged me out by my hair. I was so scared, I couldn't even scream. After he…after it was over, he just left me there in the grass by the brook. I thought he was nice, asking me if I wanted a lift 'cause it was raining. I didn't know he was going to do that to me. I didn't want him to. I'm not a whore, Arlis. Ye have to believe me!"

Minnie collapsed against her sister, hysteria overcoming her. She could still hear his voice in her head; she could still feel the weight of his body on hers. Shuddering, she drew her knees to her chest and wrapped her arms across them, weeping violently. But none of these memories were as painful—as frightening—as the memory of Father O'Toole's declaration. *Ye are a whore, and as a whore, ye must repent. I will immediately make arrangements for ye to enter the convent of the Guardians of the Penitents where ye will remain until you're cleansed of your sins.*

****

As Arlis struggled to comprehend what her sister just told her, the bedroom door opened. Limned by hallway light, the parish priest stood in the doorway, Paddy O'Shea beside him. Father O'Toole spoke quietly, his normally strong voice sounding thin and reedy. "It's time, girl."

"Da, please. Don't do this," Arlis cried as she stepped in front of her sister, who sat curled in a ball on her bed, quietly sobbing. "Minnie was attacked. It wasn't her fault she was raped."

Father O'Toole gasped and shook his head. Raising his volume and using his sermon voice, he shook his bony finger at Arlis, his eyes bulging from their sockets. "Stop! Ye shall not profane your father's ears with that ugly word, and think of the bairn in your belly, woman, screaming it like ye are. This whore must repent of her sin."

Paddy remained standing in the doorway, his head down. His silence spoke louder than any shouting in the room.

Why isn't Da listening to me? He can't let Father O'Toole take her away. Arlis screamed in anger and frustration, losing all control. "Stop calling her that! Minnie is *not* a whore. She's been raped, do ye understand? Some devil attacked her. She fought him, but he took her body. Why can't ye understand that? Why are ye punishing her? Find him. Find the man that did this." She looked at her father, tears flowing. She dropped her voice to a whisper. "Da, don't let him do this."

Her father finally lifted his eyes to look at his older daughter, raw grief in his voice. "Enough, Arlis, enough. I don't know where your mum and me went wrong. We thought we were raising another good girl." He slowly raised his arm as if it were weighted down and dismissively waved his hand toward Minnie, who continued to cower on the bed. "The tart doesn't even know the man she lay with. You're with child, for God's sake. Do ye want the whore polluting your babe? No, the girl has to repent. She goes."

Arlis was shocked into silence. *Da can't even say her name. Tart, whore, girl. Holy Mother of God, she's dead to him.* She wanted to scream again, repeating that her sister was the victim of a horrible crime. She opened her mouth, but no words came out, her begging falling on deaf ears. The priest was immovable, and her father's words—or lack of them—sealed Minnie's fate. Paddy O'Shea had already erased his youngest daughter from his life. Arlis turned to her sister, sobbing in defeat as she collapsed on a chair. She could hear her father's heavy footsteps cross the room toward the bed, but she couldn't bear to watch what was happening. She could hear Minnie's keening as she was led from the room and down the stairs. *She can't leave like this.*

Arlis gathered what little strength remained and pushed herself up from the chair, rushing to the top of the stairs. Her heart ached at the scene at the bottom— her little sister, hair hanging matted and tangled, being led out the door like a criminal going to the gallows. "Minnie! I swear to ye, Minnie. I swear to ye before God Almighty, I'll find a way to bring ye home. I promise. I promise."

Minnie raised her tear-swollen face to her sister, comforted by her words, trusting in her heart that she would save her; somehow, Arlis would bring her home.

Chapter Four

June 1966

Arlis sat on the bed, Claire's head resting in her lap as she stroked her hair, waiting patiently, hoping her daughter would tell her what happened. Her throat tightened as she recalled a similar scene when her daughter was in high school and came home crying because a boy she liked asked another girl to the school dance. Arlis held her just like this as she soothed her daughter's broken heart with gentle strokes through her luxuriant black hair, so like her father's.

This was no teenage heartbreak they were dealing with, however. Someone viciously violated Claire, cruelly taking away her innocence, her trust. Some monster had stolen that unique moment when a woman chooses to give herself to someone for the first time. Now, in an act of heinous desecration, all of that was gone—the innocence, the trust, the moment. Finally, Claire stirred but continued to lie on her bed with her head in her mother's lap. Arlis felt her daughter's chest rise as she breathed deeply and began to speak, her words coming out in a whisper.

"I was putting away some pots in the storage room before I came home. I was only in there for about ten minutes. Suddenly, a man was standing there." Claire stammered and quickly added, "I....I couldn't see him 'cause the lights were dim. I didn't see him so much as sense him." She paused again. "He pushed me against the wall and kissed me hard." Her entire body shuddered as she continued. "His hands were all over me, and then he dragged me down on the floor. I could smell whiskey on his breath, whiskey, and cabbage, I think." Claire suddenly sat up and heaved convulsively. She remained seated her legs curled to her side as she leaned on one arm. She gulped twice. "When...when it was over, he just laughed. And then he left. I didn't see him, Mum." She dropped her voice so low, Arlis strained to make out what she was saying. She thought it odd that Claire was repeating her last words. "I didn't see him, Mum. I don't know who he was. I don't."

Arlis listened to her daughter and struggled to hide her shock. *She's lying to me. She knows the bastard. She knows the man who raped her.*

She treasured the relationship she shared with her daughter. Perhaps it was because her own mother always dismissed her and her sister while catering to their father. Gwen had what Arlis considered to be an antiquated view of a woman's place in life. In her mother's defense, however, Gwen was raised in an age-old, religion-based culture that believed that women were second-class citizens, an afterthought in Creation.

Maybe society in 1966—at least in the Irish culture—wasn't ready to accept women as anything more than wives and mothers, but Arlis knew in her heart that someday, someday, women would finally claim their right to live the lives they chose.

Minnie's life and all its choices were taken from her by people she trusted—first by the man who raped her and then again by a merciless old priest and parents who thought more of themselves than they did of their suffering daughter. Perhaps it was because of what happened to Minnie all those years ago that Arlis was fierce in her beliefs about women controlling their own destinies, and she carefully nurtured the innate, independent nature she saw in Claire. That was why she was so sure Claire was lying to her about what transpired tonight. She was protecting someone or something.

There were so many similarities in the stories recounted by Claire and Minnie. How can that be? She shivered involuntarily, recalling the events of long ago as she continued to soothe her daughter with tender caresses. That would not happen to Claire; her daughter would live the life of her choosing despite the savage violation she just endured.

Claire's steady breathing signaled that she had finally surrendered to sleep. Arlis rose and gently slid Claire's head onto a pillow, covering her with a blanket. She wanted her to bathe, to thoroughly wash away any signs of the demon and his violation of her, but rest was more important right now. Sleep would allow her to bury the memories of tonight, at least for a few hours. Tomorrow, she would have to face them again, but she would not be alone. Arlis would be with her daughter, and together, they would start anew; tomorrow, Claire's life would begin again.

****

Jamie O'Brien sat dozing at the kitchen table when Arlis walked into the room. She roused him with a pat on his shoulder. "Wake up, Jamie, I'll get ye something to eat."

He opened his eyes and shook himself awake.

"Jesus, darlin. What have ye been doing? Did Minnie take that long to settle? What set her off this time, will ye tell me that?"

She busied herself at the stove, reheating the stew she made for supper. She wanted nothing more than to sit with Jamie and tell him what happened to Claire and why Minnie was so upset. She wanted to cry and scream and rant. But, of course, that was impossible. Jamie's reaction to Claire's attack would be blind rage; no man in all of Ireland would escape his wrath. No, she had to protect Jamie as much as she had to protect her daughter. So Arlis remained steady as she gripped the handle of the stewpot, holding it so tightly, her knuckles blanched white. She coughed to steady her voice, rage boiling within her.

"I told ye. It was something on the tellie. It just made Minnie sad, is all. Once I got her settled, I went to talk to Claire in her bedroom. She was telling me about some hospitals in Dublin. She should be hearing soon. Offers usually go out a few weeks after graduation."

Arlis hid a deep sigh and changed the subject. "I think I should stay in Minnie's room tonight. She might have one of her nightmares. I don't want her waking ye in the dead of night."

"Suit yourself." Jamie pouted. "But don't start making a habit of it, darlin. A woman's place is in her husband's bed. And don't threaten me again, if ye please. I understood why ye did it all those years ago, but Minnie's safe, and has been for a while now. Like ye said, something on the tellie must have set her off. And truth be told, darlin, I miss ye beside me. And that's God's truth."

Arlis nodded, remembering what her husband was

referring to. She smiled at Jamie and stroked his face. "Just for tonight, luv, I promise ye. Just for tonight."

It was a long night. Although she told Jamie she was staying with Minnie, Arlis slipped into Claire's room and slept beside her, snuggling her close, just as she did when Claire was little. As she lay with Claire in her arms, her thoughts again turned to Minnie. Her heart clenched, and tears filled her eyes as she recalled her younger sister's hellish life.

Chapter Five

November 1946

Gwen sat on the hard seat, nervously fingering her purse strap. Her eyes looked straight ahead as the bus trundled down the road. Arlis sat on the aisle seat, her body tense as she tried to control her movements when the bus hit a pothole or followed the curve of the ancient road. The sleeping baby in her arms stirred with every bump. She looked down at the precious bundle nestled close to her breast. Her daughter, Claire Minerva O'Brien, arrived three weeks earlier than expected. The doctors asked Arlis if she'd been under any undue stress over the past few months because that could sometimes trigger the early onset of labor.

If seeing your little sister being dragged off to some God-awful convent by a ferret-eyed priest and a ranting father didn't qualify as stress, Arlis wasn't sure what did. What was worse—having your sister accused of whoring when, in fact, she'd been raped—or realizing that your parents, the two people in the world who are supposed to protect you from all harm, turn out to be selfish, unreasonable, ignorant pawns of the Church? Yes, indeed, she'd been stressed.

Arlis tried to make small talk during the hour-long bus ride, but Gwen just sat there, her eyes staring into nothingness. After numerous attempts to talk to her mother, she gave up and let her mind wander.

She was surprised when her mother appeared at her house six months to the day that Minnie was sent away. Gwen grudgingly visited Arlis to ask her if she would accompany her to the convent. The O'Sheas received a letter from the mother superior of the Guardians of the Penitents, Sister Assumpta, asking them to meet with her "regarding a matter of utmost importance." Not surprisingly, Paddy would have none of it since he stated quite plainly that he didn't have but one daughter, Arlis, even though he wasn't speaking to her. Gwen didn't want to go to the meeting either, but she was more concerned about how it would look to the nuns if no one acknowledged their request. Hence, Gwen stowed her displeasure with Arlis and asked her to accompany her to the meeting.

Since that horrible day when the O'Sheas had turned their backs on their youngest child, Arlis had not seen or spoken to her parents. Even when she gave birth to their first grandchild, Gwen and Paddy O'Shea ignored her numerous phone calls and letters. At least they were all saved public embarrassment when Arlis arranged to have Claire baptized in a small church in Kilkenny, rather than the parish governed by the iron fist of Father O'Toole. When Arlis asked the new priest in Kilkenny if she could stand proxy for her sister, who was to be godmother, she conveniently left out why Minnie was now in a convent. The young clergyman was thrilled to accommodate this request thinking this newly-illumined Catholic would benefit from a nun's guidance throughout her life. Arlis was relieved by the man's naiveté.

Arlis eagerly accepted her mother's invitation to

accompany her to the convent. Although no visitors were allowed, she would try to find a way to see Minnie. The promise she made to her sister that day was a constant weight in her heart. It was not an empty vow made in a moment of extreme emotion. She would get her sister out of that prison, but figuring out how to bring Minnie home was a daunting task. She was anxious to tell her sister that she was still trying to work something out. Like being in gaol, perhaps her sister would be free after a six-month sentence; maybe that was the purpose of this meeting. Whatever the reason, Arlis would be inside the convent walls and perhaps, at least, get a glimpse of her sister.

Gwen was relieved that the bus stopped a mile from the convent; she didn't want anyone to see her entering the nunnery. The purpose of convents like this one was well-known throughout Ireland. The burden of shame she carried was heavy enough; she didn't want to add any more weight to the load.

Thankfully, Arlis had the foresight to bring along a pram for the baby. The cobbled road to the convent did not allow for a smooth ride, but the brisk air and sunshine made for a pleasant walk.

As she and her mother approached the convent, Arlis felt her heart tighten. The cluster of buildings was surrounded by a stone wall at least twelve feet high. The only ingress and egress seemed to be enormous iron gates, on which hung a thick chain and padlock. From all appearances, it was a prison, not a peaceful respite from the world. Rather than a feeling of joyful spirit, the air hung heavy with dread. She felt as though she were standing at the very gates of hell. Even a two-month-old infant seemed to feel the disquiet in the air as the baby began to cry.

While Arlis rocked the pram, her mother reached a shaky hand and rang the bell that hung on the pillar next to the gate. Gwen dabbed her eyes several times. Arlis reached out and patted her shoulder, one mother comforting another. She could not comprehend the depth of her mother's anguish—nor did she ever want to—but she wanted to convey to her mother that she did indeed feel her pain. Gwen didn't acknowledge her daughter's gesture, evidently lost in her own world of despair.

What seemed like hours were only minutes until a black-clad figure made her way along the path. She approached the gates, taking a large, heavy key from the belt around her waist as she nodded to the women. Arlis noted the belt on which the key hung tangled with a heavy wooden rosary, which also girded the nun's waist. She groaned inwardly at the irony.

Gwen held an envelope in her hand, and as she raised it, she began to speak. "Good day to ye, Sister. I'm Gwen..." The nun slowly put a finger to her lips, indicating silence. She then crooked her finger and gestured to them to follow her. Gwen and Arlis exchanged quizzical looks as they set off behind the nun.

The women headed for an enormous, dull, red brick building at the end of the path. As they walked, Arlis took in their surroundings. The private grounds, covered with a light frost, added to the starkness of the place. Two enormous stone walls flanked the building and appeared to wrap around it. Numerous lower barriers sectioned off each building within the compound. *This isn't a convent. It's a fortress.*

The small group climbed the steps to the front door, Arlis dragging the pram behind her. The silent nun took another large key from her belt and unlocked the front door. Why is the door locked from the outside? She mused. An involuntary shudder raced through her body. *I've got to get Minnie out of here.* Upon entering the building, she and her mother followed their escort down a long, dark hall, stopping before a single oak door. Rapping softly, the young nun opened the door, directing Gwen and Arlis to enter.

They now stood in a large, sparsely furnished office: a large desk, two wooden chairs, and two file cabinets were the only furniture in the room. The walls were utterly bare except for a ten-foot crucifix that hung on the wall behind the desk. Arlis noted the strategic placement of the cross so that visitors could not divert their eyes from the sufferings of Jesus Christ while sitting in the uncomfortable-looking chairs.

Behind the large desk sat the imposing figure of the mother superior. Her heavily-starched white coif covered by a layer of black crepe wholly covered her head except for her hawk-like face—sharp, darting eyes underneath heavy brows, a beak-like nose situated over a thin slit which served as her mouth. A stiff white wimple secured the coif around her neck. Her black serge tunic draped to the ground, overlaid with a white scapular hanging down her back and front. A woven black wool cincture secured the tunic. Her arms were sheathed in white so that no part of her flesh was visible except her bony hands; the sleeves of her habit were full and bell-shaped. A long, black veil trailed down her back almost to the floor, completing the nun's habit. Several adjectives came to Arlis's mind to describe the nun, but she settled on the kindest one she could think of—formidable.

The nun looked disapprovingly at the baby and then directed her comments to Gwen. Her voice was not surprising; it certainly was in keeping with her cold and detached appearance.

"Good afternoon, Mrs. O'Shea. I am Sister Assumpta, the mother superior of our convent. I was under the impression Mr. O'Shea would be with you today." She gestured toward Arlis with her hand, not even bothering to make eye contact. "Who is this young woman? This meeting is not a social visit, Mrs. O'Shea. There are important matters to discuss."

A red flush crept up Gwen's face as she wrung her hands nervously. "I'm so sorry, Mother Superior. Paddy, my husband, couldn't get off work, so my daughter here, Arlis is her name, came with me. She had to bring her bairn, ye see, because she's just a tyke." Arlis knew Gwen feared being struck dead for lying to a nun, but she couldn't admit the truth—that her husband considered Minnie dead and of no further consequence. Gwen visibly squirmed under the nun's icy stare.

The intimidation continued. "I see. Well, it is of the greatest import that I speak with you privately. I will have your daughter escorted to our sitting area while we talk." The Mother Superior pressed a black button on her desk, and another young woman, similarly clad in black, appeared at the side door. She kept her head bowed in submission. "Elizabeth, take this young woman and the child to the parlor." The nun nodded obediently and stood by the door.

****

It was obvious from the old nun's demeanor that no further discussion would be tolerated. Arlis clenched her teeth to calm her fury, and gathering the baby, stalked from the room.

As she followed her escort to the visitors' parlor, Arlis noted the atmosphere surrounding her. The absolute silence of the place struck her—it was foreboding and evil. She shook her head to dismiss such silliness. *It's a convent, for mercy's sake. It's supposed to be quiet. Maybe everyone's at chapel or reading or meditating, whatever they do in convents.* Her thoughts turned to the nun, Sister Assumpta. *Now there's a 'wagon,' truly. Is this what living a life of prayer will get ye? I'd rather have my rows with Jamie from time to time and put up with his shenanigans than live like this. I've got to get Minnie out of here.*

They finally reached a door, which Arlis assumed was the parlor. She was again surprised when the young nun, who continued her silence as they walked, reached into her pocket and withdrew a key to unlock the door. *What in blazes? Why is every door in this place locked?* The nun called Elizabeth opened the door and stood back, gesturing to Arlis to enter. "You may wait in here. I will return for you at Mother Superior's instruction." Arlis noticed a slight hesitation in the young woman's actions, as though struggling with a decision. Suddenly, she raised her head and smiled as she fled the room. Arlis shook her head in bewilderment. *Daft, for sure!*

She was relieved that Claire had been quiet since they arrived, but Arlis's full breasts signaled that it was time for a feeding. She gently lifted the baby and cradled her in her arms as she prepared to nurse her, pleased that she didn't have to explain the need for privacy to the young nun. As Claire began to suckle, Arlis breathed deeply and closed her eyes, burying all negative thoughts for the time being. She was always overcome with feelings of total love and peace when she nursed Claire; the oneness she shared with her child was so beautiful, so complete.

The baby, finally sated, was content to rest in her mother's arms. Arlis was so deep in her reverie, she didn't hear the old door creak open. It was when the baby stirred that she slowly opened her eyes. Was her mind playing tricks? Was she so overcome with emotion that her wishful thinking was taking form? She blinked quickly and concentrated on focusing her eyes. She gasped at the image before her. *Minnie?*

"Minnie," she whispered. "Minnie!" Arlis, so shocked at seeing her sister, was unable to move, unable to do anything except whisper Minnie's name over and over again. It was then that she noticed that her sister was not alone; the young novice stood to her side. The nun quickly closed the door and began to speak in a hushed whisper.

"I will be back in five minutes, Minerva. Remember, just whisper. We don't want to get caught now, do we?" Arlis was further shocked when the nun turned to her, winked, then padded out of the room.

Minnie turned and watched Elizabeth close the door and then wasted no time running to her sister and falling at her feet, burying her face in Arlis's lap. "Oh, Arlis, Arlis." She wept. "I thought ye forgot about me."

"Forgot about ye?" Arlis stroked what remained of her sister's hair. It was cut so short; spiked tufts stood out all over her head. "Oh, Min. I think about ye all the time. Well, almost all. See, I had the baby. Isn't she beautiful, Min. I named her Claire Minerva, after ye. Do ye want to hold her?"

Minnie raised her head to look at the baby. She smiled through her tears and gently touched the infant's head. "I don't think I should hold her," she whispered. "I might drop her."

"Don't be silly, Min. You're not going to drop her. Come on now, quick as ye can." It was then that she noticed her sister's fingers. A pained cry escaped her lips as she looked at her hands. Fresh, angry blisters were forming atop several burn scars on her palms and the backs of her hands, marking an ugly path up her forearms. Layers of bandages swathed several fingers on her right hand. Her thumb appeared to be at an odd angle. "Holy saints, what's happened to your hands?" Arlis whispered.

"We all have to work in the laundry. My hands get scalded in hot water; the bleach and lye sure don't help. And my fingers?" Minnie shrugged. "I haven't learned the ways of the washing machine yet. I'm always getting my fingers stuck in the rollers. Ye get used to the pain, though." She lowered her voice, her tone hopeless as she added, "Ye have to. But I don't want to talk about my hands. There's something else." Minnie stood now and pulled the dingy blue shift tight against her stomach. Arlis took in a sharp breath as she noticed the apparent swelling.

"You're pregnant? Do the sisters know? Does that Mother Superior know?"

Minnie managed a sad smile. "I don't think they know yet, but I can't keep it a secret much longer, can I? I told Sister Damien I hurt my back, so they took me off sorting through the dirty laundry for a while; I run the washers now." She raised her bandaged hand and slowly shook her head. "I'll get the hang of it—sooner or later."

Minnie hesitated a moment and then spoke in a rush. "Arlis, I want to keep the baby. Do ye think they'll let me? Will Da and Mum let me? I could live with ye, and we could raise our babes together. I know I'm young, but ye can teach me what I need to know. Can we, Arlis? Can we live with ye after I leave here?"

Arlis was still trying to process the knowledge of her sister's condition when she heard the pleading in Minnie's voice. She swallowed hard, her mind racing. She didn't want her sister to despair, but Arlis knew full well what could happen to her baby. She heard the rumors; wealthy Americans coming to Ireland to buy babies—*buy babies*! She and her girlfriends often talked about what went on in these places. Although she was upset by it, these stories didn't affect her since her sister wasn't sent here because she was pregnant. Arlis truly believed Minnie would "atone for her sin" and leave this hell she was living in and return home.

She now scoffed at her naiveté. What was she thinking? That Minnie would "repent" and then everything would be like it was? Her head had been up her arse this whole time. Now she was faced with the reality of it. What could she say to her little sister who stood before her, her belly swollen with child, her eyes pleading? *Holy Mother, help me.*

The Holy Mother did help her at that moment as the novice Elizabeth quickly opened the door. "Minerva, we have to go, or they'll miss you. Come now. Hurry!" She caught Arlis's questioning look and offered a brief explanation. "When I saw you accompany your mother, I knew Minerva would want to see you; she talks about you all the time, you see. I told Sister Damien that I had to tend to Minerva's fingers; instead, I brought her to see you. And now, we really must go."

Minerva planted a small kiss on Claire's cheek as she hugged her sister. "I know ye can get us out of here, Arlis, the baby, and me. I'll wait to hear from ye. I love ye." And then she was gone.

****

Once again, the bus ride passed in silence. Arlis's thoughts were reeling with her sister's news. She was careful not to mention that she saw Minnie. Although she wanted to tell her parents how poorly Minnie was being treated at the hands of Catholic nuns, she kept this knowledge to herself lest they report back to the mother superior because of some perverted sense of loyalty to the Church.

She was very curious about the subject of the meeting with Sister Assumpta. As her mother sat staring out the window, she snuck a sidelong glance toward her, trying to assess her mother's mood. "Mum, would you like to hold Claire for a while? I always find that I feel better when I hold her close."

Her mother declined the offer with a firm shake of her head, avoiding looking at her granddaughter. Arlis pushed on. "Mum, what's wrong? What did Sister Assumpta want?"

"Nothing's wrong, nothing atall. There were some papers to sign, tis all. No more questions, Arlis. I'm tired. I'll be closing my eyes till we're home."

It was clear the conversation was over. Arlis

continued to watch her mother closely after Gwen closed her eyes. The strain on the older woman's face was evident, as though she had aged since meeting with the mother superior.

I can't begin to imagine how difficult it must be to sign over the care of your daughter to people you don't even know. A profound sadness enveloped her. She pulled her child closer to her breast and closed her eyes. *What will they do when they find out Minnie's pregnant? I've got to get her out of there before she has the baby. But how? Holy Mother Mary, how?*

Chapter Six

February, 1947

It had been almost three months since Arlis had seen Minnie, and she had yet to come up with any viable plan to get her sister out of the convent and back home before her baby was born. She was running out of time.

Her blood still boiled as she recalled her husband's tirade when she tried to broach the subject of bringing Minnie home. Jamie sounded just like her father. "Are ye daft, Arlis? We can't have your sister with her bastard child living with our Claire. Minnie can't even tell ye who got her that way. I'll be damned if I'll have her living here. What'll my friends say? I can see them all now, smiling at me with a wink and a nod. No. She won't be coming here, and that's final, Arlis. That's final!"

****

Claire just settled for her afternoon nap when the phone rang. Arlis hurried to answer it before the shrill sound woke the baby. The voice on the other end spoke in a panicked whisper, "This is Elizabeth—at the convent. Minerva had the child. You must come now. They're going to take it. You must come now." The line went dead. She stood still in shock, her heart pounding, thoughts of Minnie racing through her mind. She heard the novice's hushed voice—*They're going to take it. You must come now.*

Panic clawed in Arlis's stomach as she tried to make sense of the words whispered on the phone. *They're going to take it.* Fury surged through her as the meaning of those words burned through the panic. *They have no right to take my sister's baby! I'll tell Da. He'll stop them.*

She donned her jacket as she ran into the parlor. Grabbing an afghan from the sofa, Arlis hurried to the nursery, quickly scooping up the sleeping infant and wrapping her tightly in the blanket. She laid the baby in the pram, carefully covering the hood with another blanket to shield her from the bracing wind as she walked out the door. Claire began to stir but was soon lulled back to sleep by the carriage movement as Arlis sped along the sidewalk. What was usually a fifteen-minute stroll to her parents' home today became a seven-minute sprint. Rounding the corner, she was stunned to see Father O'Toole entering her parents' house.

She slowed, struggling to make sense of the old priest's presence. Was he here to tell them about Minnie's further *transgression*? Was he telling them that their new grandchild had arrived and was about to be taken from them? Was he going to help them stop this crime? She was relieved that she would be with her mother when the priest broke the news to her. Gwen would be devastated.

Since the visit to the convent with her mum, Arlis made an effort to visit her parents more often, so the visit today wouldn't raise any alarms. She couldn't tell her parents about the young nun's phone call; she couldn't tell them that she knew Minnie was pregnant, so Arlis entered the house with all the nonchalance she could muster.

"Hi, Mum. Hi, Da. I thought I'd bring little Claire over for a visit." She feigned surprise as she nodded to Father O'Toole, who was seated on the divan. "Oh, good day to ye, Father O'Toole. I hope I'm not interrupting something." She glanced at her father and noticed the hard set of his jaw, his teeth so tightly clenched, the muscles spasmed beneath his leathered skin. *Sweet Jesus. They know.*

Gwen was sitting in her rocker, weeping, the knitting she was working on lay forgotten at her feet. Arlis looked questioningly at her mother. "Mum, what is it? Is it Minnie? Is she all right?"

Father O'Toole looked at Paddy O'Shea and then at Gwen as though urging them to answer their daughter.

Paddy opened his mouth to speak, but no words came out. He raised his right arm and waved his hand in a gesture of futility. Gwen continued to sob as she rocked in her chair. When neither spoke, the old priest cleared his throat and began to talk. "Perhaps it's not for me to tell ye, but ye should know. Your sister has birthed a male child. Since all the papers were in order, the adoption has already gone through. The babe is on his way to America."

The priest's last words *on his way to America* burned into Arlis's consciousness, momentarily robbing her of all rational thought. Her breath came in shaky gasps. She struggled to comprehend what she just heard. *Minnie's baby—Minnie's son—on his way to America? They took her baby already? How can this*

39

be?

"Da, is this true? How could they take Minnie's baby away from her? They have no right, Da! They have no right. We should call the authorities, Da. They can't do this. They…"

Finally, her father spoke. His voice so full of despair, she halted in mid-sentence. "Enough, girl, stop. They can do this. Your mum signed the papers months ago. It's done—it's over, Arlis. It's over." Paddy O'Shea hung his head and covered his face with his hands.

Arlis wondered if her father was hiding his grief—or his shame? Fury welled inside of her. "What do you mean Mum signed the papers?" Her head swiveled toward her mother, white-hot anger fueling her words.

"Mum, ye knew Minnie was going to have a baby? Ye did this?" She now recalled the visit to the convent, when that old nun insisted on speaking to Gwen alone. They knew then that Minnie was pregnant. Those were the papers Gwen signed that day. "Ye let them take Minnie's baby, your own grandchild? How could ye, Mum? What kind of a woman are ye? What kind of heartless bitch are ye?"

Through Arlis's tirade, Gwen's sobbing increased with every one of her daughter's words. Her pathetic keening, coupled with the baby crying from all the yelling, was finally drowned out by Paddy's own painful roar. "I *said enough*, Arlis. Ye will not speak to your mum like that, and ye will not speak those words in front of the Father. The girl did this to herself. She laid with a man, and she paid the price. By God, look at us, will ye? We've all paid the price."

"You're damn right, we've paid the price. And the

price you'll be paying is that neither of you will ever see my child or me again. Ye haven't lost one grandchild this day, Mr. and Mrs. O'Shea, you've lost two." Arlis picked up the yowling infant and turned toward Father O'Toole, sitting quietly on the divan, watching the emotional scene unfold before him. The fury and hatred she now felt she gladly directed to him. Her voice came out in a deadly whisper.

"And ye, ye self-righteous prig. This is all your doing. My sister was raped. She told ye that, but ye wouldn't believe her. Look what you've put this family through." Arlis visibly spat out her next words. "You're a vile excuse for a man, let alone a priest of the Church. Shame be on ye, old man. Shame be on ye. I know what goes on in that hellish place ye call a convent. I hope ye all burn in the fires of hell."

Paddy O'Shea sat in his chair, slack-jawed, shocked by his daughter's vehemence. Gwen's crying finally ceased, but she continued her rocking, staring trance-like into space. The old priest's face contorted in rage, his eyes black pools of fury as he watched Arlis settle the baby in the pram and stalk from the house.

The fresh air helped Arlis rein in the raw emotion unleashed by the news of Minnie and her child. Although she felt justified in her anger toward her parents and that vile little man in the black cassock, most of the rage she was experiencing was for herself. It was because of her inaction that her sister lost her son. There must have been something she could have done to avoid the tragedy that just occurred. This was her fault. She couldn't even begin to imagine what Minnie was feeling now. This was her fault. She should have pushed Jamie harder to accept Minnie and her

child into their home. This was her fault. This was all
her fault!

Chapter Seven

After his shift, Jamie arrived home to find his wife pacing around the kitchen, arms folded across her chest. The stormy look on her face quelled his desire to question her mood. Wordlessly, he removed his heavy work boots, hanging his jacket on the clothes hook, carefully placing his badge on the shelf above. He leaned his back against the counter, crossed his ankles, folded his arms, and braved her ire.

"Let's have it then, darlin. What's got ye all hot and bothered? Shall we talk now, or can it wait till after I've had my tea?"

"No, Jamie, it can't wait. It's waited long enough, and now my sister has lost her babe. We can't ignore it anymore, Jamie. I have to bring Minnie home."

"Well then, bring her and her bas...her baby home—to your da's and mum's. She's not coming here, Arlis. We decided that before."

"No, Jamie, ye decided that. Ye know how I feel about Minnie coming to live with us. And now, it will only *be* Minnie as the blessed Church has somehow coerced my mum into signing adoption papers, and now the bairn is on his way to America to some family who fancies Irish babies."

"Whoa. Back up, girl. What's this you're saying? They just up and took Min's baby? Is that even legal?"

"It's legal by their say so." Arlis knew she was

making little sense. She inhaled and slowly expelled her breath, feeling her body relax somewhat, and told Jamie about the phone call from the young nun at the convent.

"I went over to my parents' to see if they knew anything. When I got to the house, Father O'Toole was there. I could see that Da and Mum were upset. The priest told me that Min had a baby boy and that he was already on his way to America with his new parents. Mum signed some papers giving up Minnie's rights as a parent. I guess since Min is only fifteen, Mum could do that. I realized that was why she went to the convent for that meeting—it was to sign papers giving away Min's rights to her baby. Now, Minnie is still at the convent, and by God, I'm getting her out of that hellhole. I mean it, Jamie. My sister is coming here. I'll take care of her from now on; she doesn't have anyone else."

Arlis could tell from her husband's body language that he wasn't about to budge on his original decision, so she risked it all. She walked across the room and boldly stood in front of him. She straightened her shoulders and raised her chin in defiance, making sure he understood her resolve.

"Jamie, before ye say anything, I want to make something crystal clear to ye. I love ye, Jamie O'Brien. I've loved ye since I was sixteen years old. I wanted to be your wife then, and I want to stay being your wife— in all ways. But I love Minnie, too. She's my little sister, and she's been through hell these past nine months. Da and Mum deserted her for God-knows-what reason, but I can't do that. I'm all she has. And she will come to live with us."

Jamie's face clouded in anger, and he opened his mouth to speak. But Arlis anticipated his reaction and responded quickly. She gently placed her hand on his mouth and held his gaze. Her voice was just above a whisper, but her husband heard every word. "Jamie, if ye will not agree to bring Minnie here, we will no longer live together as husband and wife. Ye will never again be welcome in my bed. Ye may have me whenever you wish, but it will just be my body you'll be taking; my heart will no longer be yours. I will not respond to ye in any loving way. Ye will be making love to a corpse because all the feelings I have for ye will be dead. I cannot love a man who could be so cold and cruel so as not to give refuge to a broken soul like Minnie."

"And what about your vows to the Church?" Jamie's voice dropped to a raspy whisper. "The vows ye took on our wedding day? That ye would be my obedient wife? Do those vows mean nothing to ye, then?"

Arlis calmly whispered her reply. "The Church be damned."

Jamie stood glaring at his wife. It was evident from the look on his face that he was shocked by his wife's intensity and had no retort. "I'm going to the pub," he grumbled, pushing away from the counter and grabbing his jacket and boots.

As he passed her, Arlis put her hand on his arm. "Ye go to the pub, Jamie," she spoke quietly. "But I'll not be put off, do ye hear? It's in your hands now."

Silently, he started for the door but stopped as she began to speak again. "I lied to ye just now, Jamie. I haven't loved ye since I was sixteen."

Jamie closed his eyes and swallowed hard as he turned back to face his wife. "Ye lied about that? Ye haven't loved me all this time?"

Arlis fought the hot tears welling in her eyes as she saw the pain on her husband's face. "I lied when I said I've loved ye since I was sixteen. I'll confess to ye now. I've loved ye since I was six. I remember the day like it was yesterday; we were all playing by the creek. I slipped and fell in. There were crayfish all around, and I was in fear for my life. I can still see ye running up to me and helping me up. I turned my ankle when I fell, so ye pulled me home in your cart. I knew from that very day that you would protect me forever, and I loved ye for it, and I love ye still."

Jamie slowly released the breath he'd been holding, hanging his head as he walked silently from the house.

Chapter Eight

Arlis spent a fitful night after Jamie left so abruptly for the pub because she'd given him her ultimatum. He never came to bed. Other than the six days she stayed in the hospital after Claire's birth, she never slept alone; she spent every night nestled in Jamie's loving arms. Even when they had silly newlywed spats, they never went to bed angry with one another.

Jamie and Arlis were married soon after he returned from the war. A year later, Claire came along. Their marriage was a happy one; this breach in their relationship was unexpected, leaving both of them feeling angry and confused.

She would readily admit she could never follow through with her threat to Jamie about the absence of any future marital unions if he didn't allow her to bring her sister home. No, their physical relationship was as important to her as it was to him, perhaps even more so. Nevertheless, Arlis knew the possibility of that part of their marriage vanishing made Jamie think twice about his initial decision. She knew that decision was just a knee-jerk reaction based on his upbringing and years of conditioning in a male-dominated society. She had to bring home the point that Minerva had been a victim, and what remained of her life had to be protected by the only person in the world who cared—Arlis.

As she lay pondering all this in her mind, she heard

Claire begin to fuss, ready for her morning feeding. Arlis started to rise from her bed, and as she slipped on her robe, the baby abruptly ceased her crying. Thinking the baby found her thumb to comfort herself, she smiled and tiptoed into the nursery. Her heart tightened with emotion as she beheld the scene before her.

Jamie's muscular frame was squeezed into the seat of the rocking chair. Their daughter, dwarfed by his size, was nestled snugly in his arms. The baby held Jamie's gaze as she cooed in response to his soft crooning. Whether it was the squeak of the floorboard or the scent of her mother's milk, Claire squirmed in her father's arms, and Jamie glanced toward Arlis and then quickly back to his daughter. "Well, darlin, I'll be handing ye off to your mum now. Time for breakfast." He heaved himself out of the chair and walked toward his wife, handing her the baby. He averted his eyes as Arlis took the child in her arms.

A lump formed in Arlis's throat as Jamie began to walk past her. She swallowed hard and managed to whisper one word—"Jamie?" A strange mix of relief and alarm swept over her as he reached the doorway and then turned to face her.

His usual strong voice was low and raspy. "Ye tend to Claire. I'll make tea, and then we'll talk."

*****

Arlis fed and changed Claire and carried her downstairs, settling her in the cradle in the parlor. She had quickly tended to her morning ablutions, applying some powder, trying in vain to hide the dark circles below her eyes. She entered the kitchen and found Jamie sitting at the table, his head lay atop his folded arms, his eyes closed. Two cups sat at their usual places, tea steeped in the pot. Once again, her heart lurched at the sight of him.

Jamie heard her slippers scuff on the cold linoleum, and he slowly raised his eyes to look at his wife. "Sit down, Arlis. Please." He cleared his throat as if to buy himself a few more minutes of preparation.

"I want ye to know, darlin, that I heard every word ye spoke last night—*every* word. I don't think much of your usin our lovin time as a negotiatin tool, but I understand why ye did it and why ye felt ye had to go to such lengths. What I do agree with ye about, though, is how poorly Minnie's been treated all these months. Whether she was raped—like she sez—or she lay with a fella of her own free will, I don't think anyone has the right to take a woman's babe from her, even if she is only fifteen years old.

"I can't imagine our Claire comin to us when she's grown and, God forbid, tells us a story like that. I hope I will believe her. But even if I didn't, I don't think I could turn her over to the likes of Father O'Toole and those ladies at the convent. The whole village has heard stories about the goins-on in that place. Christ Almighty, we all grew up hearing those stories. I think our mothers made sure we knew 'em to keep us all on the straight and narrow. And I'm sure whatever Minnie has told you about that place is God's truth. So, the long and short of it is that I agree that Min should come and live with us. And I need to say this—I'm sorry I was such a stubborn arse. If I hadn't been so pig-headed, maybe we could have gotten to her before they took her boy."

Arlis swallowed hard and closed her eyes in relief. To her surprise, Jamie continued to speak.

"Now that bein said, there's something else I want to make clear to ye. I love ye, darlin, and I love lovin ye. But if I ever for one minute thought that I could take your body while not having your heart, that would be the end of it. I confess it does hurt me that ye could think so little of me, but like I said, I understand why ye thought ye had to go that far."

He sighed in sorrow. "Mebbe I don't say it, darlin, but you are the music of my heart, the reason I get up in the morning. Ye—and now, Claire—are life to me." Arlis released a sob as Jamie repeated his last words in a tear-filled whisper. "Ye are life to me."

The chair she was sitting on toppled over as she jumped from her seat. In three short strides, she was on his lap and in his arms, smothering him with kisses all over his face, the sharp, day-old whiskers going unnoticed by her frantic lips. "Jamie, Jamie, I'm so sorry I hurt ye. I love ye. I'm sorry I hurt ye."

Jamie silenced her teary pleas as he caught her mouth in a deep kiss. He finally pulled away as they both became aware of the insistent yowling of their daughter. Before letting Arlis off his lap, Jamie wrapped her tightly in his arms and buried his face in her hair, inhaling the scent he knew so well. "I'm sorry for being such an arse. Now, settle Claire. I have to get cleaned up. We have a visitor coming soon."

Arlis looked at him questioningly and turned, hurrying to the parlor to tend to the baby. As she rocked Claire, she heard Jamie in the bathroom above her as he ran water for his bath. She pictured him stripping and easing himself into the steaming tub. The vapor in the bathroom would be so dense; it would look like the steam room at O'Shaughnessy's bathhouse.

As she sat rocking her daughter in her arms, Jamie's words were still echoing in her mind, and she began to relax. Of course, she was relieved that Jamie was allowing Minnie to come live with them. But more than that, his beautiful and heartfelt profession of the depth of his love overwhelmed her.

She had feared that they had already started to take each other for granted, as most married couples do. Even though they'd only been married a short time, maybe they'd fallen into the marriage rut without realizing it.

When she got together with her girlfriends, the conversation was always three-tiered: first, they talked about their little ones, comparing notes on teething, potty training, walking, and talking. None of her friends had children over the age of two, so comparisons were easy. It was a relief to know your child was on track with the others in the group. Then the talk would turn to the latest town gossip: any hanky-panky going on, who among their unmarried classmates was about to take the plunge, did Old Man McShane ogle you when you shopped in his store? Did Mrs. McShane know? And then the conversation inevitably turned to their marital relationships; Brenda was sure her husband was stepping out on her. Molly was tired of picking up after her slob of a husband—didn't his mum teach him anything? Grace thought she might be *in that way again*, and she wasn't happy since she already had two, and the oldest wasn't even twenty-three months old yet.

When that discussion started, Arlis remained silent. Her marriage to Jamie was damn near perfect compared to her friends'. She never worried that Jamie would be untrue to her, and much to her embarrassment, he was neater than she was. The only topic that made her uncomfortable was when one of the girls announced they were expecting again. Arlis believed that Claire was a one-time gift; there would be no others. Doc Madden told her there was no medical reason, but it was something that she knew in her heart to be true.

She heard the water draining from the tub and pictured Jamie wiping the steam from the mirror as he prepared to shave. He would lather his face with his shaving brush, take the straight razor and expertly remove his whiskers, leaving his face smooth and handsome, once again. A lump formed in her throat as she repeated the heartfelt words he just spoke to her. *"Ye are life to me."* At that moment, she promised herself that she would not take her husband—or their marriage—for granted ever again.

The sound of Jamie descending the staircase broke through her musings. She rose, settling Claire in the cradle as she walked into the hallway to meet him at the base of the stairs. Just then, the doorbell rang.

Jamie checked his pocket watch. "Well, he's prompt. I'll say that for him." He gave Arlis a measured look and opened the door.

Chapter Nine

Arlis saw a man standing on the threshold. Jamie held out his hand in welcome. "Come in, Thomas, come in. You're right on time." He turned to Arlis for an introduction. "Darlin, this here is Thomas Brady. Thomas, my wife, Arlis."

She had no idea who this man was or what he was doing here, but she knew her husband. She knew this meeting was significant by the look he had just given her before opening the door and his body language now. She had also noticed the look of apprehension on the man's face. She forced a smile. "Good day to ye, Mr. Brady. Welcome to our home. Please, come in."

Mr. Brady nodded stiffly and followed Arlis into the parlor. She gestured toward one of the chairs that flanked the divan, and he sat. Jamie took a seat on the sofa and held out his hand for Arlis to join him. There was a moment of uncomfortable silence; no one seeming to know what to do next.

Jamie took control as he softly cleared his throat. Unexpectedly, he turned to his wife. "Arlis, I met Mr. Brady here, Thomas, that is, at the pub last night." She caught the unmistakable tone in his voice as he continued. "Seems it was providential that I visited Mac's last night, seeing as it's not usually the place I spend my Friday nights now, is it?" She noted the look in his eyes and reddened.

"As luck—or fate—would have it, Thomas had been looking for me. Well, he'd been looking for you, but he didn't think it proper to show up here unannounced. We started to talk and...well... Ah, Thomas, I think ye should take over from here."

As the man shifted in his seat, Arlis noted that in addition to the hat balanced on his knee, he carried a small business-like satchel. She thought it odd because there was nothing business-like about Thomas Brady. He was about Jamie's age with coppery-red hair and pale skin, looking more like a teacher than a businessman. She raised her eyes and looked expectantly at their visitor.

"I'd like to thank you both for seeing me on such short notice." At this point, he unclasped the satchel and removed a slender envelope. His hand noticeably shaking, he stood and walked over to Arlis and handed it to her. "After reading this, I'm sure you will agree that time is of the essence. I'll be happy to answer your questions when you are finished. I'm sure there will be many."

Arlis was stunned—but intrigued—by their visitor's comments. She looked to Jamie, trusting he would know what to say, what to do.

He smiled gently and took her hand, holding it tightly to reassure her he was there for her. "Go on, darlin. Read the letter."

"May I read it aloud?" she asked.

Thomas Brady nodded vigorously. "Oh, yes. I don't know the exact words she used, but I know the gist of it. Yes, please. Read it out loud," he said encouragingly.

She? Arlis was intrigued. Overwhelming curiosity

took over, and she unsealed the letter with shaking hands. Resisting the urge to turn the message over and see who signed it, she took a deep breath and began to read.

"February 13th
Dear Mrs. Arlis,

Please forgive the familiarity with which I address you. I only know you as "Arlis," so I hope the honorific will salvage any rules of decorum that I have breached.

The bearer of this letter, and its accompanying package, is Mr. Thomas Brady, in whom I have the utmost trust. He will be happy to answer any questions you will most certainly have after reading this epistle.

My name is Alise Ewing of the Dublin Ewings. I am writing to you with a strange request, but one of the most considerable importance. To avoid undue confusion, I shall begin at...well, I suppose I shall begin at the beginning.

Four years ago, my husband, Edward Ewing, signed a marriage contract for our daughter with Dennis Lassiter, the principal landowner of a neighboring county. The agreement stated that, upon coming of age, our only daughter—and only child— would enter into marital union with Mr. Lassiter's profligate son, Declan Lassiter. The contract was based solely on economics and was most assuredly never agreed upon by myself, nor my daughter.

Rather than be forced into such a barbaric and antiquated tradition, Liza chose to break the contract the only way she knew how. She allowed herself to be found in flagrante delicto with a young man with whom she had genuinely fallen in love, Mr. Thomas Brady, who stands before you now.

In retribution for my daughter's defiance, my husband—who is well known to be heartless and cruel—sent her away privily to that horrid nunnery, The Convent of the Guardians of the Penitents. It is there that she has spent the last four years in despair and hopelessness. You know my Liza as the novice Elizabeth.

Liza has told me that your sister, Minerva, has great trust in you that you will somehow gain her release into your care. Although Liza's letters are sporadic at best, I just received her latest missive yesterday. She confided in me the horrific account of how they mercilessly took Minerva's child from her when the babe was only days old. I am ashamed to admit that, over the years, I have heard stories of such atrocities, but they seemed too heinous to believe. Now, hearing first-person accounts of these stories, I can no longer hide behind my naïveté.

My dear Arlis (if I may be so familiar), I now come to the purpose of my letter. If—no, because I have the utmost confidence in you, I will say when—you gain your sister's release from that hellish place, would you consider aiding my daughter in her escape as well? I know I am audacious in suggesting such a drastic endeavor, but I feel I have no recourse.

You see, madam, I am dying. I do not have long for this world. When Liza was taken from me four years ago, my heart could not bear the shock or the agony of losing the only person I have ever truly loved. Since the day Mr. Ewing took her away, I have been dying a slow, agonizing death, emotionally and physically.

Hearing of your existence from my Liza was the answer to my prayers. You will be her deliverer; I know it.

And now to explain Mr. Brady's part in this. I bear no ill will toward this good young man. Although he was the reason my daughter's reputation was compromised, he allowed himself to be a participant in their encounter only to make sure the proposed marriage arrangement would never occur. Alas, no one could have foreseen the depths of my husband's anger or cruelty. Upon finding Liza and Thomas together, he went so far as to put a bounty on the poor boy's head, forcing him to leave the county. He has been living very near Teaghlach these four years past on a relative's farm. Rather than allow Liza to marry a man of good character, albeit not of her social standing or religion, instead of the reprobate son of a reprobate father, my husband destroyed his family and the life of an innocent young man. I am sorry to say that I will go to my grave hating him for what he has forced our daughter and this good young man to endure.

I have digressed. Please forgive me. Mr. Brady has all of Liza's papers in his possession, which will be necessary for travel. There are also some family mementos I think she would like to have along with my last letter to her. And finally, I have included a small dowry. I have been putting a bit aside every week since the day she was born. It isn't much—just whatever I could manage while avoiding a miser's scrutiny. I think it is essential for a woman to have some independence, no matter how good her husband is. Perhaps my own marriage has jaded me.

I can now die in peace. I know you are the answer to all my prayers. God sent you to us, dear Arlis.

Although it was a painful journey for you and your sister, I believe that you are His instrument of deliverance. May God bless you and your family now and always.

I remain your most grateful servant,
Alise Ewing"

Chapter Ten

The ticking of the mantel clock was the only sound in the otherwise silent room. Even Claire remained asleep. Arlis sat staring at the letter she had just read, questions flooding her mind. Jamie switched his hands, continuing to hold hers tightly while he slipped a strong arm around her shoulders and drew her to him. She took comfort in the nearness of him and silently whispered a prayer thanking God that her husband was sharing this new burden with her.

And it was a burden. *Holy Mother Mary!* She was trying to rescue Minnie from the jaws of hell. Now, another poor soul needed saving. The novice Elizabeth? She could barely remember what she looked like, but she did remember the young nun's kindness to her and her sister the day she and her mum visited the convent. She also remembered the risk Elizabeth took in somehow getting to a telephone to call Arlis and warn her about what was happening.

Elizabeth is a nun. Am I even allowed to help a nun leave a convent? Won't I be damned to hell or something? Of course, after the language she used to Father O'Toole, calling him a self-righteous old prig, her one-way ticket to hell was probably already bought and paid for...and no refunds. *Well, maybe a hundred Our Fathers and a hundred Hail Marys along with a few Glory Bes could clean the slate. But helping a nun escape a convent? That might be one of those unforgivable sins.* Who could she ask?

Jamie's deep voice broke through her daze. "Darlin, Thomas wants to know if ye have any questions. Ask 'em now 'cause then it's my turn, and I've got a few."

Arlis sat upright, looked at Jamie, and then turned to face Thomas Brady. "I'm not sure where to start, Mr. Brady. The first question that keeps popping up in my head is this—is Elizabeth a nun? Aren't novices just early nuns who haven't taken their vows yet?"

"Mrs. O'Brien, please call me Thomas. Liza is most definitely not a nun, not even a novice. She and I were engaged—albeit secretly—for almost two years before…well, before the *incident.* You and Mr. O'Brien must understand, Liza and I planned the entire *in flagrante delicto* scene; it was staged. We made sure to be seen by Mr. Ewing and that horrible man, Dennis Lassiter. I swear before Almighty God, nothing untoward ever took place between us. As I said, the entire scene was an act.

"Liza and I knew that her father would force her into a loveless marriage to Declan; it didn't matter that he was a known womanizer—like his father—or that he was a drunkard. Declan Lassiter isn't welcome to any gatherings of polite society in all of Ulster. Mr. Ewing knew all this, and still, he was willing to sacrifice his only daughter—his only child—on the altar of almighty power. It was only ever about power—and money." Thomas spat out the last words as he choked back a sob. He struggled to regain control of his emotions.

"I love her, Mrs. O'Brien. And I loved her enough to sacrifice her reputation and mine to save her from unimaginable suffering. Little did either of us know the lengths to which her father would go to punish us for embarrassing him and ruining his plans for a *Ewing/Lassiter empire.*

"The very day after they found us together, Ewing packed Liza off to the convent and sent a letter to my headmaster. Oh, I forgot to tell you. I'm a teacher of science and mathematics at a private school in Belfast. At least, I was a teacher. As I was saying, the day after the incident, I was dismissed for lewd behavior when the headmaster read the account of our liaison. Mr. Ewing also put a bounty on my head for sexual deviancy. I had to flee Ulster immediately to save myself from a public beating and imprisonment. I've been staying at my cousin's farm outside of Teaghlach for the past four years under my mother's maiden name, working as a farmhand.

"I was quite surprised to receive a letter from Liza's mother and the package she mentions in her letter to you. I've had no contact with Liza since that horrible night, four long years ago. I couldn't imagine how to contact her and had all but given up hope when Mrs. Ewing's letter arrived yesterday morning." The man's strength left him as he finished telling his story. He shrugged in hopelessness and leaned back into the chair.

Once again, silence hung heavy in the room. Jamie gathered his thoughts and spoke first.

"Well, that's some story, Thomas. I can't say as I blame the girl's da for wanting you beaten to a pulp." He glanced at his precious daughter in the cradle. "If ye compromised my Claire, I would have beaten ye myself—I wouldn't need a bounty to find ye. That

61

being said—and knowing the rest of the story—I understand your reason for *staging* it, as ye say. But I can't get my head around this Ewing fella doing something like that to his own daughter, or anyone's daughter, come to that.

"Well, sir, what's your plan? If ye can get Liza out of that place, what's your plan for tomorrow? For the day after? What's your plan for the future?"

Thomas Brady set his gaze past Jamie, as though he were looking into the future. "I want to take Liza to America so that we can start anew. I know I can find work there as a teacher."

Arlis had been quiet, listening first to Thomas Brady's story and then to Jamie's comments. She took a deep breath and shifted to face their visitor.

"Mr. Brady, I'm genuinely sorry for what happened to Elizabeth—to Liza. But we have no authority to barge in there and take her out. And even if we did try, don't ye think Sister Assumpta would contact Mr. Ewing in a blink? And then he might send the Ulster constabulary, his goons, or whoever, to stop us. You might be putting Liza in worse danger, not to mention yourself. Do ye have a plan for that?

"And while I'm thinking of it, was there a *sentence* of some kind imposed on Liza? Was she told she had to stay there for a certain length of time? I know with my sister, Minnie, I was under the impression—and now I see, wrongfully so—that her time of *punishment*, if ye will, would be about six months, something like a gaol sentence. Doesn't it seem strange that your Liza's been there four years? Maybe she does want to become a nun; maybe she's gotten used to it there, though, for the life of me, I can't imagine how anyone could get used to that place."

Thomas was nodding in agreement. "Yes, Mrs. O'Brien, I understand your thinking. I thought the same thing, too, until Liza's mother explained it to me. You see, when Ewing took Liza to The Guardians of the Penitents, he made a deal with the mother superior. In exchange for keeping Liza behind the walls of that convent for the rest of her life, Ewing would make monthly payments—directly to Sister Assumpta. Those payments aren't going into any church treasury; they are going directly to the mother superior. And from what I gathered from Mrs. Ewing, the payment is twenty-five pounds a month."

Jamie slapped his open palm on his forehead and fell back against the divan in shock. "Jesus, Mary, and Joseph!" he shouted in disbelief. "Twenty-five pounds? A month? By God, she's got more money than the King of England." His reaction jarred Claire from her slumber, and she reacted in kind.

Arlis jumped from her seat, silently admonishing her husband with a stern look as she scooped the bawling baby from the cradle.

"Sorry, darlin—sorry," Jamie whispered in apology. "I wasn't expecting that now, was I?" He continued to shake his head in disbelief. "That Ewing fella must be richer than Croesus. How do you fight someone like that? Someone with that kind of wealth and power?"

Thomas looked crestfallen as he spoke. "From what I learned from Liza, the Ewings are an old family of landowners in Ulster, old family, old money. That's why he was so eager to merge his family with the Lassiters. Together, they would have owned most of the land in Derry, Fermanagh, Down, and Tyrone Counties, with their eyes cast on the rest of the province, to be sure."

Pacing the room, Arlis gently patted Claire to settle her after Jamie's outburst, pondering on all Thomas Brady had told them. A kernel of a plan began to take root as she mentally sifted through all that she had learned that day about Edward Ewing, his cruelty, his wealth, and his grand scheme, using his daughter as the deal-closer. She finally stopped pacing and turned, furrowing her brow and chewing the inside of her mouth as though mapping a plan in her mind.

"You're Church of England, am I right, Thomas?"

Jamie stood in frustration. "Arlis, what does it matter what religion the man is at a time like this? From what I hear from ye, you're not too happy with our Church right now. Let's figure something out to get this Liza out of there—and fast."

She ignored him and kept her eyes on Thomas. "Thomas, you're an Orangeman, are ye not?"

"Aye, I am. Church of England, my whole life. Why does that matter now?"

Smiling slyly, Arlis looked from Jamie to Thomas. "Because, my fine gentlemen, we're going to threaten to expose the convent and their nasty goins-on to the Orangemen in the North. How do ye think the archbishop will feel when he sees one of his sacred convents exposed for what it is—the convent's mother superior, no less, keeping donations for herself? Why, he'll never be able to raise a penny for the Church."

"Darlin, ye can't take on the whole Catholic Church because of one nasty nun and her convent. Holy Mary! You'll get us all excommunicated."

"Aw, Jamie. To quote the good book—'O ye of little faith.' "

Chapter Eleven

1966

Arlis woke before Claire and slipped quietly from the room. After a quick trip to the bathroom to wash her face and brush her teeth, she hurried down to the kitchen to start breakfast. Everything had to appear normal this morning; there could be no hint of the drama that was upon them. How could this be happening again—after all these years?

She had lain awake most of the night, hugging Claire close to her. She was overwhelmed with guilt that she hadn't protected her daughter from her attack last night, but, by God, she would protect her from any future assaults she might face. Although Claire's attack bore a striking resemblance to Minnie's so many years ago, that was where the similarities ended. There would be no priest invited into their home to question their daughter. There would be no recriminations, and there would most definitely be no incarceration in the Convent of the Guardians of the Penitent to *cleanse* her daughter of any defilement.

Heavy footfall sounded on the stairs signaling her husband's imminent presence. She shook her head sharply and brought herself back to the tasks at hand— frying a rasher of bacon and acting as normal as possible. "Good morning to ye, husband. Did ye sleep well?"

Jamie nodded in acknowledgment and took a seat at the breakfast table. "Would have slept better if my mate were lying beside me. I meant what I said last night, Arlis. Your place is beside me—all night, every night."

"I know, Jamie. And I'm willing to sleep in our bed, as long as your snoring doesn't keep me awake. And that's the truth." Arlis put his breakfast before him and added a light kiss on his cheek to appease him. As she turned away from him, Jamie grabbed her wrist and gently pulled her down on his lap. He slid his hand tenderly along the shape of her body and pulled her to him in a deep kiss. He let his lips linger on hers as he looked deeply into her eyes. "That's the proper way to greet me in the morning, darlin, not a quick peck."

After he finished his breakfast, he rose from the table and headed for the clothes rack to don his jacket, patting his wife's shapely derriere. "Now, that should keep me going for the rest of the day. I'll see ye tonight." As he pinned his shield to his jacket, he looked at his wife questioningly. "Shouldn't Claire be down by now? Is she keeping late hours with her latest fella?"

She struggled to keep her smile bright. "Ye should know how long it takes a young girl to make herself presentable to the rest of the world, Jamie. She'll be down soon. I'll be sure to tell her ye asked after her. Have a good day, darlin. Be safe." Jamie, seemingly satisfied by her vague excuse, gave her a cheerful wave and was gone.

Arlis's legs were shaking so badly, she barely made it to one of the kitchen chairs. Her heart was throbbing, and her chest was heaving. Ever since she brought Minnie home from the convent, Arlis had made it her life's mission to actively help many young girls escape the clutches of Sister Assumpta and the Guardians of the Penitents. She was always calm and clear-headed when planning these *escapes*, but this was different. The girl at the forefront of this latest rescue mission was her own daughter, Claire.

The sheer number of these tragic women was astounding. Arlis realized early on that a life dedicated to hating and vengeance was a wasted life. Of course, she had moments of anger, but they were fleeting. She decided long ago that she would take her anger and sadness and use them to fuel a new purpose in her life—to do her utmost to make sure no girl was so blatantly robbed of her life as Minnie had been.

But this was Claire—and her father was a copper! How could she tell Jamie about Claire's attack? No man in Ireland would be safe from his wrath. He would be the one who wound up in gaol for murdering someone. But she couldn't keep this from her husband. She would have to tell him. She thanked God he wasn't like her father, Paddy O'Shea. No, Jamie loved her and their daughter more than life itself. She would have to tell him everything, but not until she worked out every detail. Her heart ached for the pain this would bring him. He would, of course, blame himself. She would have to help him heal as well as Claire. As strange as it might sound to someone who wasn't a parent, Arlis knew that Jamie's pain would last long after his daughter's healed. And she would be there for him, just like he was always there for her. Her mind wandered back eighteen years, to the day her doctor gave them the heartbreaking news that there would probably never be another child for them.

****

There was no real medical reason; it was just God's will, as the doctor put it. They had no trouble conceiving Claire, but that was when Arlis was twenty-one years old. Although they'd never tried to prevent pregnancy—and risk the damnation of their souls, according to the Holy Church—they were careful to do some natural family planning, as best they could. It wasn't until Claire was approaching her second birthday that they began in earnest to have another child—and began in earnest to worry that something was wrong. Jamie never cast any blame. He just accepted it as the way things were and told Arlis that she and their daughter were all he wanted. He adored his wife and daughter, and they were happy.

****

Her breathing finally returning to normal, she rose and started to clear Jamie's breakfast dishes from the table when she heard the stairs squeak. She walked quietly through the kitchen and stood in the hallway, her head cocked toward the stairs. "Good morning, Min. Are ye ready for breakfast?"

Minnie sat on the stairs midway up the staircase, her legs pulled to her chest, her nightgown taut around her thin body, her ever-present baby doll clutched in her right hand. Arlis thought she looked so tiny sitting there with her baby doll, more like a little girl than a thirty-five-year-old woman. "Is Jamie gone?" Minnie whispered.

She smiled tenderly at her sister and walked up the stairs to sit with her. "Yes, Min. Jamie's gone.

Everything's going to be okay. I promised ye last night, didn't I? We just have to figure some things out, is all. Why don't ye go into the kitchen and pour your tea? I'll go wake Claire, and then the three of us will have breakfast. How does that sound?"

Minnie studied her sister's face and, as usual, found the comforting strength that made her feel safe and secure. She smiled shyly and nodded her head. "I'll wait for ye and Claire in the kitchen."

Arlis gently pulled her fingers through her sister's now-thinning hair and cupped her cheek. As always, her heart ached for her younger sister. She inevitably felt a mixture of deep sadness and intense anger in Minnie's presence: sadness for the innocent child who endured so much suffering; anger at the people who caused it; the rapist, her parents, her priest, and the nuns at the convent. These people were responsible for the person Minnie was today—a thirty-five-year-old child who had her life and her baby stolen from her. Arlis quickly admonished herself and let the anger go, but the sadness would always remain. "That's me girl. Off ye go now. We'll be right there. And, Min, remember— Jamie isn't Da."

Minnie managed a tremulous smile and nodded again as she rose from the stairs.

As she watched Minnie walk through the hallway to the kitchen, Arlis recalled her first *rescue*. It was the day she brought Minnie home from what she referred to as the first circle of hell.

Chapter Twelve

1947

The day dawned with all the promise of spring; birds chirped gaily as the warm air ruffled their new feathers. By noon, the sun shone brilliantly in the cloudless sky. The O'Brien family, with their visitor from Belfast in tow, headed out of the village in the borrowed truck of one of Jamie's cousins. Arlis and Thomas were crammed tightly in the front seat next to Jamie at the wheel. Little Claire was seated snugly on her mother's lap, her eyes wide with the new experience of riding in a moving vehicle.

A feeling of anticipation charged the air— anticipation, and dread. What if her plan didn't work? What if Sister Assumpta stood her ground and called Edward Ewing—or even worse, the constabulary? And the most dreaded *if* of all—what if Liza refused to leave with them?

There was no concern that they would face any difficulty freeing Minnie. She was of no use to them any longer. And even if that horrid mother superior contacted the O'Sheas—what did it matter? Paddy didn't have the financial wherewithal to keep Minnie shut up in the convent, not like Edward Ewing.

"Now, Thomas, remember. Just stand there, close to the gate. Ye have your notebook and pencil with ye?" Ye have to look official. Everything depends on ye looking like ye mean business."

"Yes, Arlis," Thomas nodded nervously. "I just stand near the gate, holding my notebook and looking serious."

She glanced sideways at Thomas, and her resolve faltered. Although this man was as old as Jamie, he had the soft face of a boy. His cheeks were flushed, making his freckles stand out across his slender nose. His cinnamon hair lay in damp curls around his face.

"Holy Mary, Thomas, furrow your brow or something. Ye look like we caught ye with your hand in the biscuit jar. When we get there, just follow my lead and don't say anything. I'll do all the threatening there is to be done. You just stand there and look serious. Ye have to look like ye mean every word you're saying, or I'm saying, that is."

She turned to her husband. "Jamie, ye know what ye have to do? Just lean against the truck and look mean. Try to remember how mad ye were last year when Finn McMahon asked me to dance at the ceili. Ye remember that, don't ye, luv?" A smile played at her lips as she looked intently at her husband.

"Very funny, darlin. Ye want me to look that mad, do ye? I might frighten those ladies in black to death, and then what?"

Arlis patted Jamie's knee, which was pressed tightly against hers in the truck's cab. "Well, that would surely make it a whole lot easier, and that's God's truth." She sucked in a deep breath as the walled convent came into view.

Jamie burst out laughing as Arlis made a quick sign of the cross upon her body. "Seriously, darlin? Don't ye think that's a bit hypocritical?"

"Indeed, I do not, Jamie O'Brien. I know the good Lord is on our side—don't ye? Just because I'm going to war with the likes of Sister Assumpta, doesn't mean I don't love the Lord Jesus."

Jamie chuckled and shook his head as the truck pulled up in front of the gates. Heaving a sigh to expel all joy and laughter from his mind, he fixed an angry look on his handsome face as the rescue team exited the vehicle.

****

As planned, Jamie lounged by the truck, looking fierce and bored.

Arlis held Claire at her shoulder as they approached the gate. Thomas stood to her right, near the gate hinge. Doing a quick check of positions, she squared her shoulders as she pulled the thick bell chord.

Time stood still as they waited for someone to answer the bell. Finally, they heard the creak of the side door and saw a small figure clad in black hurrying toward them. The woman raised her eyes timidly.

Arlis began to speak in a firm but gentle voice. "Good day to ye, Sister. My name is Arlis O'Brien, and I've come for my sister, Minerva O'Shea. Please tell Sister Assumpta I'm here."

She felt a moment of pity for this young woman—a girl, really—who stood inside the gates. Her look was one of utter confusion as she continued to stare at Arlis.

"Sister, I know from being here before that ye are not allowed to speak, so just go tell Sister Assumpta I'm here to take Minerva home."

When the nun did not move, Arlis realized her tone was too gentle. She squinted her eyes toward the young nun and hardened her voice. "Do as I say, girl, go and get Sister Assumpta. *Now!*" The severe tone of the command shocked the nun as she turned and hurried back toward the convent.

Arlis felt a pang of sorrow; the girl could only respond to harsh commands. It had probably been ages, if ever, that this poor little thing had been the recipient of one kind word. *How do these women survive in a world without love?*

It was only minutes later that the novice returned with another nun, much older and severe-looking. Arlis steeled herself. Thomas and Jamie remained in character, both silent but watchful.

Arlis went on the offensive. "Good day to ye, Sister. As I told this novice here"—gesturing with a wave of her hand—"my name is Arlis O'Brien, and I've come to take my sister, Minerva O'Shea, home. So if ye would be so kind as to let me in so that I might gather her, we'll be off in a jiffy and will be troubling ye no further."

"I am Sister Agatha. I know of no arrangements to remove Minerva from our care. Indeed, the girl is in no state to leave. She has been ill since the birth of her child. Even now, our mother superior is away from the convent, visiting a nearby asylum for the mentally ill to seek accommodation for your sister. I daresay, moving her now is most ill-advised."

Although Arlis listened intently, only three words caught her attention—mentally ill and asylum. All other thoughts drained from her mind. Her heart pounded in her chest, and she fought to control her breathing. Somehow, she dug deep within and gathered her strength. There was more than just Minerva's life to think about; there was Liza, too. If she could save only one more person from this hell on earth, then by God, she would.

"I beg your pardon. Sister Agatha, is it?" The nun nodded tersely. "I'm sorry, Sister Agatha, where are my manners? This nice gentleman beside me is a reporter from the Belfast Press. He's doing an article about the rumors of girls being kept against their will at convents like this one." She lowered her voice to a whisper and moved closer to the gate as though her words were for the old nun's ears alone. The nun inched toward the entrance to hear her.

"I know this is a nasty business, Sister Agatha. But, ye see, there are so many rumors tossed around by those godless Orangemen up north. A story like this— not allowing Minerva to leave by her own free will—is certain to leave quite a black mark on the Holy Church. And how will that affect the bishop and the priests hereabouts, not to mention the wonderful nuns such as yourself who have devoted yourselves to helping these poor penitents."

Arlis stepped back and glared at the nun. She raised her voice. "Now, as I asked before. If you would be so kind as to let me pass these gates, I'll gather my sister and be away quick as a wink. I assure ye, I take full responsibility for my sister's health—mental and otherwise."

Sister Agatha continued to stand inside the gates, returning the young woman's glare. It was several minutes before she conceded defeat. She nodded stiffly to the young novice, turned on her heel, and walked quickly back to the gloomy building. The girl carefully removed the large gate key from the pocket of her habit. Arlis noted how the girl's hand shook as she unlocked the gates.

Clutching Claire tightly, she followed the novice into the convent. This time, they used the side entrance, rather than the front door they entered on her first visit.

The young nun remained silent, but she looked back several times to make sure Arlis was following her. Climbing three flights of stairs, Arlis found herself in a large room littered with several occupied beds. The infirmary, she surmised.

Most of the girls huddled in fetal positions in their beds; one girl was sucking her thumb. Arlis's heart tripped. Finally, at the back of the room, under the window, was a lone bed in which lay Minnie, sleeping like an angel.

She forced herself to keep her control as she approached her sister. "Minnie, Minnie luv, it's me, Arlis. I've come to take ye home, darlin."

Minnie's eyes opened slowly. "Arlis, is this a dream? Am I dreaming? Can we take Brian, too? I haven't seen him for a while, Arlis. Can we take him, too?"

"Come on, darlin, up ye go." She helped Minnie to stand on shaky legs. It was apparent that the girl hadn't been out of bed for a while. She was weak from inactivity. "There now. Let's get your shoes on. Never mind the stockings. Just your shoes. Is there anything else ye have, Min?" Her heart broke at her sister's reply.

"Just my baby. I think Brian's in the nursery. I'll ask Sister Elizabeth to get him."

At the mention of Liza's convent name, Arlis replied quickly. "Yes, let's ask Sister Elizabeth to help us."

Arlis remembered that Liza provided medical attention to Minnie's hand the last time she was there. Perhaps she worked near the infirmary. By this time, a large group of girls, women of all ages, gathered around. The young nun who guided Arlis to the infirmary had disappeared.

She struggled to keep her voice light and calm. "Good day to ye, girls. I'm here to take my sister home. I was wondering if you might find Sister Elizabeth for us. Do any of ye know where she might be on this lovely day?"

The zombie-like group just stood, staring with lifeless eyes. Arlis choked back tears, thinking that would be Minnie's life if she were left here. Movement in the back of the room caused Arlis to hold her breath. Was it Sister Assumpta? As the crowd parted, a small figure in black emerged.

The novice Elizabeth stood wide-eyed as she beheld a miracle. "You came!"

"Yes, I came, thanks to ye. Now Li…Sister Elizabeth, as ye can see, my hands are a bit busy with my little one. Would you be so kind as to help Minnie outside? I have a truck waiting to take us home."

Elizabeth hesitated as she looked around. "I should ask Sister Assumpta for permission."

Arlis pressed on. "I can't manage my babe and my sister. Please, Sister. It will only take a minute."

Elizabeth shook her head sharply. "Of course. Of course, I'll help you." She slipped her small arm around Minnie's waist as Minnie wrapped her arm around the novice's slight shoulders. "Here, Minerva, lean on me. We'll get you home."

Minnie offered a weak smile. "Can we stop and get Brian, too?" Sister Elizabeth shared a sorrowful look with Arlis then quickly looked away. "Let's get you out of here first."

****

It seemed like an endless walk down the three flights of stairs, through the long hallway, and out the building's side door. All the while, Arlis prayed fervently that Sister Assumpta would not appear. The path from the building to the gate was short, but today, Arlis felt it stretched for miles.

Sister Elizabeth kept her head down, concentrating on keeping Minnie's feet moving, so she exited the gate before lifting her eyes toward the truck. She saw the big, fierce-looking man standing guard by the door of the vehicle. There was another man on the other side, but she took little notice of him.

Jamie opened the door and helped Minnie into the cab as she stumbled into his arms. Arlis quickly passed the baby to Jamie and turned to the young novice.

"Thank ye, Liza."

At the sound of her given name, Liza jerked her head up and looked at Arlis. "What did you call me?"

"I called ye Liza. That's your name, isn't it?"

"How did you know?"

Thomas came slowly around the back of the truck. "Because I told them, Liza."

Liza's legs collapsed beneath her, but Thomas was there to catch her. He eased her to the ground. "How? Why? I don't understand, Thomas. Why are you here? You must go. If Father finds out, he'll kill you." She began to sob in fear—and joy.

Arlis knelt beside her. "Listen to me, Liza. Listen

to me. We can explain everything on the road, but now we have to leave before Sister Assumpta returns. Do you understand? We have to leave now."

"But I can't leave." Liza choked. "Father will kill Thomas. I can't leave. I love him. I can't let Father hurt him. And where will I go? I have nothing."

Arlis put her hands on either side of Liza's face and held her firmly, forcing the hysterical girl to look at her. "Liza, listen to me, please. We don't have much time. Thomas is here. He's safe—ye'll both be safe—once we leave this place."

Clutching Thomas's hand, Liza's hysteria continued. She shook her head in hopelessness. "Father will find us. Where will we go?" she repeated.

Jamie was sitting in the cab of the truck holding Claire when he glanced in the rearview mirror and saw a car making its way down the narrow road. "Holy Mother of God!" He beeped the horn. "Darlin, we've got company." As if in slow-motion, the small group turned in unison.

Chapter Thirteen

The taxi pulled up behind the battered truck, and the tall, reedy nun with the hawkish face slowly exited the hired car. The look on her face quickly turned from confusion to comprehension as she took in the scene before her—Minnie sat huddled in the cab of the truck, very close to a rather large man who, oddly enough, was holding a baby at his shoulder.

Minerva's sister was kneeling on the ground a few feet from the truck. She appeared to be talking to the novice Elizabeth who, Sister Assumpta noticed, was weeping violently as she, too, knelt on the ground, clutching the hand of a well-dressed man. The nun chose to direct her comments to whom she considered to be the weakest link in this disparate group.

Quickly dismissing the car, the black-clad woman glared at her target. "Sister Elizabeth, what is the meaning of this? What are you and Minerva doing outside the gate? Both of you return at once behind the convent walls." The mother superior turned toward the gates, confident that neither Liza nor Minerva would dare to defy her.

****

The woman's lack of acknowledgment and total disregard for what was happening was the fuel Arlis needed to face her enemy head-on. She spoke quietly to Thomas and Liza as she rose slowly and strode toward the truck. Reaching into the passenger's side, she grabbed a white envelope from her purse and walked toward the mother superior.

Speaking in a firm voice that belied the terror she was feeling, she raised her voice. "Hold on there, Sister. The only place anyone is going is away from here. I've come to take my sister home. She's of no use to you, now that you've stolen her child." She continued to walk toward the nun and stopped when Sister Assumpta abruptly halted her steps and whirled around, her black veil whipping in the breeze.

"Young woman, you would be wise to watch your tongue. You are speaking to a woman religious of the Church, and you will show me the respect I deserve. Is that clear?"

Catching the nun off guard, Arlis lowered her eyes and spoke softly in reply. "Oh dear, Sister, I must have lost my head for a moment. I will, indeed, show ye the respect ye deserve."

The nun glared at her, nodded sharply, and turned to enter the gates.

Arlis continued to speak as she raised her eyes and returned the nun's glare. "Ye see, I get like that sometimes when my temper's up. And, by all that's holy, it's up today. As I said, I'm here to take Minerva home. She doesn't belong here or in an asylum. She's not mentally ill; she needs care and love. She needs to heal from the loss of her child—the child you stole from her."

The mother superior opened her mouth in retort, but Arlis continued. "Don't try to deny it. I know what goes on here." She enunciated her next words very carefully. "Everyone knows what goes on here. I promise ye, if it takes me the rest of my life, I will find Minnie's son; if it's the last thing I do, I will find him."

She gestured with her thumb, indicating Thomas. "Ye see this nice man, Sister? This gentleman is from up north. Ye know, the Orangemen are just waiting for him to write his story about what goes on behind these proper convent walls. Ye try to stop me from taking my sister, and her tragic story will be appearing in all the papers up north in the blink of an eye. So ye just go on about your business, Sister. I'll be taking Minerva now." Arlis continued to stare at Sister Assumpta. It was evident from the black look in her eyes that the nun was struggling to control her fury.

The mother superior raised her voice. "Sister Elizabeth, inside the gates—*now*!"

Liza had remained crumpled on the ground, her head in Thomas's lap, her sobbing quiet but relentless. Her body jolted at the sound of the nun's voice, and she attempted to stand.

Arlis spoke in a rush. "Oh, I knew there was something else. In all the excitement of taking my sister home, I almost forgot to tell ye, Sister. Elizabeth is also coming with me. I've been in touch with her mother, and to her way of thinking, four years is long enough to keep the poor girl walled up inside that place. So, she's coming home with me."

Sister Assumpta began to speak, an evil smile on her lips. "Elizabeth is not going anywhere with you. Her mother has no authority here. I deal directly with her father, Mr. Edward Ewing. It is his wish that Elizabeth remain here with the Guardians of the Penitents, where she will soon take her final vows and spend the rest of her life in this convent. If you insist on removing her, I will contact her father immediately, and I assure you, neither you nor Liza want to deal with him."

Arlis closed her eyes as Liza's keening grew louder. She breathed deeply to control her temper, which now coursed hotly through her veins. She began to speak slowly, but with such force, even Jamie was astonished by her intensity.

"Liza is leaving with me. And before ye go threatening me, ye old wagon, ye would be wise to heed *my* threat." She raised the white envelope she'd been grasping and waved it in the air. "I have here a full accounting of all the money you've received from Liza's father over the past four years. The bank has verified the accounting, so there will be no denying it—from him or ye."

Sister Assumpta sneered at Arlis. "Any money that Mr. Ewing has seen fit to gift us over the past four years is just that—a gift. That money is to feed and clothe his daughter. And I have detailed records to prove it."

Arlis shook her head, smiling in derision as she walked up to the nun. She now spoke in a whisper so quiet, Sister Assumpta had to bend her head to hear what Arlis was saying. "If ye interfere with me taking Liza today—or if ye contact her father, now or in the future—I will give this information to the Archbishop. Ye see, Sister, the report I have here"—she waved the envelope again—"clearly shows that not one pound, not one shilling, not one penny has gone anywhere but into *your* pocket. All that money over the years and not one penny has gone into the Church coffers or the convent accounts. Now, I'm no solicitor, but I think that might come under the heading of fraud or some such thing. That could mean gaol, I'm thinking. Not to mention how the Church would see it. And the press? Especially up north?"

Arlis enjoyed seeing all the blood drain from the wretched woman's face as panic replaced the fury in her eyes. She continued whispering. The nun was so close now, Arlis was speaking directly in her ear.

"Now, believe it or not, ma'am, I'm not a vengeful person. I just want to take my sister home with me so I can care for her. And I want Liza here to have a chance at a normal life, not cooped up behind those walls with the likes of ye. So how about we make a deal? I'll take Liza today, and ye won't tell Mr. Ewing that she's gone. He will continue to send ye your monthly *payment* like always, and no one's the wiser. Ye can do with the money what ye will. I promise ye here and now that I will tear up this report—in front of ye, if ye like—and it will ever just stay between the two of us women—a sacred bond, so to speak. We both get what we want. I get freedom for Liza, and ye…well, ye remain in the good graces of the Holy Church and out of gaol—and ye keep getting your nice, generous allowance." Arlis stepped back and smiled sweetly at the nun.

"How do I know you're not just making all this up to take Elizabeth away from here?"

"Well, I guess ye don't." She shrugged her shoulders, arching her eyebrows and raising her voice. "But I will tell ye that since May of 1943, you've been receiving payments, in cash, from Mr. Edward Ewing, twenty-five pounds a month to keep his daughter a prisoner behind those walls there. That's three hundred pounds a year if my mathematical skills are still up to snuff. Does that sound about right to you? And goodness, three hundred pounds a year for four years, along with all the money you're skimming off the top from those American adoptions? My, my, Sister Assumpta, you're probably the richest woman in all of Ireland. Come to think of it, I should just give this little envelope here to that nice young man yonder, and have done with it. Ye don't deserve to get away with anything."

As she turned to walk away, the nun's arm shot out and grabbed her, digging her claw-like nails in Arlis's arm. "Destroy that damn thing and take the girl. Go. Now! But first, I want to see you rip that to shreds." She pointed to the envelope in Arlis's hand.

Arlis yanked her arm out of the older woman's grasp and backed away. "I'll do better than that." She turned and strode over to the truck, struggling to calm her breathing and regain some control of her hands, which now shook uncontrollably. She whispered something to Jamie and waited for him to hand her something. She walked back to the nun, and standing defiantly before her, opened her palm to reveal a small match. Scraping it over the sole of her shoe, Arlis watched a tiny flame erupt from the end of the slender piece of wood. She held the nun's glare and lit the envelope in her hand, twisting it to make sure it completely caught fire. She held the envelope until flames devoured it. As an act of final disdain, she tossed the flaming paper at the nun's feet and watched as it disintegrated into ash and smoke.

Turning, she sauntered back to Liza and Thomas. Raising Liza to her feet, Arlis guided her into the bed of the truck, Thomas climbing in behind her. She gently removed the black muslin veil that encased Liza's head and tossed it carelessly onto the dusty ground. As she closed the tailgate, Thomas covered Liza with a blanket and held her close.

Without looking back, Arlis opened the passenger door and slid in next to her sister, who, mercifully, had fallen asleep. Jamie passed the baby into her outstretched arms.

From all outward appearances, Arlis looked calm and serene; only Jamie could see beyond the façade she carefully erected. He squeezed her shoulder in love and admiration as he started the truck and pulled back onto the road.

She rested her head against the seat and closed her eyes. She spoke quietly. "Jamie, I think I'm in some trouble here."

Jamie gave her a sidelong glance and chuckled softly. "Ye think? By all that's holy, darlin, from what I heard, ye just blackmailed a nun. I think that might be cause for excommunication, to be sure. And you're telling me ye *think* you're in trouble?"

Arlis blew out a breath she had been holding and buried her face in her baby daughter's soft curls. "I am. That envelope contained a copy of my recipe for soda bread that I promised Brenda I would drop off this afternoon. Now, I have to go home and re-copy it. I'll be late getting to Brenda's."

Jamie swerved the truck as he glanced at his wife. He stared at her briefly, shocked into silence. Shaking his head, he laughed deeply, in awe of his wife's courage and tenacity. "Darlin, ye are the music of my heart, and that's God's truth."

Arlis looked lovingly at her sister sleeping beside her. She gently brushed her hand on the girl's cheek and closed her eyes, a peaceful smile on her face.

Chapter Fourteen

1966

Arlis quietly opened the bedroom door and tiptoed across the room. Claire was lying on her side, her back to the door. She sat on the edge of the bed and gently rested her hand on her daughter's slender hip. "Luv, are ye up to having some breakfast? Maybe just some tea and toast? Minnie's waiting to see ye downstairs."

"Is Da gone? I can't see him, Mum." Claire choked back a sob. "I can't have him see me like this."

In one motion, Arlis stretched out next to Claire and turned her around so that her daughter was nestled close to her, her head resting on Arlis's bosom, just like last night. She held her as, once again, both mother and daughter poured out their grief in the safety of one another's arms. Both took comfort in the familiar touch, both grieved the things that would never be the same.

They lay like that until all their tears were spent. Claire was the first to speak, her voice hoarse from crying.

"I can't seem to put two thoughts together because I can't get last night out of my mind. The memories won't let anything else in. Oh, Mum, Mum. What am I going to do? I don't know what to do."

Arlis stroked her daughter's hair and kissed the top of her head. "Claire, we'll get through this, I promise.

It's not what you're going to do; it's what we're going to do. Luv, always remember. It's us—together. Now, we can't undo what happened last night. But we can't—we won't—waste another minute wishing it didn't happen. For the time being, I'll do the thinking for both of us until those memories fade—and they will fade, luv, they will fade.

"Now, why don't ye go wash up and come downstairs? I left some makeup out in the bathroom, in case ye want to use it." She hesitated a moment, taking a deep breath before she spoke. "Darlin, I think I know your answer, but I have to ask it just the same; shall I call Doc Madden?"

Claire gave a hopeless shrug. "Why? It's just bruises now. He can't undo what's been done, what's been lost."

"No, he can't do that. I just thought I'd ask." Arlis stroked her daughter's arm and gave it a gentle squeeze. "Just thought I'd ask. Now, why don't you take a nice hot bath and soak for a while? I set out some bubble soap for ye. Minnie and I will wait for ye in the kitchen." A final kiss to the top of Claire's head and she walked from the room.

As she passed through the doorway, she heard Claire's small voice. "Mum?"

Arlis turned and cocked her head.

"Mum, thank ye. Thank ye for believing me. I don't know what I'd do if ye didn't believe me. And thank ye for not asking questions—questions I can't answer. I love ye, Mum."

Arlis worked her mouth, chewing the inside of her lip. "Luv, I do believe ye. And I know ye would tell me everything if ye could. And ye will when you're ready.

I believe ye, and I love ye. I'll always be here for ye, and so will your da. I promise ye. We'll get through this, Claire darlin." She managed a tender smile and closed the door.

****

Minnie, the ever-present baby doll clutched in one arm, was bustling around the kitchen when Arlis entered the room. "Is Claire coming down, Arlis? I made a pot of tea for her. See. I even put her favorite cup out, jam for the toast, too." She smiled proudly at her accomplishment.

"Oh, Minnie. The table looks grand—truly." She beamed with pride at her sister. "Claire's going to take a bubble bath this morning. She'll be down soon. But let's not wait. Let's us enjoy a cuppa. How would that be?"

Minnie nodded and took her seat at the table. Arlis noticed that she was toying with the teaspoon. "Min? Is everything all right? Do ye want to talk about something?" After years of caring for her, she was adept at reading her sister's frame of mind. Since bringing her into their home, Arlis and Jamie had both been very aware—and very careful—to shield Minnie from undue tension and stress. Perhaps because of this awareness, the O'Brien home was always filled with love and security. Because of his sincere love and concern for her over the years, Jamie had gained Minnie's trust.

Arlis knew Minnie was upset last night. Her sister saw Claire's physical state when she came home. She might be emotionally-stunted from her past traumas, but Minnie was also perceptive. She might not have seen the bruises, or the torn clothes and blood, but she saw the look in Claire's eyes, heard the terror in her niece's voice. Minnie's instincts told her what Claire suffered, and Arlis knew that at that moment, the long-buried memories of her attack slithered back into her sister's fragile mind.

But she was surprised—and relieved—this morning to note that Minnie was trying very hard to fend off those old feelings of her own terror and betrayal.

Minnie smiled and put down the teaspoon she'd been twirling nervously in her hand. "Yes, Arlis. I want to tell ye something." She carefully laid her doll down on the table beside her teacup. "Give me a minute. I want to say this right." She pressed her lips together as her eyes darted back and forth, as though she were trying to gather her thoughts. As she began to speak, the emotionally-stunted woman-child faded away, and in her place, a woman appeared.

"When Claire came home last night, I saw how she looked, and I got scared—scared for Claire and me. It all came back—all of it. And ye know what the worst memory was, Arlis? It wasn't that man on top of me; it wasn't the convent or the laundry or my hurt hands. It wasn't even losing Brian, though I miss him terrible. No, the worst memory was Da and Mum, not believing me. Right then, I got scared that, maybe, Jamie wouldn't believe Claire, and he would send her away to that place.

"And then, it was like an angel came to me in my sleep and told me to look inside myself and see. I did like the angel told me, and somehow, I looked deep inside. And do ye know what I saw, Arlis? I saw Jamie's face, smiling at me and teasing me and taking

91

care of me, and I realized that Jamie isn't like Da. He would never desert his daughter like Da did to me. He's your husband, Claire's father, and my friend. He loves all of us, truly."

Arlis sat in rapt attention, silently weeping at the simple truth of her sister's heartfelt words. Neither she nor Minnie noticed the door open or the man standing in the doorway until they heard Jamie's stifled sob. "Arlis? Where's Claire?"

****

Jamie sat at the kitchen table, crying unashamedly and trying desperately to quell the rage boiling within— rage at the man who assaulted his daughter, rage at Arlis for keeping this from him, rage at his helplessness. He sat with his head in his hands, gripping his hair as if to rip it out by its roots. "How could ye not tell me last night, Arlis? How could ye not?"

Arlis sat across from him, head bowed in sorrow, in guilt. "I was going to tell ye tonight, Jamie, after I thought things through."

"Thought things through? What things would they be? How to keep this from me? How to hide my own child from me?" His voice rose. "What things, Arlis?"

"Da?"

At the sound of Claire's voice, Jamie jumped up and ran across the room to his daughter. He enveloped her slender body in a gentle embrace. His voice, wracked with sobs, moaned her name. "Claire, Claire. I'm so sorry, darlin. I'm so sorry. This shouldn't have happened to ye. I'm supposed to protect ye, and I didn't. Forgive me, darlin. I...I..."

"No, Da. Don't. It wasn't your fault. It just happened." Claire stood in her father's arms, sobbing, as she patted his shoulders and the back of his head, trying to comfort him. "And don't be mad at Mum. I couldn't let ye see me like that last night. I just couldn't. I didn't want Mum to see me either, but she did." She pulled away to look up into her father's eyes. "Da, ye can't be mad at Mum. I need ye both, Da. I need ye both."

Jamie eyed the ugly bruises on her neck and her swollen lower lip. His stomach heaved, and he fought hard not to gag. His vision blurred as his fury burned hotter than the fires of Gehenna. From somewhere far away, he heard a small voice calling his name over and over. He felt two thin arms wrap around his waist from behind as someone laid their head on his back. The gentle voice and light touch calmed the savage beast within him as he struggled to regain some control.

"Jamie? Jamie?" Minnie soothed. "It weren't your fault. Like Claire said, it just happened. But now, you're here, and you'll take care of us, won't ye, Jamie? You'll take care of all us, won't ye?"

Arlis remained seated at the table, allowing Jamie and Claire this moment together. She felt sorrow and shame for not sharing this horror with him last night. Jamie had every right to know. She secretly admitted to herself that she feared he would react as her father did all those years ago. How could she think that of Jamie? He loved her and cared for her and their daughter—and Minnie—for all these years. And yet, in this, their darkest moment, her trust in him faltered. What could she say to him now? She lowered her head to her folded arms on the kitchen table, her chest heaving in unrelenting sobs.

She felt Jamie's strong hands on her elbows as he

lifted her into his arms. Collapsing against him, she lay her head on his broad chest as he buried his face in her hair. No words were needed as they shared their agony in the tears they shed, wrapped in each other's arms, comforted by the two women for whom they wept.

Chapter Fifteen

Arlis lay entwined in Jamie's arms, the silent night encompassing them like a warm cocoon. Neither slept—nor spoke; happy memories of days gone by, coupled with the tragic events of the last two days, crowded their thoughts. The sound of their soft weeping broke the long moments of silence as they held each other close. They wept as they remembered all the happy moments of their life together. Each felt the agonizing pain of the horrors their daughter endured at the hands of a monster. No feelings of blame passed between them, no recriminations, just a sense of deep sorrow for what Claire had gone through. It was in those moments of weeping that Jamie and Arlis clung together, drawing strength and comfort from each other. Finally, Jamie spoke.

"Darlin, you're going to have to help me; help me to let go. I know ye know how to do it. Ye have to teach me to let go of the hate. God forgive me, I have so much hate in me, Arlis, I'm choking on it. Now I know what ye felt all those years ago with Minnie. I'm so sorry, darlin. I'm sorry I didn't understand your pain or your hate then. But I know it now, God knows, and, Arlis, along with all the hate I feel, I'm filled with so much pride in ye. Ye let it all go. Ye took all that hate and all that pain, and ye turned it around to help girls ye didn't even know. Ye took all that hate and pain and, somehow, ye turned it into love—love for those girls who didn't have any place else to turn.

"I see what letting go has done. Because ye refused to let the hate eat at ye, ye raised a fine woman in our Claire. Ye taught her right, and because of what she saw in ye, I know she'll survive this.

"I thought I was proud of ye all those years ago when you took on that old Sister Assumpta. But that was nothing compared to what you've done since then. Your strength—and your courage—shame me a bit, darlin. And that's God's truth. But now that this has come to us, I won't hide behind shame or hate. I understand why ye didn't tell me straight away. Ye knew I'd go off half-cocked and maybe kill somebody. And I'll confess to ye now, I'm still thinking of all the ways I want to kill that devil. But I love ye too much, Arlis darlin. I love ye and respect ye too much to do that. But I'm weak, too, luv, so ye have to show me how to let go." Jamie sobbed as he pulled her closer to him. "Please show me how."

Arlis's heart swelled with love and respect for her husband. She always knew the depth of his love for her and their child. But she was in awe of the complete honesty and humility he now revealed to her. Long ago, she learned that hate could feed on itself forever and continue to grow, destroying all the light and love in your life. Long ago, she'd chosen love over hate, life over death. Together, she and Jamie would make the same choice.

She raised herself to look at the man she'd loved since she was six years old. She brushed his thick black hair off his brow and looked deeply into his eyes. There she caught a glimpse of his soul burning bright with love and hope. She pressed her lips to his, and in that kiss, she offered him love, forgiveness, and salvation.

Chapter Sixteen

Rays of early summer sun slanted through the bedroom curtains. Arlis woke with a start. She looked at the bedside clock and was shocked to see the time. Eight thirty? *Is it Saturday?* No, it's Tuesday, she thought. Suddenly, memories of the past two days made their way through her muddled, sleep-filled brain. She bolted upright and looked to Jamie's side of the bed— empty. Grabbing her robe, she dashed to the bathroom, ran a comb through her hair, splashed water on her face, and hurried down into the kitchen.

Minnie sat alone at the table, sipping her tea and murmuring to her baby doll. "Good morning, Arlis. Jamie and I already had breakfast. There's some bacon left for ye and Claire. Jamie said not to wake ye, but I was to give ye this note when ye came down." She carefully slid a small envelope from under her napkin and offered it to her sister.

"Thank ye, Minnie." She smiled at her sister and kissed her on the top of her head. "And how are ye this morning?" She was concerned that her sister might be upset about everything that happened yesterday, but Minnie appeared unfazed as she cradled her ever-present doll in her arms.

"It's so pretty outside; I think I'll take Brian in the backyard so we can swing a bit. Would that be all right, Arlis?"

Arlis smiled. "Yes, Min. I think that's a grand idea. Ye go on now. I'll just sit here and read Jamie's note. He's probably telling me what he wants for tea." She waited until Minnie walked outside, then wasted no time tearing open the envelope.

Darlin,

We'll talk (the three of us) when I get home tonight. There are some things we should discuss. And call the restaurant and tell them Claire quit. She should take some time off right now, I'm thinking. I'll be home by seven or so.

Jamie

Ps: I love ye, darlin

She smiled and closed her eyes, remembering last night. She shook her head to bring her thoughts back to the present. Yes, she would call Mannion's Restaurant right now and tell them Claire quit. There always seemed to be job openings at the restaurant, so they would probably be caught short, but her daughter didn't need the added burden of a job right now.

She just finished the phone call when Claire entered the room. Arlis tried not to stare at her daughter's fading bruises, but the yellowish marks stood out in stark contrast to her creamy skin.

"Good morning, luv. How are ye feeling today? Da made bacon before he left if you're hungry. Sit down and have your tea."

Claire sat obediently as if in a trance. The dark shadows under her eyes were evidence that she hadn't slept well again last night. She cleared her throat and began to speak.

"Mum, was Da all right last night? He was so upset. I thought he would be mad, but it wasn't that kind of upset. Da was so sad, Mum. He was so sad, he broke my heart. I'm sorry he was sad, Mum. I'm so sorry for everything." Claire started to sob uncontrollably, her breaths coming out in short, deep gasps.

Arlis stood quickly and dropped down to her knees in front of Claire. She placed her hands on either side of her daughter's beautiful face, gently forcing Claire to make eye contact.

"Look at me, Claire. Look at me, luv. Ye have nothing to apologize for now, have ye? Your da's pain yesterday was for ye, it's true. It's natural for a parent to hurt when his child is hurt. Do ye remember when ye were little and ye fell off your bike? Why, your da cried with ye, remember? And he laughs with ye, too, doesn't he?" Claire nodded and managed a shaky smile through her tears.

"Of course, he does," Arlis continued. "Yes, I'll not deny he's sad, but he'll work through it—just like ye will—just like we all will. I told ye, luv, there's nothing we can do about what's happened. So we're going to put all the energy that goes into being upset, and we're going to focus it on something positive."

"Like what?" Claire hiccupped.

"Well, like ye starting your nursing career somewhere. We can't have ye just lolling around here indefinitely." She waved Jamie's note in her hand. "See, your da's already thinking about it. He says right here in this note that we three are going to have a good chat when he gets home from work tonight."

Arlis stood and pulled Claire up with her, wrapping

her in a warm embrace. "I promise ye, luv. We will get through this."

****

It was shortly after seven when Claire heard Jamie's car pull up in front of the house. Her heartbeat quickened with the dread of seeing her father. She knew the words he spoke to her yesterday were sincere, but she also knew whenever he looked at her now, he would think about what happened.

He would never again be able to think of her as his pure, untarnished angel; no, now, and for a long time to come, Claire would be his tarnished angel. Could she bear to see the pain in his eyes, day after day, to see the unwarranted guilt she knew he held in his heart? She lay on her bed, wishing she could erase the last two days, knowing that it was just that, a wish—and Claire was too old to believe in wishes coming true. She heard the light rap on her door and the timid voice of her aunt. "Claire, your da's home. Your mum said to call ye for tea."

Claire smiled at the sound of her aunt's tiny voice. Minnie—a child when she was raped, a child when she was abandoned by her parents and her church, and a child when she bore a child. And yet, here she was twenty years later, surviving as best she could, Claire mused. But Minnie did survive. She might have escaped to the safety of a child's mind, but she was happy. She survived through the unconditional love of Claire's parents, and Claire would survive through their unconditional love, as well.

Although they never discussed it, Claire knew of her mother's tireless efforts over the years, helping so many girls begin to mend their shattered lives. Arlis had, somehow, made contact with a couple in New York, who helped those girls settle in America. Claire was never sure how her mother knew anyone in America, but she did. And she knew that much of her mother's success was because she had the full support of Claire's father, Jamie. They were a pair, those two. Neither of them realized how much they were loved and respected throughout the entire county.

Claire knew she would survive this tragedy, just like her mother told her. But her heart broke because of the pain it caused the two people she loved most in the world.

"Claire? Ye coming?"

"Yes, Auntie. I'll be right there."

Chapter Seventeen

When Claire entered the kitchen, Arlis was relieved to see that her daughter made use of the makeup she left out for her. Although her neck bruises were still quite visible, the cover-up toned down the ugly hues of yellow, green, and purple but did little to disguise the apparent bite mark to her lower lip.

Jamie was seated at the table, reading the evening newspaper. He glanced up as Claire took her usual place at the table. He smiled and spoke quietly. "Hi, luv. How ye doing today?" He forced himself to keep all emotion from his face as he noted the evidence of the attack.

Claire met his eyes and returned his smile. "I'm fine, Da. How are ye doing?"

Minnie, who quickly reverted to her childlike persona after her heartfelt speech yesterday, smiled brightly at Jamie and Claire. "I'm fine, too, Jamie. I took Brian in the yard for a while this morning. I saw pretty birds back there. I'm glad you're feeling fine, Claire. Arlis, can I pour the tea now?"

Arlis turned toward the range, pretending to busy herself as she quickly wiped the tears from her eyes. She chuckled at Minnie's innocence. "Yes, Minnie, ye go ahead and pour the tea."

The meal passed with the usual small talk of the day. Everyone was making an effort to have some semblance of normalcy when, in fact, there was nothing ordinary about the unexpected turn of events of the last few days.

Finally, the meal ended, and Arlis rose to clear the table. "Min, why don't you go in and turn on the tellie. *Quicksilver* is about to start, and I know how much ye like Bunny Carr. He always makes ye laugh."

Minnie looked to Arlis to make sure it was all right to leave the table first. "It's fine, luv. Ye go on. Jamie and Claire and I have some things to talk over. We'll join ye in a few minutes." Minnie smiled joyfully and darted from the room. Arlis turned from the sink and beheld her family—her husband and her daughter—the music of her heart.

Jamie sat with his elbows on the table, his left hand fisted into his right one, his chin resting on them. His eyes were closed, and it was apparent he was trying very hard to control his breathing. Claire was sitting with her hands in her lap, head bowed, eyes closed.

Arlis pulled her chair close to her husband, softly pulling her fingers through his hair as she stroked his cheek. "Jamie, darlin. Ye said in your note that we would talk tonight. Do ye want to start?"

He remained as he was for a moment longer, then placed his large hands together and brought them to his lips, exhaling slowly. He then folded his hands and lowered them to the table as he began. "Aye, darlin. I have something I want to say. Like the both of ye, I've thought of nothing else today, but this situation we find ourselves in—a situation that was not our doing, to be sure."

Jamie stretched out his hands and offered them to his wife and daughter, who responded eagerly. He held their hands in his. "Now, I can sit here and dwell on the bad things—we all can—but, Claire luv, if I've learned nothing else from your mum these twenty-plus years, I've learned that dwelling on things ye can't change, won't change 'em. 'Course, I've learned many a thing from your mum besides that, and that's God's truth. I've learned that loving is better than hating. I've learned that love builds, and hate just destroys. I've learned that even though we belong to a Church, we have to use the brains the Good Lord gave us to think for ourselves and not follow someone—or something—blindly. And, luv, from watching your mum, I've learned to have the courage to do the right thing, even tho' it scares the begeezuz out of us. And finally, and probably most important, I've learned that loving someone means doing what's best for them, even if it shatters your heart to pieces.

"So, all that learning I've done these past twenty-odd years has brought me here—to this moment. I hope I don't disappoint ye by telling ye I don't have any answers. I think I can speak for your mum when I say that any decisions ye make about the days and years ahead are just that—your decisions. We can advise ye, sure, and we will. We can suggest and point out the ayes and the nays of it, but only ye can make the life decisions that are upon ye now. We were hoping that we still had some years left to guide ye and...and protect ye." His voice cracked, and his words faltered. "But that wasn't to be. It wasn't your fault, Claire—and that's a truth you have to hold close to your heart, darlin, always and ever.

"And one last thing. Your mum and I will love ye, completely and unconditionally, until the day we close our eyes for the last time on this earth and open 'em in the Hereafter. The Lord saw fit to give us one child, but He sure gave us the greatest blessing of all when He picked ye to be our one and only." In turn, Jamie raised their hands to his lips and softly kissed one, then the other.

Claire stood and wrapped her arms around her father's neck. "Thank you, Da. But you're wrong about one thing."

Jamie patted her arm and chuckled. "Just one thing?"

Claire smiled through her tears. "Yes, Da, just one thing. The Lord gave the greatest blessing to me. All the people in the world, and He chose ye and Mum for me. And I want ye and Mum to know something—no matter where I go, no matter what the future holds for me, one moment of horror won't change who I am or what I believe because I know without any doubt that your love will carry me through anything. I see Auntie in there, and I know what she went through. Her life changed because she didn't have parents to love her and believe in her like I do.

"And something else—some feeling I've been having all day. Because I know the Lord blessed me with both of ye, I think He might have a plan for me, and maybe, just maybe, what happened might be a part of that plan. I don't mean that He made this happen, but maybe He's waiting to see if I can make something good come out of it—like ye did, Mum. Because of what happened to Aunt Minnie, you've been helping girls all these years, and, Da, you've been right there with her. And maybe ye wouldn't have if ye didn't know, firsthand, what would have happened if ye didn't help them."

Claire kissed Jamie's cheek, then rounded the table to hug her mother. "Thank ye, both of ye. Thank ye for loving me and teaching me to love back. Well, time for bed. Lots to think about. Good night."

Arlis and Jamie watched their daughter leave the kitchen, a different person than when she entered. No, Arlis thought. She was the same person. It was just that she and Jamie were seeing her in a different light.

Jamie continued to stare at the doorway through which Claire just passed. His voice was thick with emotion as he grasped his wife's hand. "By God, she's just like you, darlin—the music of me heart."

Chapter Eighteen

Jamie pushed himself away from the breakfast table as he drained his coffee cup. "I best be off, darlin. Have to drive down Kilkenny way to see about some poachers, but maybe I'll stop by for a cuppa around noon." As was his habit, he reached for his shield, but it was not where he put it yesterday evening. Furrowing his brow, he tried to remember what he did with the badge when he came home last night. He heard Arlis laugh as she began to speak.

"Is this what you're looking for, husband of mine?" She smiled as she walked toward him and pinned the metal badge on the thick chambray. She slowly ran her hands across Jamie's broad chest, smoothing out the front of his shirt before trailing her hands up to his shoulders. She didn't stop there as she wrapped her arms around his neck.

He automatically responded by sliding his arms around his wife's waist and drawing her to him. Their lips met in a chaste kiss. The kiss ended, and Jamie lifted his head as Arlis opened her eyes. They held each other's gaze, each silently conveying to the other that at that moment, more was wanted—more was needed. Jamie's arms tightened around her waist as Arlis drew his head down to meet her welcoming lips.

There was nothing chaste about this kiss as their lips parted and their tongues played a quick Hide 'n

Seek. Jamie's hands moved slowly around Arlis's back as her fingers enjoyed the luxuriant softness of her husband's thick hair. Somewhere, in the distance, a small voice brought them back, reluctantly, from the precipice of passion.

"Good morning, Jamie. Good morning, Arlis. Can I have toast and beans this morning?"

Jamie and Arlis ended their kiss, both quietly laughing at the interruption. Jamie smiled at Arlis and kissed her brow.

"Well, now, that's the way to start my day, to be sure." He glanced at his sister-in-law. "Good morning to ye, Minnie luv. I think toast and beans sound grand. Why didn't I think of that?" He patted her shoulder as he headed for the door. "Have a good day, my ladies." He turned, sharing a knowing smile with his wife.

Arlis's heart tightened as she watched Jamie walk out the door. Something had changed between them since their daughter's attack. Perhaps it was their shared grief that brought them closer than they had ever been before. But she believed that it was more than that. It was the realization that their love created their daughter, an incredibly strong woman who would weather the storm in which she now found herself.

Through the years, Jamie's love and desire for Arlis never waned—nor hers for him.

Their only regret was that Claire was the sole product of their union. Seeing the beautiful, courageous woman she had become left them both in awe. Now, in a blink of an eye, Claire stood on the threshold of whatever new life she would choose for herself. And neither Jamie nor Arlis doubted what her choice would be.

****

The week passed quietly—almost normally. The only thing out of the ordinary was the feeling that change was coming; even Minnie knew things were going to be very different in the weeks and months to come. But rather than feeling apprehensive, Minnie was experiencing an inexplicable sense of calm and happiness.

She always enjoyed a special relationship with Claire. Perhaps it was because Claire filled the gap left by the absence of Minnie's child. In Claire, Minnie found an infant she could dote on, a child she could play with, a young woman she could call a friend.

But it was also because Claire was Arlis's daughter, and Minnie loved Arlis more than she loved anyone else in the world. Arlis was her mother, her sister, her friend, her savior, literally. Minnie's life could have been a lonely one, but Jamie and Arlis and Claire worked through the years to ensure that she lived a happy, full life—in spite of the permanent scarring on her psyche. When Claire finally left home, would Minnie be able to emotionally survive the loss of someone who'd been a part of her life since she was a young girl?

****

Sunday morning dawned, and the birds chirped happily with the promise of a new day.

Arlis lay entwined in Jamie's arms, awake but resting contentedly in the warmth of his embrace. A light rapping broke her reverie.

"Yes, come in, Minnie." She experienced a moment of surprise when Claire peeked her head into the room.

"Morning, Mum. I thought since it's Sunday, we could all go to church together in Kilkenny. It's a lovely day, and I know Minnie would enjoy the ride. Do ye think ye can roust Da from his beauty sleep?"

Jamie sighed and pulled Arlis closer to him, keeping his eyes closed as he began to speak in a husky, sleepy voice. "Da doesn't need beauty sleep; he's pretty enough. But if my girls want to nourish their souls a bit, who am I to stand in their way? Give me thirty minutes, and we'll be on our way, luv."

Arlis smiled and scooted out of bed as Jamie gave her hip a playful tap. "Is Minnie awake? Tell her to dress for church, Claire. I'll be down in a jiffy."

"Minnie's all dressed and waiting for us on the front swing."

Arlis noticed that Claire hesitated for just a moment, a tender smile on her face as she stood gazing at her parents.

"Claire? Is everything all right?"

"Grand, Mum. Everything is grand. We'll be waiting downstairs."

Arlis joined Jamie in the bathroom as he lathered his face. She stood behind him, wrapping her arms around his bare midriff as she laid her head on his back. He brought his razor to his throat, looking at his reflection in the mirror. "And what do ye think this is all about, darlin?"

She smiled sadly and sighed. "I'm thinking, dear husband, that our Claire has come to a decision, and I think we need the good Lord to give us the strength to live with it." She gave one final squeeze around his waist and walked into the bedroom to dress.

****

After Mass, Jamie joined Claire and Minnie in the car while Arlis stopped every few feet, receiving a hug from this person or exchanging niceties with that one.

"I didn't know Mum knew so many people in Kilkenny, Da." Claire commented.

Jamie watched his wife greeting people as she made her way to their car, his heart swelling with pride. "Well, luv. I'll tell ye the truth. Your mum has helped a good many people over the years; it's just her way."

Claire heard stories about these rescues, and she knew her mother was the one who orchestrated them, with the help of her father. She felt a moment of sadness that now she was one of those girls who needed rescuing, but at the same time, she felt incredible pride that it would be her own mum—and da—who would rescue her now.

****

As Minnie helped Claire clear the table that evening, Jamie and Arlis sat, sipping their tea, knowing that Claire was on the brink of making an announcement. They shared a sad smile observing their daughter rinse every plate with exceptional care as she played for time. Arlis finally spoke.

"Claire luv. Sit and have your tea. Your da and I are thinking you've come to a decision. Will ye share it with us?"

Minnie continued to wash the dishes as Claire sat down across from her parents.

"Minnie, would you like to sit with us? There are some biscuits in the tin."

"No, thank ye, Arlis. I'm going to sit on the front swing with Brian for a while. Would that be all right?"

Arlis shook her head in wonder. She knew that

Minnie was aware of the forthcoming conversation. Although her sister had the emotional development of a child, sometimes her perceptiveness and intuition gave Arlis pause. "Yes, Minnie. Ye go and enjoy the sunset."

Minnie hung the towel carefully on the rack by the sink and turned toward Arlis. "I love ye, Arlis. I love ye and Jamie—Claire, too. And we'll all be fine. We'll all be just fine. You'll see."

Arlis was shocked into momentary silence as she shared a look with her husband and her daughter.

Claire smiled. "Thank ye, Auntie. I'll come out later and watch the sunset with ye. How will that be?"

Minnie walked through the doorway, smiling over her shoulder. "That would be grand, Claire. I'll be outside."

"Out of the mouths of babes," Jamie said quietly. He raised his eyes to his daughter, silently urging her to begin.

"Right ye are, Da. Sometimes I think Minnie is wiser than all of us." Jamie and Arlis nodded in agreement.

Claire took two deep breaths, reached for her parents' hands, and closed her eyes, as though she were gathering her courage. The touch of their hands gave her the strength she needed to speak. "Well, I've made my decision. I've thought about moving to Dublin, but somehow it doesn't feel right; I'm sorry to say that nothing here in Ireland feels exactly right just now. I've thought about staying here and putting things on hold for a year or two until I feel more natural about everything, but then I think about staying here—so close to...well, to what happened, and I realize I'm not brave enough to do that. I don't want either of ye to think me a coward, but I have to go away." She choked back a sob. "Please understand. I can't stay here; I just can't." She took a steadying breath and continued.

"As I told ye the other day, I feel, somehow, that God has a plan for me in all this. In church this morning, I felt it again. I feel my life is in America now." She gulped and quickly added, "It's not that I want to leave Ireland. I love this place; everyone and everything I love is here, but I can't rid myself of this feeling that my life is over there, waiting for me.

"And I want to be completely honest with both of ye. Since the attack, I don't think I could ever be with a man...in a married way, I mean. I know ye told me the memories would fade, Mum, but what if they don't? And then everyone in town will know something happened. I could never live down the rumors—or the truth."

Jamie closed his eyes and hung his head. Arlis held her tears in check as Claire continued.

"In America, I could *get lost in the crowd*, as they say. America is so big; it will be a lot easier to get lost. I know it's going to be hard for all of us, but I truly believe it's the only way."

She squeezed her parents' hands in turn. "Please, Da, don't be mad—at yourself or me. And Mum, I'm sorry I don't have your strength to stay and work things out, but I don't, and that's the truth of it."

At her last words, Jamie abruptly lifted his head and opened his eyes. "Mad at ye? How could I be mad at ye? And don't say ye don't have your mum's strength. It takes a person with real courage and strength to leave all she knows and travel to a foreign place. I would never have the courage to do that."

He chewed his lip, fighting tears. "Claire, your mum and I both support your decision. It's the right decision for ye. I told ye the other day, your mum and I love ye beyond our own lives. You're the music of our hearts, to be sure."

While Claire was speaking, Arlis was remembering the countless girls she helped flee Ireland for America in hopes of starting anew. Never did she imagine that one day her own daughter would be doing the same thing. Her heart was shattering into a million pieces. How would she bear her child's absence? How would she make it through the day without seeing Claire's beautiful face? Without hearing her lilting voice, her laughter? How could she make it through the night without a goodnight kiss? Without snuggling with her in bed during a storm? Jamie was right when he said Claire was the music of their hearts. And when Claire left for America, Arlis knew her heart would never sing again.

Chapter Nineteen

Brooklyn, New York, USA, June 1966

The family stood waiting patiently as the steady stream of passengers walked through the doorway after clearing Immigration. The young boy twirled the sign he held in his hands.

The petite redhead glared at her brother. "Mom, tell Sean to hold the sign still. What if she walks right past us 'cause he's got the sign backward or something? Honestly, Sean, act your age."

Fourteen-year-old Sean Brady crossed his crystal blue eyes and twirled the sign even faster in response to his sister's chastisement. As he opened his mouth for a rude retort, his father intervened.

"Enough, you two. Sean, Bridget's right. Hold the sign steady. I'm sure there's more than one passenger named O'Brien coming through that door, and we don't want her to walk past us."

Tom Brady reached for his wife's hand. "Nervous, luv?"

Liza Brady smiled up into her husband's face as she clutched the small photo. "Not nervous, exactly. I guess excited would be what I'm feeling just now." She took another quick look at the image in the picture and continued to scan the crowd.

Suddenly, Bridget started pointing and waving her

hand. "I see her, I see her. She looks...she looks...oh, man she's drop-dead gorgeous! Mom, do you see her?"

Liza rose on her tiptoes, attempting to see over the crowd of people in front of her. Her breath caught in her throat. Although Arlis sent them a picture of Claire so they would recognize her, the photo didn't do the girl justice. Dressed in a simple black skirt and a white blouse with a pale blue sweater tossed carelessly over her shoulders, the statuesque beauty walked with her head down, totally unaware of the glances and more prolonged stares from people as she passed.

Sean Brady followed the direction of his sister's waving hand. His eyes opened wide as his heart skipped a beat. He could only manage a raspy whisper. "That's her?"

Tom Brady smiled at his son's reaction. "Sean, close your mouth, and let's go help the young lady get her bags." Still grasping Liza's hand and giving his son a gentle nudge, Tom wended his way through the throng of humanity. Bridget Brady had no thought of politely wending as she pushed her petite frame through the crowd.

Claire had just raised her head when she spied a tiny teenager with a mass of copper-colored curls running toward her, her arms outstretched, her cheeks flushed with excitement, and a broad smile decorating her Irish Colleen face. Any trepidation Claire was feeling about meeting her parents' friends, Tom and Liza Brady and their family, vanished as the young girl flew into her arms and hugged her tightly. She was talking so fast, Claire was having trouble following her.

"Claire, hi. I'm Bridget, Bridget Brady. Oh my gosh, you're beautiful...and tall." She turned and looked over her shoulder. "Oh, here come my mom and dad." She grabbed Claire's hand and pulled her toward Liza and Tom, who were drawing near. "Mom, Dad, c'mere. It's Claire."

As Tom Brady approached, he grinned broadly and kissed Claire lightly on the cheek. "Hello, Claire dear, I'm Tom Brady. It's so nice to meet you finally. The last time we saw you, you were just a tyke in your mother's arms." He looked from Claire to Bridget and furrowed his brow. "I see you've already met our daughter, Bridget." He gestured to the gawking boy with cinnamon hair standing next to him. "And this is our son, Sean. Sean, can you find your tongue and say hello to Claire?" Sean continued to stare, wide-eyed, at their guest. "Sean, say hello." The boy nodded mutely but managed a shy smile. Tom chuckled and shook his head.

Claire felt almost giddy with relief. These people were so welcoming; she smiled warmly to each one in turn. Looking past Sean, she saw a woman standing alone. Claire recognized her mother's long-time friend from a photo Arlis had given her.

Liza didn't speak, just opened her arms wide, silently offering Claire a place in their family. Claire stepped eagerly into Liza's warm embrace. She might not be in Ireland, but, somehow, Claire felt that she was home.

****

Tom Brady took Bridget and Sean aside while they waited for Claire's luggage to come off the plane. He cautioned them on overloading their guest with questions about herself or information they wanted to share with her about themselves.

"You must both understand that Claire just finished an extremely long trans-Atlantic plane trip. She left her home in Teaghlach almost twenty-five hours ago. She traveled to Shannon Airport to catch the plane, which then crossed the ocean and went on to Montreal, Canada, and from there to Chicago, where she changed planes for New York. I'm exhausted just thinking about it.

"Also, there's the time-change factor, not to mention being in a foreign country for the first time. And don't forget, Claire just left her entire family—her dad and mom and her aunt. I hope you'll understand if she's a bit reticent about joining in conversation for the first few days."

Bridget nodded in understanding. "I'll take care of her, Dad. Mom said Claire's here because there are more opportunities for young people in America, not so much in Ireland." She shook her amber locks and looked away, a slight tremble to her chin, her voice thick with emotion. "I don't think I'd be brave enough to leave you and Mom and everything I know to start a new life in a new country."

"Aw, Bridget the Gidget's gonna cry...boohoo." Sean rubbed his eyes in feigned sadness.

"I'd be happy not to see you again," Bridget shot back. "Hey, I have a great idea. Why don't we send you to Ireland to live with Claire's parents? They don't have any other kids. They might like a son." She looked at him and sniffed. "Maybe not. Nobody's that lonely."

"Enough, you two." Tom turned toward the luggage carousel as it began to move. "Claire said there are five bags, and they all have ribbons with red, white, and blue stripes on the handles." He chuckled. "Arlis's idea, I bet—red, white, and blue for the old USA."

Sean spotted them on the second turn. "Bridge, get the smaller one." She quickly nodded in compliance. "Dad, I have those two; you get the last two."

Tom Brady was relieved that his children were finally working together. With all of them cooperating, they headed out the door to the taxi stand in minutes.

****

When they exited the terminal at LaGuardia Airport, Tom hailed a cab. Claire had just a moment to take in her surroundings before she slid into the back seat of the taxi, next to Liza. The activity going on around her overwhelmed her senses; people of all nationalities hurried to their various destinations, taxis honked, buses beeped, and planes soared overhead. There was an excitement in the air—unmistakable electricity that was at once both terrifying and exhilarating. New York City.

The taxi ride from the airport to the Brady's Brooklyn home was brief and, much to Claire's relief, made in almost complete silence. She closed her eyes and heard her father's voice as he whispered his parting words into her ear. I *love ye, Claire darlin. You're the music of my heart.*

Chapter Twenty

The taxi pulled up in front of an enormous chocolate-brown building with a steep flight of stairs leading up to a small stoop. On the way from the airport, Bridget explained that they lived in what was called a *brownstone*. Each brownstone connected to a replica building on either side.

As they exited the cab, Claire gazed in wonderment at the activity on the street—children playing, people walking by, and taxis constantly honking. Flower boxes decorated every window of the building. She noticed an older woman sitting on the stoop of the next brownstone. The woman smiled and waved as, one by one, the Bradys trudged up the stairs, each carrying one of Claire's bags.

Bridget spoke first. "Hi, Mrs. Sabella." Gesturing to Claire, she continued. "This is Claire. She's from Ireland—my mom's best friend's daughter. She'll be staying with us for a while." Turning back to look at Claire, she gestured her head in the older woman's direction. "Claire, this is our neighbor, Mrs. Sabella. She lives next door."

"Bridget. Enough." Liza shook her head and laughed. "Good day to you, Maria. We'll stop over tomorrow for proper introductions."

Maria Sabella, who had been patiently waiting on her stoop for two hours to get a look at her neighbors' guest, beamed at her neighbors. *"Bene, bene! Domani!"* Her eyes lingered on the tall beauty who nodded to her and smiled shyly. As Maria turned to enter her home, she smiled and whispered to herself in Italian, *"Bella ragazza,* beautiful girl."

****

After a light snack, Liza gave Claire a quick tour of their home. As they climbed the stairs to the second floor, Liza told Claire how she and Tom emigrated to America twenty years ago. "Tom found a teaching position in Brooklyn, so that's why we settled here. We've made a good life here, Claire. I know you can do the same." As Liza opened the bedroom door, she smiled at Claire. "I hope you'll be comfortable here, luv."

Claire slowly looked around the room. It reminded her of her bedroom back in Ireland; it was apparent that Liza might have left Ireland, but Ireland hadn't wholly left Liza. The cheery floral wallpaper with matching curtains and bedspread, the braided oval rug, the small writing desk in the corner, the chair with the tufted back and skirted bottom all spoke of Ireland. Claire was sure the room was decorated just for her, and Liza's efforts deeply touched her.

She sighed and sank onto her bed as Liza quietly closed the door behind her, finally leaving her alone. Claire welcomed the solitude just now. She would try not to think of her mother and father and Minnie. She couldn't dwell on *what if*; she had to deal with the reality of the situation. The decision to make this drastic change in her life was hers and hers alone. So Claire was determined to make a success of the choice she made. Although she missed her parents terribly, Claire couldn't deny the excitement she felt from the moment she landed in New York. She was determined to start her new life here.

Her thoughts turned to the other members of her new *family*. Liza's husband, Tom, was very nice, very gentle. Seventeen-year-old Bridget was like sunshine on a dreary day; she made everything sparkle with her enthusiasm. Although they had just met a few hours ago, the two had bonded like long-lost sisters. She always wanted a younger sister to talk to, to share things with—maybe not everything, she thought sadly.

Claire smiled as she thought of Sean. Although he was a gawky tween right now, someday he would be a nice man like his father. The Bradys were all warm and welcoming.

She slid off the bed and knelt. Putting her hands together and bowing her head, she began to pray. *"Thank ye, Lord, for bringing me here to these good people. Please take care of Da and Mum and Minnie, and take away their anger and their sadness. And please take away my anger and my sadness. Thank ye for all that you've given me. And please have mercy on that devil's soul. In Jesus' name. Amen."*

A light rap on the door interrupted Claire's meditation. "Claire, Mom wanted me to tell you supper's ready. You coming down?"

A quick sign of the cross and Claire rose and walked across the room and opened the door. "Yes, I'm coming, Bridget. Thank ye."

"Oh, I just love the way you talk, Claire. The guys are going to go nuts when they meet you."

Claire's stomach clenched as the smile froze on her face. It took all her concentration to hide her reaction to

Bridget's innocent comment. The thought of some man putting his hands on her made her feel faint.

"Claire, are you okay? You got pale all of a sudden."

"Oh, it's nothing, really, Bridget. Just that long plane ride and I haven't adjusted to the time difference yet. I'm fine, truly." She smiled sweetly, willing all negative thoughts from her mind. She patted Bridget's shoulder and followed her to the dining room.

Tom Brady and his son rose from their chairs as Claire and Bridget entered the room and sat at the table. Liza bustled in from the kitchen with a steaming pot roast. After Tom said grace, Liza began to pass the food, and conversation started. Claire felt as though she'd been sharing a meal with this family her whole life.

"Oh, by the way, family," Liza began. "Maria Sabella invited us over for dinner tomorrow. She's very eager to meet Claire."

Bridget put her fork down and casually twirled a lock of her hair. "That sounds like fun. You'll like the Sabellas, Claire. They're all nice."

Sean rolled his eyes and whined. "Oh, yes, Claire, they're all really nice, especially Frankie Sabella. He's really, really nice, isn't he, Gidget?"

Bridget's naturally pink cheeks flamed red, almost matching her hair. "Shut up, Cee-ann. You're such a jerk. You're—"

Tom Brady's quiet voice rose quickly. "That will be enough from both of you. If you can't behave with any decent manners, you may leave the table— immediately. Shame on both of you. What must Claire think of us?"

Liza began to speak quietly. "Sean, apologize to Bridget for teasing her. And Bridget, apologize to your brother for those remarks. Or, you may choose to leave the table as your father said and go to bed without supper."

"Sorry, Bridget. Just having some fun." Sean blushed as he mumbled his apology.

Bridget glared at her brother. "Sorry, Cee—Sean."

Tom looked sternly at his children. "Well, neither of those apologies will win any awards, but let's try to finish our meal as civilized people, shall we?" He looked at Claire. "We three apologize to you, Claire. Your first night in America, and we've shown you, first hand, that we are uncivilized colonists."

Claire was sitting quietly, biting her lip to keep from laughing at the siblings' exchange of insults. She kept her eyes downcast as she began to speak. "Well, I guess what they say is true. Ye can take the person out of Ireland, but ye can't take Ireland out of the person. That good old Irish dander was flying tonight, to be sure. Ye would all be welcome in Teaghlach any time."

She slowly raised her eyes and looked at Tom Brady and then at Bridget and Sean. In unison, the family burst out laughing in relief.

Liza shook her head in feigned disgust. "Welcome to our family, dear. We sit before you, warts and all."

Claire smiled. "Thank ye for the warm welcome. I think I love ye already—warts and all."

Chapter Twenty-One

"Somebody answer the phone, will ya?" Pete Callahan hollered from the storeroom.

"Yeah, yeah. I got it. Hello, Engine 250, Raimy speaking." Joe Raimy stifled a yawn as he stretched his back, waiting for a reply. "Hello? Joe speaking. Can I help you?"

"Hallo? I speak to Antonio. I wait."

Joe covered the receiver with his hand and chuckled. He quickly dismissed the laugh before answering the caller. "Just a minute, Mrs. Sabella. I'll find him for you." He covered the mouthpiece again, and in his best singsong voice, he called out. "Oh, Antonio. An-ton-i-o Sa-bel-la. Your grandma's on the phone. An-ton-i-o?"

Tony Sabella came around the corner of the fire station, broom in hand. "What? Who's calling?"

"It'sa you nonna, Antony. Come on, *paison*, don't keep her waiting."

Joe shared a smile with his friend as he crossed the room. Tony grabbed the phone, keeping his hand over the mouthpiece. "Nice accent, Raimy. Remind me to teach you a few choice words in Italian sometime."

Joe grinned. "*Bene*, Antonio, *bene.*"

Tony raised the phone to his ear. "Hi, Nonna. Everything okay?"

Maria Sabella smiled when she heard her favorite

grandson's voice. "Antonio, you come for dinner tonight, after work."

"What's up, Nonna? Do you need something fixed?"

"Yes, yes, I need something fixed. You come."

"Okay. Just so I bring the right tools, what am I fixing?" He waited. No response. "Nonna? What am I fixing?"

"I don't know. I think of something. You just come after work."

Tony heard a soft click as the call ended. He smiled and shook his head. *Here we go again. Nonna, Nonna. Are you ever going to give up?*

Pete Callahan joined Joe at the table in the kitchen of the fire station. He gestured to the coffee pot on the stove as Tony hung up the phone. "Fresh pot, Sabella. What did your grandmother want?"

Joe noted the look on Tony's face. "Oh, Antonio. Does Nonna have another Italian dish for you? Jeez, I should be so lucky as to have my grandma looking out for me like that."

"Stuff it, Raimy. You might think you'd like it, but my grandmother isn't going to rest until some breezie has me roped, tied, and branded. How about we trade places for a while?"

Pete tipped back his chair and laughed. "She only wants to see you happy, Tony boy. Any guy here— except for us happily-married men, of course—would gladly change places with you if your nonna would keep bringing those good-looking chicks home."

Tony forced a good-natured laugh and went back to sweeping the sidewalk in front of the fire station. *Yeah, sure, trade places...if only.*

Joe and Pete exchanged looks as Tony walked away. They joked about his grandmother always trying to fix him up, but his friends were seriously concerned about him. Ever since he got back last year, it was apparent he wasn't the same Tony they knew before going to Vietnam; to say he changed was an understatement.

When they were teenagers, Tony was the Romeo of the group. There wasn't a skirt that was safe when Tony was around. He never forced himself on a girl—he didn't have to. One look from his seductive brown eyes, one mischievous smile, and girls practically melted in his arms.

Friends always surrounded Tony; he was smart, he was funny, he was loyal—an all-around good guy. He was also a considerable chick magnet—a big plus because wherever Tony was hanging out, there were always scads of cute girls around. It didn't bother any of his friends that they got Tony's cast-offs. If you couldn't get 'em one way, you'd get 'em another.

But that was then. Since Tony got back, he stayed pretty much to himself. He might go for a beer with the guys, but girls? Never. He was still friendly with them; he might even flirt a bit, but he steered clear of the opposite sex for the most part.

He never shared his experience in Nam with his friends. The guys knew he had been injured; his unit took a beating in a place called Pleiku. Several of his buddies were killed, and about one hundred twenty-five had been seriously injured, Tony included.

There were no visible scars, but his friends knew not all wounds were visible; Pete's brother-in-law had lost his mind over there after a raid on a village where dozens of Vietnamese women and children were killed.

Since returning home, Tony's friends decided to stay close to their buddy, kidding him, sure, but always staying close in case he finally broke and needed someone to listen. So far, that hadn't been the case, and Tony remained silent about Vietnam.

The first shift ended, and the firefighters of Engine Company 250 headed home—to their wives, to their girlfriends, to their solitude.

"Got time for a short one, Tony boy?"

"Naw, thanks though, Pete. I'm going to head home and clean up before I go to my grandmother's. Besides, I have to get my toolbox—you know, for whatever she needs fixed. I wonder where she found this one. The niece of the cousin of the aunt of the brother of the guy who works in the butcher shop? Who knows? Maybe she's right off the boat from Italia. You have to love my nonna's tenacity, that's for sure." Tony laughed and sighed. "I just wish she'd give it up, already. I'll see you tomorrow. Have a good night, Pete. Kiss Katie for me and the little guy, too."

Pete Callahan slapped his friend on the back. "See you tomorrow, *paison.*" As he started to leave, a thought popped into his head. "Hey, Tony. This one might turn out to be the love of your life. Have a little faith."

Tony smiled and waved absently to his friend, his mind dwelling on Pete's last comment. *That ship has sailed, my friend. Even if I meet the love of my life, how will anyone love what I am? No, this is as good as it gets; having an occasional beer with my friends and visiting Nonna a couple of times a week until she's gone...or I am.*

He crossed the street without looking, his thoughts turning to a dark place he was beginning to visit more often. *Could I do it? Could I? It would kill Nonna. Mom and Pop would never get over it. What would Frankie think? I'm supposed to set the example. I'm supposed to be the strong one—the man. Man? Now, that's a laugh. I can't make love to a woman anymore; kids are out of the question. What good is a man if he can't be a man? Maybe they would understand if I—*

"Bro, wait up."

Tony abruptly left the darkness when he heard his younger brother's voice. "Hey, Frankie, what's happening, man? You going to Nonna's later? Mom and Pop, too?"

Frankie smiled up at his big brother, his hero. He not only looked up to Tony literally—Tony towered over his little brother with his six-foot three-inch muscular frame—Frankie idolized Tony. He was everything Frankie thought a man should be: funny, smart, smooth with the ladies, a sharp dresser—and a war hero.

"Oh, yeah. It's gonna be great. The Bradys are coming over, too. Nonna wants us all to meet Mrs. Brady's friend from Ireland."

Tony glanced sideways at his brother. "And their little red-haired cutie is coming, too, I suppose?"

"Who? Oh, you mean Bridge?" Frankie shrugged nonchalantly. "Yeah, I guess."

"Take care there, little bro. Don't let things get out of hand if you know what I mean—and I know you do. I'm not going to preach to you like Mom and Pop do. I'm just saying be cool. And be nice. Don't break her heart."

"I know, I know. Sheesh, you sound like an old man. Where's my love-'em-and-leave-'em brother? Did you leave him back in Nam?"

Tony stopped abruptly. "Is that what you think I did? Loved 'em and left 'em? God, I hope that's not what they think of me." He stood gazing into space, lost in thought.

Frankie squinted his eyes and looked curiously at Tony. "Hey, man. I was just kidding, honest. But you do kinda sound like an old man."

"Frankie, I didn't leave myself in Nam. I came home with something, though. I came back understanding a couple of things—that the world is more than just what I want and that life can be over in the blink of an eye—at any age. Life is precious, and you only go around once, so, man, don't screw it up, okay?

"I'm sorry I sound like an old man, but that's the way I feel. Just be kind and forget about what you want, what makes you feel good. Be more concerned with helping people. I guess that's why I became a fireman, like Pop. I want to help people and protect them. It doesn't matter if I risk my life to save them. Even if I don't know them, their lives are important to somebody, so they're important to me. Love, buddy, not kissy-kissy love, but love for each other. That's the kind of love that makes the world go round."

"I hear you, Tony, and I understand what you're saying, but you still sound like an old man."

Tony laughed, wrapping his arm lovingly around his brother's neck as he mussed his curly black hair, so much like his own. "Maybe I should borrow Nonna's cane tonight. Whaddaya think?"

Chapter Twenty-Two

Claire dressed carefully for dinner at the neighbors'. She wanted to make a good impression on the first real Americans she would be meeting. She didn't consider the Bradys *real* Americans because they hailed from the same part of the world as she did. These neighbors, the Sabellas, were born here in America—well, at least the younger Mrs. Sabella was born here along with her children.

Liza had told her the older Mrs. Sabella, Maria, emigrated with her husband and three small children when she was a young woman in 1925. Maria had been a widow for almost fifteen years. Although she lived alone, her children and grandchildren were practically daily visitors to her home. They were a close, loving family, but her reputation as the best Italian cook in Brooklyn certainly was one of the reasons she rarely spent an evening alone.

The sleeveless black linen sheath flattered Claire's lithe figure, the broad white collar bordered the scoop neckline and graced her swan-like neck. The dress length fell just above the knee, accentuating her long shapely calves and slender ankles. Because of her height, five feet eight inches, Claire always shied away from high heels. Her simple black pumps with a stack-heel complimented her dress. A single string of pearls—a gift from her parents for her sixteenth birthday—and tiny pearl earrings completed her outfit.

Claire wore her black hair in a simple flip that skimmed her shoulders. Her only makeup was a light coral gloss. She just finished applying the lip gloss when Bridget knocked on the door.

"You ready, Claire? Can I come in?"

"Come in, please."

Bridget bounced into the room. It suddenly occurred to Claire that Bridget bounced everywhere. Immediately, the room came alive with movement—and it was all Bridget.

Her cornflower-blue eyes opened wide in surprise.

"Oh…my…God."

Claire looked down at her dress, then glanced in the mirror of the dressing table. "What? Isn't this proper? Too much color on my lips? Bridget? What? Tell me."

A broad grin appeared on the teenager's flushed face. "I'm going to ask mom if we can walk down the street before we go next door. I want all my friends to see you. Claire, you look like a movie star. Maybe we could make up a story about you, you know, a mystique." As she spoke, she became more excited.

"Oh, let's not tell anyone who you are. Let them guess. We can make them think you're a rock star from England or something. We could tell them you're one of the Beatles' girlfriends. Yeah, that's it. John Lennon's girlfriend. This is going to be so cool."

Just then, Liza appeared in the doorway. "What's going to be so cool, Bridget? You girls ready?"

"Mom, let's not tell anyone who Claire is. I'm going to try and pass her off as John Lennon's girlfriend. Cool, huh?"

Liza shook her head. "No, Bridget, not cool. Gracious, Claire is our guest, not your plaything. When she does meet your friends, our friends, anyone, you will introduce her properly. She is the daughter of my dearest and oldest friend from Ireland. Do you understand?"

"Yes, Mom. But I think John Lennon's girlfriend is so much cooler."

Once again, Claire found herself stifling a laugh at Bridget's shenanigans. "Thank ye for the compliment, Bridget, but I'm not a big Beatles' fan."

Bridget stood in shocked silence, her mouth gaping, her eyes bulging. Finally, she found her voice. "You're not a Beatles' fan? Who do you like? The Rolling Stones? The Supremes?"

Claire smiled. "I hate to disappoint ye, Bridget, truly I do. But I like Perry Como and Jerry Vale."

The disappointment on the Irish colleen's face was laughable. Liza struggled to keep a straight face as Bridget began to speak. "Come on, then. You're going to fit right in with the Sabellas." She turned and slowly walked out of the room, shoulders slumped, her pretty mouth turned down in a severe frown.

Liza called after her. "Frankie will be there with his brother."

Bridget sighed. "Well, there's that."

****

Sean barely lifted his hand to rap on the door when a tall, broad-shouldered man opened it. He wore a crisp white shirt, sleeves rolled midway up his forearms because of the August heat. He extended his hand in greeting.

"Tom, Liza, come in, come in. Mama told me she

heard your door close, and she didn't want you waiting outside—too hot. Bridget, you and Sean go find Frankie. He's with some neighborhood kids. They're waiting for you on the roof. I guess they have a radio up there, too."

"Thanks, Mr. Sabella." Bridget turned to her parents. "Is it okay, Mom?" Can we go up to the roof, please?"

Liza exchanged a meaningful look with her daughter. "Yes, you may go."

Bridget and Sean hurried toward the door.

Tom called after them. "Behave, the two of you. I don't want any complaints from our neighbors in the other buildings about any loud music."

"Yes, sir. We'll be good little kiddies." Sean waved his arm as they headed out the door.

The layout of the Sabella apartment was the mirror-image of the Brady home. Claire found it fascinating that two places could be identical in design but so different in decor. Where the Brady home was light and airy, heavy, traditional furniture decorated Maria Sabella's apartment. Pictures covered every square inch of wall space: landscapes, reproductions, and family photos. Heavy brocade curtains framed the floor-to-ceiling windows, which were now open, allowing the city's sounds into the large living room.

Claire felt surrounded by warmth—and it wasn't because it was eighty-five degrees outside. No, the warmth she felt was an emotional warmth and a genuine welcoming feeling emanating from the people to whom she was now being introduced.

Liza slid her arm around Claire's slender waist. "Maria, Enzo, Angie, this is Claire O'Brien. She's the daughter of my dearest friends back home. We're so excited that she's here." She gently pulled Claire closer to her in a gesture of sincere affection. "Claire, these are our friends, Mrs. Maria Sabella, and Mr. and Mrs. Enzo Sabella."

Enzo beamed and nodded to Claire. "Hello, Claire."

Angie Sabella smiled warmly and extended her hand. "Claire, it's wonderful to meet you. Liza has spoken of you and your parents often. I feel as though I know you already." She gently squeezed Claire's hand with both of hers.

Claire smiled shyly, nodded to Enzo, and returned Angie's gesture. "It's lovely to meet ye, Mr. and Mrs. Sabella." She turned to the older woman dressed entirely in black, who had been standing behind her daughter-in-law.

Claire trembled slightly under the woman's scrutiny. She was hoping her voice wouldn't betray her nervousness. "How do ye do, Mrs. Sabella? Thank ye for inviting me to your lovely home. It's charmin'." She tentatively offered her hand.

****

Maria Sabella had, indeed, been studying her guest. Once again, she was struck by the girl's beauty; it was natural, and it wasn't just skin deep. But Maria sensed there was something more, something Claire was careful not to display—the girl had been hurt, and hurt deeply, and recently. Just like her Antonio. *So much pain for people so young. Deo!*

She watched as the girl extended her hand in politeness. Maria cocked her head to one side as Claire spoke. The Irish lilt was the tipping point. She gently pushed Claire's hand aside and gathered her in her arms, a broad smile lighting her wrinkled face. "*Benvenuto in casa mia*! Welcome to my home."

Chapter Twenty-Three

Maria and Angie disappeared into the kitchen as Enzo led the group into the living room. "Come in and sit down. How about something to drink? Tom, a beer?"

Tom Brady smiled and nodded in appreciation. "Thanks, Enzo. I'm genuinely parched."

Enzo grinned in response. "One beer coming up. Liza? A beer? I'm getting one for Angie, too."

"Yes, Enzo, that would be grand." She turned to Claire. "I don't usually drink beer, but it's been so hot, it sounds just right." The group nodded in agreement.

Enzo glanced at Claire. "What can I get you, Claire? Along with the beer, I have soda, lemonade, and water."

"Lemonade would be grand." Claire spoke softly. "Thank ye, Mr. Sabella. May I help ye serve?"

"Sure, I never refuse an offer of help. Come on."

Tom and Liza watched Claire follow Enzo out of the room. Tom reached for his wife's hand and whispered, "She'll be fine, honey. It's just going to take some time, that's all."

Liza's gaze lingered at the kitchen doorway. "I know, dear. She hasn't told me anything yet, but it's bad, I fear. It's bad."

"She'll tell you when she's ready, Liza. And you'll be there when she is ready. You always are."

138

"Thank you, Tom. I have to help that girl. I owe her mother everything. I'm here with you and our two rapscallions up on the roof. What more could I ask for?" Liza leaned over and kissed her husband softly just as Angie and Enzo entered the room carrying their refreshments.

"Enough of that, you two. We leave you alone for a few minutes, and you're all over each other." Angie laughed.

Liza colored slightly and smiled. "Where's our charge? I'd hate to tell her mother we lost her already."

Enzo grimaced slightly. "I think you did lose her, Liza. Mama has certainly taken to that young beauty. I don't know if you'll ever get her back."

"Well, at least I can assure Arlis she'll be in good hands. I can't imagine anyone or anything getting past Maria."

Just then, the phone rang. Enzo picked up the receiver. "Hello, Sabella's."

"Pop, it's me. Tell Nonna I'm sorry, but I can't make it for dinner tonight. Big sixer just got called in—a warehouse in Harlem. I'm heading back to the station now. Tell her I'll stop by after, if it's not too late."

Enzo's heart tightened. "I'll tell her, Anthony. And son, be careful. God bless you."

"Thanks, Pop. Will do. Give Nonna and Mom a kiss for me. I love you."

Enzo stood holding the receiver to his chest.

"Is everything okay, En? Is Anthony all right?"

"Yeah, hon, he's okay. He got called back to work. Six-alarm in Harlem. I'll go tell Mama he'll be missing dinner." He replaced the phone as he headed to the kitchen. He stopped in front of his wife. "Oh, yeah, this is from Anthony." He bent down and kissed his wife on the cheek. He started to raise his head but lingered for a moment before putting his finger beneath Angie's chin and gently lifting her head. "And this is from me." His lips touched her uplifted mouth as she smiled.

Angie spoke in a quiet voice. "Thank you, honey. Tony will be fine, Enzo. God will take care of him. It's not his time, just like it wasn't his time over there. He has a full life ahead of him. I know it. Besides, he hasn't given us a grandchild yet."

Enzo traced his finger down his wife's cheek. "Okay, sweetheart." He turned to Tom and Liza. "It's so nice to be married to someone who can see into the future." He glanced back at Angie. "It doesn't take a fortune teller to tell me how Mama's going to react. Here goes..."

Angie watched him walk into the kitchen. "I don't think my husband realizes how I felt every morning when he left for work. He was a fireman for forty years, and not a day went by that I didn't worry that he wasn't going to make it home in one piece. Why can't my men have chosen safer careers?"

Liza smiled in sympathy. "It must be so difficult for you, Angie. I guess all we can do is pray that, as you said, it's not their time yet. At least Anthony made it home safely from Vietnam. All his injuries have healed?"

"Well, his physical injuries have healed completely; we're not so sure about the emotional trauma. Anthony's changed since coming home. You remember how he was as a kid—gregarious, always chasing the girls, or rather, they were chasing him. Enzo and I used to worry that Tony would screw up his life. But then, he went to Vietnam, and when he returned, he was different.

"He stays pretty much to himself. He rarely goes out with his friends, let alone on a date. He's so introspective now. And he seems driven to help people. It's like he's making up for some past wrong." Angie sighed and swallowed hard.

"On the bright side, we see him more now than we did when he lived with us. He goes out of his way to spend time with Frankie, and he always tells us he loves us. He's very attentive, especially to Mama. He makes sure he visits her often. You see him here, right?"

Liza and Tom nodded in unison. "You're blessed with a wonderful son, Angie," Liza said softly. "I've dealt a lot with emotional trauma. And I can tell you, it takes time; it takes time and lots and lots of love."

"But how much time? Weeks? Months? Years? And will our love for him be enough?"

"Each person is different," Liza offered, "so they react to their trauma differently. And I'll be honest with you; it could take weeks, months, or years.

"I know the kind of man Anthony is. He doesn't appear bitter or angry; he just appears sad. With your love—and, I'm sure, the love of the right girl—Anthony will, as you told Enzo, lead a full life, a happy life."

Angie Sabella rose from her chair and walked to Liza. She bent over and hugged her. "Thank you, dear friend. Your words of wisdom are a balm to my troubled heart. Now, let me see what's happening in the kitchen. Tom, would you gather the kids from the roof?"

"Sure. And, Angie, you and Enzo did a great job

with Anthony. He'll make it through."

"Thanks, Tom. You're a dear." She turned as the front door opened, and three flushed faces appeared. "Oh, look who's here. Just in time, kids. Go wash up. I'll tell Mama everyone's here."

"Hi, Mr. and Mrs. Brady." Frankie looked around the room. "Where's Tony? I thought you said everybody was here."

Enzo walked through the kitchen door, his arms laden with an enormous platter. "Anthony just called. There's a big fire in Harlem. He'll try to make it later. Wash your hands. Nonna and Claire have everything ready." Enzo stopped suddenly. "Oh, that's right. Frankie, you haven't met Claire yet."

Claire followed Enzo through the door, carrying a basket of freshly-baked bread. When she heard her name mentioned, she put the basket on the dining table and walked into the living room.

Bridget sputtered. "Oh, let me introduce Claire, Mr. Sabella." He smiled and nodded. She turned proudly to Frankie. "Frankie, this is my friend, Claire O'Brien. Claire, this is Frankie."

From the conversations she and Bridget had over the past two days—along with the teasing Bridget endured from Sean—it was clear to Claire that Frankie Sabella held a special place in Bridget's heart. Claire smiled as she offered her hand. "Frankie, it's lovely to meet ye. I hear you're a great baseball player as well as a wonderful dancer. Your reputation has reached as far as Ireland."

****

Frankie was disappointed when he realized Tony wasn't going to join them. He wasn't listening to

Bridget when she was introducing him to her friend from Ireland. But he knew his parents wouldn't like it if he was impolite, so he started to raise his head as the girl stuck out her hand and began to talk. Her voice sounded like someone was reciting poetry or something. It was like a soft song, and the hairs on the back of his neck started to tickle.

He blinked and swallowed at the same time as he looked at the girl standing before him. *She's tall. Her hand's soft. Her hair's shiny. Her eyes are dark. She's tall. Her hand's soft.*

Finally, he found his voice. "Hello. Welcome to New York." He cringed as he heard his father's deep voice.

"Well done, Frankie. Why didn't I think of that? Better late than never. Yes, Claire, welcome to New York."

Chapter Twenty-Four

Bridget was lying on Claire's bed, twirling her hair and staring at the ceiling as she recalled the evening. "Isn't Frankie dreamy, Claire? All that curly black hair and those brown eyes. All the girls think he's dreamy. I think he liked what you said about him playing baseball and being a good dancer. I'm glad I told you that." She giggled. "It was hilarious when you told him that his reputation reached all the way to Ireland. I think he believed it for a minute."

Flipping onto her stomach, she sighed. "Why do we have to be so young? If we were older like you, we could really be in love, and people wouldn't laugh at us and call it *puppy love*. Have you ever been in love, Claire? I mean, real, *hot* love? You must have had tons of guys falling in love with you in Ireland. You're so beautiful and sexy."

Claire removed her pearls and slipped out of her dress. Not ready for bed, she donned a light blue top and a pair of white shorts. Claire enjoyed Bridget's company; all her incessant chattering kept her from dwelling on her sadness. She settled herself comfortably in her chair. "Well now, let's answer those questions in order, shall we?

"First of all, be happy you're only seventeen. Ye don't want to grow up too fast 'cause once it's gone, Bridget, it's gone forever. And, sometimes, it can be real love when you're only seventeen. My mum told me many times that she fell for my da when she was very young. Of course, they waited until she was out of school, but they were in love. I think love can come to ye any time, young or old. The important thing is that ye watch what you're doing, so ye don't mess up your life. If it's true love, it will still be love when you're old enough to handle it.

"Now, ye ask me if I have ever been in love? No, I don't think so. I've had crushes on lots of boys, but never in love with one of them where I wanted to give myself to him and spend the rest of my life with him.

"And no, I did not have *tons* of boys falling for me. My last boyfriend dumped me for my best friend. Now, *she* was beautiful! She had long blonde hair—he didn't seem to care that it was from a bottle, just that it was blonde."

Bridget sat up and fidgeted with the bedspread. She chewed her lip and started to twirl her locks again. She spoke almost in a whisper. "Claire, can I ask you something? I feel like you're my big sister now, so I think I can ask you."

Claire smiled and cocked her head to one side. "What is it, luv? You can ask me anything."

Bridget took a deep breath and let it out slowly. "Claire, have you...have you ever done it?"

"Done what, Bridge?"

"You know. Have you ever had sex with a boyfriend?"

Now it was Claire's turn to breathe deeply. She closed her eyes, willing her racing heart to slow. She struggled to shut out the familiar feeling of terror that was rapidly growing in her mind. She spoke softly, slowly, desperately trying to hide her pain. "No, Bridget. I can honestly say that I have never had sex with a boyfriend."

A light tap sounded on the door, and Liza peeked her head inside the room. "Honey, leave Claire alone for a while. It's time for bed anyway. Come away now."

Reluctantly, Bridget slid off the bed and walked over to Claire, who still sat on the overstuffed chair in the corner. "Okay, okay." She bent down and kissed Claire on the cheek as she wrapped her arms around her shoulders. "Good night, big sister. Thanks for the words of wisdom."

Claire smiled up into Bridget's open face. "Good night, luv. I like having a little sister—I always wanted one. I'll see ye in the morning."

Liza stood in the doorway, watching the exchange between the two girls. "And what words of wisdom did your *sister* impart?"

"Mom, some things are just between sisters. I never had a sister. I'm glad Claire's here." She placed a light kiss on her mother's cheek and walked from the room. "Good night, Mom. "I love you."

"Good night, sweetie. God bless you. I love you, too. I'll see you in the morning."

After Bridget closed the door to her room, Liza stepped into Claire's and closed the door. "I know I shooed Bridget away, but are up for a chat, luv?"

"Yes, Aunt Liza, I'd like that. Please take the chair. I'll sit on the bed."

It seemed so natural to hear Arlis's daughter call her *aunt*; Liza smiled at the title. As Claire rose from the chair, they passed one another. Liza reached out and gave a gentle squeeze to Claire's forearm.

A few minutes of silence passed between them, each seeming to gather their thoughts. Finally, Claire spoke. "I want to thank ye for taking me in like this. Ye and Uncle Tom are very generous to do so. I know I've only been here for a couple of days, but I already feel like one of the family. I think ye have a right to know the whole story as to why my mum called you and asked if I could stay with you."

Liza smiled at the girl who was undoubtedly a mixture of her parents, her mother's stunning features, and her father's dark coloring. Arlis had thick chestnut brown hair and large, periwinkle blue eyes that flashed when she was angry. Her skin was the color of rich cream. Claire's hair was raven black, her eyes a deep violet accentuated with long, thick lashes. Like her mother, Claire was blessed with flawless skin. It was when Claire smiled that Arlis appeared before you, Liza thought.

Liza closed her eyes and pictured her friend all those years ago. How brave she was that day at the convent, standing up to Sister Assumpta as she did, fighting for her sister's life—and Liza's, too. Her courage didn't end there; from that day on, Arlis dedicated her life to protecting victims of abuse.

When Liza arrived in America, she took some American history classes to learn more about the country she now called home. In studying the American Civil War, she learned about the underground railroad and how, through a network of brave people, escape routes and safe houses were established to help slaves escape bondage and live lives of freedom. This is what Arlis had done for dozens of girls over the years. Liza was proud of the part she played in this modern-day, trans-Atlantic underground railroad. Arlis and Liza were always very careful not to call attention to their work.

Liza stood and walked to the bed. She sat down next to Claire and grasped her hand. "In your own time, luv, tell me your story."

Claire drew a shaky breath and hung her head as the tears began to flow. As she recounted her attack, Liza wept with her. The similarities between Minnie's assault so many years ago and Claire's recent attack were striking. How could that be? Liza thought. It was almost the exact "MO," as they said in the police shows her son watched on TV.

Another curious point was that neither Minnie nor Claire would admit to knowing their attacker. Could it have been someone they both knew? All these years later? It defied comprehension. What good would it do now to dwell on the who or the why? The important thing was that Claire healed emotionally and psychologically. Minnie never had that chance, and she spent her life emotionally and mentally damaged beyond repair. Liza shared Arlis's determination that Claire would never have to suffer as Minnie did.

It was close to eleven o'clock, and Claire, emotionally spent from the retelling of her violent attack, lay with her head in Liza's lap. Liza stroked Claire's hair as she gently massaged her scalp and her temples. During her years as a trauma counselor, Liza heard countless stories of sexual assaults, but Claire's attack was, by far, one of the most vicious. This man, whoever he was, was a maniac, and Liza could not shake the feeling that Claire's and Minnie's attacks were somehow related.

Claire stirred and slowly sat up. "Thank ye for listening, Aunt Liza. I wouldn't have thought so, but telling ye—talking about it to ye—makes me feel better. Sharing it with someone eases the pain somehow."

Liza nodded. "Luv, over the years, I've learned that talking about your pain, sharing it with someone, is an important part of healing. First, it's important to understand that you hold no blame in something like this. The blame is solely on one person—whoever attacked you. Then you must share your pain, your grief, with someone. And finally, and I think this is the most difficult, you must find it in your heart to forgive. That's what your mum learned all those years ago. Because Minnie didn't have the mental capacity to do so, your mum had to do the forgiving for her. Arlis knew that to continue to hate would just keep the pain festering, and the hate would spread like cancer. And believe me, Claire, hate is as deadly as cancer. Even more so because it not only destroys you, it destroys everyone around you."

"Thank you, Aunt Liza. Talking to you is like being with Mum." Claire looked toward the window. "I heard them talking about the roof this evening. Would it be all right if I went up there for a while? I'm feeling a bit homesick just now, and I think looking at the stars will make me feel closer to Da and Mum."

"Of course, luv. I think that's a grand idea, and it's a beautiful night for it. Just to warn you, though, it certainly won't be as quiet as Teaghlach."

Claire smiled. "I just want to be close to the stars for a while."

"I understand. But put your robe around you. It's dreadfully hot, I know, but sometimes the humid breeze can give you a chill."

"Yes, Aunt Liza. I'll put my robe on. Ye do sound just like Mum."

Chapter Twenty-Five

Tony knew it was late, but he also knew his nonna would be waiting for him with a warm plate of food. Maria Sabella firmly believed that food was a cure-all.

The old mantel clock chimed on the half-hour as Tony walked through the door of his grandmother's home. Just as he thought, Maria sat in her rocker, dozing. He smiled and tiptoed over to the chair. "Nonna? I'm sorry I'm so late."

Maria slowly opened her eyes to the light of her life, her Antonio. "*Il mio tesoro,* my treasure. You're here. I get you something to eat."

As she started to rise, Tony gently pushed her back into the chair. "No, Nonna. I'm fine. Let's just sit here together, okay? It was a nasty fire. A couple of hobos camped out in an abandoned warehouse. Both of them died. I just need to sit for a minute."

The old woman had seen the change in Antonio since he returned from Vietnam. She knew his soul was hurting. He was too gentle to see so much suffering and death. He never spoke about what happened over there, but she knew her Antonio, her treasure. He was suffering so much inside—just like that sweet girl tonight.

Maria was glad she spent time with Claire this evening. She prided herself in being able to read people, to see inside their hearts. And she was rarely wrong in her assessment of others. This girl from Ireland had been hurt, but not romantically. No, her soul was hurting, just like Antonio's. They would be good for each other. Her plans to have them meet tonight failed, but there would be other dinners, other things that needed to be 'fixed.' She would find a way to have them meet. She glanced at her grandson as he sat in the chair, his arms on his knees, his head hanging sadly.

"Antonio, you don't have to sit with me. You're tired. You go home and sleep. I see you tomorrow."

Tony smiled, conveying his thanks for her understanding. "What needs to be fixed, Nonna? Maybe I can look at it now."

Maria raised her eyebrows and opened her eyes wide as she looked around the room. "I forgot. I think of it tomorrow. You go home now."

Tony chuckled. "Right, Nonna. You show me tomorrow. By the way, is she pretty?"

Maria looked at him in feigned confusion. "Who?"

He took her hands and raised her to her feet. Wrapping her in a warm embrace, he kissed the top of her head. "Nonna, you're something. I'll stop by tomorrow. Oh, before I leave, would it be okay if I head up to the roof? It's a nice night, and I need some fresh air after all that smoke."

"Yes, go to the roof. Talk to God, Antonio. He's closer up there."

"Thanks, Nonna. I'll see you tomorrow. I love you, Nonna."

Maria watched Tony walk out the door. "God bless you, my treasure," she whispered.

****

Tony made his way up to the roof. When he was a teenager, his grandmother let him and his friends hang out up here. He slowly walked the perimeter. Every hidden nook, every drainpipe, every inch of that roof brought back a memory: his first cigarette, his first beer, his first peek at Playboy, his first kiss, his first...

He stood at the edge of the roof, looking out at the city. He smiled as he recalled earlier today when his brother, Frankie, told him he sounded like an old man. Frankie would have been surprised how close to the mark he came. Tony felt like an old man. He was only twenty-six and already, he was tired; he was tired of the pain, tired of the loneliness, tired of living. Nam took away his youth, his innocence. Nam took away his manhood.

He seemed to be dwelling on all the bad stuff more than usual. He knew he was getting worse. More and more often, he was going to that dark place—that place where there was no light, no hope, only the promise of no more pain, no more loneliness—no more anything.

Tony wasn't into drugs. He didn't see the point. Why make yourself sick getting a temporary high just to wake up to reality when the stuff wore off? Same with alcohol. Lots of guys thought they could drink their memories away, but after a while, nothing helped. Drugs and alcohol were not the answer for him.

He raised his eyes to the stars. He believed that God existed; he'd tried prayer, too. Maybe he was too impatient waiting for an answer to his prayers. Why would God listen to his pleas for help? And besides, God had His hands full with that mess in Nam.

There were a lot more guys worse off than he was. At least he came back with all his parts. Maybe all his

153

parts weren't working, but from what the VA docs said, his 'parts' weren't working because something wasn't working in his head. They told him to talk to somebody.

He couldn't bring himself to talk to anybody— anybody—about what was wrong with him. He would try to figure it out on his own, and if he couldn't, well…there was always that last resort.

Another comment Frankie made this evening came to mind. *What did he call me? His love-'em-and-leave-'em brother.* Maybe God was punishing him for being a little bit too *active* in his youth. He cringed thinking about the girls he'd known. Tony was so busy chasing skirts; he didn't bother to concentrate on any one girl for longer than a few months. He was young, sure, but lots of his friends dated their current wives when they were in high school. Had Tony already met *the one*, and didn't know it? Had he missed it? Well, it wouldn't have worked out anyway. No woman would stay with a guy who couldn't perform like a guy.

Tony knew he would get used to not having sex, but he didn't think he'd ever get used to the loneliness. He just wanted to hold someone—and be held. He wanted to feel a woman's soft body against him, smell her hair. He wanted to taste a woman's mouth again. He wanted to feel that electricity, that jolt that goes right through you when the flame is lit, and the passion starts as a slow burn. He wanted… He wanted…

There were lots of guys who got all these things from hookers, but that wasn't Tony; at least that wasn't this Tony. This Tony wanted to come home to the same woman every night. He wanted to nestle beside her. He wanted to talk about his day with her, and he wanted her to talk about her day with him. He wanted to make a life with her, to have children with her. He wanted to share his pain with her. He wanted to grow old with her. He wanted... He wanted...

Tony sat down, drawing up his knees and resting his back against one of the storage sheds. He heaved a hopeless sigh and closed his eyes. He was so tired. He was just so damned tired of wanting.

Chapter Twenty-Six

Claire reached the top of the stairs and slowly opened the door, not knowing what to expect. They talked about the roof, but was it slanted? Could she actually walk out there? It must be okay; Bridget and Sean and their friends were up here for quite a while this evening.

As she opened the door, she caught sight of the star-lit sky. It took her breath away, and she smiled. There weren't as many stars as you could see in Teaghlach, but these would do nicely. She wrapped her light robe around her and walked to the edge of the building. She was amazed by the view—starlight above her, streetlights below her. Liza warned her about the noise, but it didn't take away from the peace she felt up here.

She stood at the low wall and breathed deeply. It had been difficult to recount her attack to Liza, but she felt better after she did. She agreed with Liza that she would heal emotionally from the assault, but something Claire didn't tell Liza was how she felt about any future relationships with men. Her stomach roiled at the thought of any man putting his hands on her.

She tried to remember how much she enjoyed the feel of Rory's lips on her mouth. Rory was her steady boyfriend through high school until he threw her over for Sharon O'Malley. Those innocent days seemed like a lifetime ago—they were, indeed, a lifetime ago. In that lifetime, she was a virgin; she was pure and fresh. Now, in just a few weeks, she'd become damaged, sullied, used. Even if she could desire a man again, what decent man would want her now?

Claire felt hot tears sting her eyes as she thought about all she lost on that horrible night. Not only had she lost her virginity, but any hope of sharing her life with someone was gone—love, marriage, children—all gone. The tears began to flow freely now, her breath coming out in small sobs.

She struggled to quell her anger, chiding herself for losing control. Her mother was right. She shouldn't dwell on what she couldn't change, but she just wanted her life back. She wanted to love someone. She wanted someone to love her. She wanted children. She wanted... She wanted...

****

Tony thought he heard the door open, but he kept his eyes closed and stayed seated on the ground, hoping no one would interrupt his peace. He waited a few minutes and then opened his eyes and looked skyward. It was a beautiful night; just a whisper of a breeze cooled the night air, and the sky was unusually clear tonight. What would Nonna call a night like this, he pondered. *Oh yeah. Bella Notte, beautiful night.* Tony felt he could stay up here all night, but he knew it was past eleven, and he was working the first shift tomorrow. As he started to rise, he thought he heard a woman's soft sobbing. He stood utterly still, straining his ears to hear it again. *Mrs. Brady? Her kid, Bridget?* He knew that his brother, Frankie, and Bridget Brady were having a thing of sorts. And he just warned

Frankie about hurting her. *Oh man, if it's Bridget crying, I'm gonna deck that kid when I see him.*

He wasn't sure what to do. Should he try to leave without saying anything? He didn't want to embarrass whoever was up here, but maybe they were hurt or something. Maybe he could help. He took a deep breath and walked around the corner of the shed.

A woman dressed all in white, was standing by the low barrier wall near the edge of the building. Her arms were crossed over her chest as if she were hugging herself. Her dark hair hung forward over her bowed head, masking her face.

Tony noticed the starlight shimmering on her hair. He thought for a moment that she might be an angel, but he dismissed that quickly. *I must be losing my mind. I don't think I rate an angel's help.* He coughed softly to signal his presence, and the woman looked up.

His heart tripped in his chest when he saw her face. *Oh, God, she is an angel. A beautiful, dark-haired angel dressed in white.* It was then that he noticed the *angel*'s shapely legs exposed under the white robe she was wearing over a blue top and white shorts. *Well, it is the sixties.* He shook his head emphatically, forcing himself to return to reality. He took a step toward her.

****

Wiping her tears, Claire raised her head abruptly at the sound of a quiet cough. Someone stood in the shadows. The person began to approach her. Her breath caught in her throat as panic tore through her brain. It was a man—a tall, dark-haired man. She automatically took a step back, quickly scanning the roof for an escape route. It would not happen to her again. *Oh, Lord, deliver me from evil. Help me.*

Knowing she was close to the edge of the building, she took a step sideways; her eyes never leaving the man's face, a face which she thought somehow looked familiar. A small voice from somewhere deep inside broke through her fog of fear. The voice uttered just one word. *Trust.* Her breathing slowed as the panic receded. "Who are ye?" she whispered.

"I'm so sorry I startled you, miss. I'm Anthony Sabella, Tony. My nonna—my grandmother, that is— lives downstairs. I was visiting her, and I just came up to the roof for a few minutes before I headed home. I'm really sorry I startled you."

"You're Mrs. Sabella's grandson, Antonio? You're the fireman?"

Tony raised his eyebrows in surprise. "Yeah, that's me. Antonio, the fireman. How do you know that? Do you know my grandmother?"

Claire recovered quickly from her initial fear when she realized who this man was. She recognized him because his brother, Frankie Sabella, looked like a smaller version of him. He didn't look threatening. He seemed nice; his voice was warm and kind.

"Oh, I'm sorry. I'm Claire O'Brien. I'm staying with my friends, Tom and Liza Brady, your grandmother's neighbors. We were supposed to be introduced tonight at supper, but then ye were called away to a fire." She studied his face. He looked sad. "Did it turn out all right? The fire, I mean." She stammered. "I mean, is it over? Was anyone hurt?"

****

Tony stood trance-like, listening to her voice. He decided he could listen to that Irish lilt forever. As she talked, his eyes devoured the exquisite woman standing before him. She was tall, leggy, and gorgeous. This was the woman his grandmother wanted him to meet? *Nice going, Nonna.*

Her last words finally came through. *Was anyone hurt?* "Huh? Oh, yeah. Sorry to say a couple of hobos were overcome with smoke. They both died on the way to the hospital. We didn't get there fast enough."

Claire cocked her head and looked at him. She spoke softly. "I'm sorry, but I'm sure ye did the best ye could. Sometimes things happen for a reason. I'm learning—slowly, mind ye—but I'm learning, that we can't blame ourselves when bad things happen. Sometimes there's a reason, and sometimes there's not." She put her hand to her mouth as if to silence herself. "Sorry. Didn't mean to preach to ye. We haven't even been properly introduced, and here I am giving ye advice to live by." She smiled and shrugged her graceful shoulders.

Once again, her voice enveloped him like a warm blanket. He smiled at her. "Well, let's remedy that, shall we? The introduction, I mean." Tony took three long strides and stood before her, close enough that he could see her riveting violet eyes staring back at him. His ordinarily strong voice withered to a hoarse whisper. "How do you do, Miss O'Brien? I'm Anthony Sabella, but my friends call me Tony."

Claire giggled softly and extended her hand. "How do you do, Mr. Sabella, Tony? My name is Claire O'Brien, and my friends call me Claire."

As they clasped each other's hands and looked into each other's eyes, both were astonished by the magic in that first touch; both felt peace encompassing their troubled souls—peace and hope.

Claire continued to smile as she looked down at her hand, still clasped in Tony's. Reluctant to break the unexpected enchantment in the simple touch of his hand, she allowed her hand to linger in his a moment longer and then slid her fingers from his grasp.

He hadn't noticed he was still holding Claire's hand in his. At that moment, he didn't know where his fingers ended, and hers began. Tony just knew that he'd never experienced the feeling of complete serenity and contentment that he was feeling now, just holding her hand. He continued looking at her, totally lost in the fathomless depths of her eyes. As he felt her hand slip from his, he smiled and took a step back.

"Nice to meet you, Claire. Welcome to New York." He was caught off guard as this vision standing before him laughed softly.

"That's what your brother said to me this evening—'Welcome to New York.' " Claire smiled up at him. "All this welcoming from the Sabella boys is impressive, to be sure. Maybe ye should both get a job at the airport, welcoming people when they get off the planes."

Tony found himself breathless as he spoke. "If I knew you were coming, I would have been there to welcome you."

Claire spoke so quietly, Tony had to lean forward to hear her. As he did, he caught her natural scent, and his heart tightened.

"Well, ye welcomed me now, and it was grand. Thank ye, Tony." She made a move to leave. "I should be getting back. Aunt Liza will be wondering what's become of me. Good night, Tony."

"Good night, Claire."

161

As she walked away, she turned and gave him a brilliant smile. For a moment, Tony thought that stars exploded in the sky, showering down their light, filling his senses.

"Maybe I'll see ye the next time ye visit your nonna."

Smiling, he raised his hand in a small wave as her Irish lilt played in his head. He whispered under his breath, "Oh, to be sure."

Chapter Twenty-Seven

Claire opened her eyes and stretched deeply as the summer sun peeked through her bedroom window, promising another sweltering day. Although she had trouble falling asleep, Claire slept soundly. Once again, she mentally replayed her meeting with Tony Sabella last night.

One minute she was mourning her loneliness and hopelessness, and the next, this gentle man appeared out of the darkness and brought light back to her heart. She marveled that with the sound of his voice, her fear and loneliness vanished. With the touch of his hand, hope rekindled in her soul. She smiled, recalling the feeling that somehow her new life was meant to be in America. Was Tony Sabella meant to be part of that new life?

She had to know more about him. She was astonished that she could even think of him romantically. After her attack, she was convinced that she could never be with a man. But then Anthony Sabella came out of the shadows, literally, and simply took her hand, and the shroud of fear lifted as a small flame of hope began to burn.

Liza had already gone to bed by the time Claire returned from the roof, so they didn't have a chance to talk. Claire was anxious to tell her about Tony. She knew she would have to tread carefully, but now, she had a friend—a man friend. And somehow, Claire knew that no matter what, Tony would always be her friend. Even if nothing romantic ever came of their relationship, in her heart, she knew he would always be her friend.

****

Liza was enjoying her morning coffee and newspaper when Claire entered the kitchen. She glanced up. "Good morning, luv. How are you this morning? Did you enjoy the solitude of the roof last night?" As she returned to her paper, she noted the lack of a response. "Claire? Everything all right?"

Claire poured herself coffee and joined Liza at the table, absently playing with the teaspoon. "Good morning, Aunt Liza. I'm fine. Thank ye for asking. And, yes, I did enjoy being on the roof last night. I think it was just what I needed."

It was apparent to Liza that, indeed, it was what Claire needed. The young woman sitting across from her was not the same melancholy person of last night. There was something—a light in her eyes? She seemed more peaceful. Hopefully, she was beginning to settle in. "I have to do some shopping. If you'd like to join me, we could stop for tea later. It'll be good for you to get to know the neighborhood, too. Would you like that?"

Claire smiled broadly. "Yes, Aunt Liza, that would be grand. I'd like to see something of the neighborhood. Will Bridget be joining us?"

Liza laughed. "Bridget? Food shopping? Tea?" No, luv. Bridget has a full day of cheerleading practice. She left just before you came down. She'll be home later. Sean is at the park, hitting some flies."

"Flies?" Claire furrowed her brow in confusion. "How do ye hit flies? How big are they? At home, we just swat at them."

Liza laughed. "No, not bugs. He's playing baseball in the park. 'Hitting flies' means hitting the baseball high in the air and then catching it; at least, that's the main idea."

Claire giggled at her ignorance. "For speaking the same language, there's so much I don't understand when Americans are talking." She laughed again. "All I could picture was Sean and his friends running around trying to hit giant flies."

Liza shared in her laughter. "I know. I'm still learning. You go and get dressed. We'll leave when you're ready."

"I'll be back in a jiffy." Smiling brightly, Claire glided out of the room.

Liza washed the coffee cups while envisioning her son running around the park with a baseball bat in his hands, swinging at giant flies. *I'll have to share this one at dinner.* The phone rang, and Liza answered, a smile in her voice. "Hello? Good morning, Maria. How are you this morning?"

"Hallo, Liza, I'm good. Are you shopping today?"

"Yes, actually, Claire and I are leaving soon. Do you need anything?"

"Claire? *Bene, bene.* I have some lemon granita. I make for Antonio. You take it to him at fire station, yes? Something cold for the boys on such a hot day. You take to him, okay?"

"Of course we'll take it to him. I'll bring my cooler, so it stays frozen. We'll be over in about half an hour."

"Okay. I keep it in freezer. *Ciao*...bye-bye."

Fifteen minutes later, Claire entered the kitchen. "All set, Aunt Liza." She spied the small box on the table. "Do ye carry your groceries in that? We just use sacks back home."

Liza smiled. "No, it's a small cooler—an insulated box to keep things cold. Maria Sabella called and asked us to take some lemon ice to the fire station where her grandson works. In this heat, it would melt before we got a block; the cooler will keep it frozen. And to tell you the truth, I think Maria just wants to make sure you meet her grandson."

Claire absently toyed with the handle of the cooler. "That would be Tony, then?"

Liza caught the breathlessness in Claire's voice. "Yes, luv, that would be Tony. Why?"

"We met on the roof last night."

Things were beginning to make sense to Liza now. The light in Claire's eyes, her mood this morning. *Act casual, Liza.*

"Did you now? Would you like to tell me about it?"

Claire looked at her, her face radiant. "Yes, Aunt Liza. I'd like that very much. It was like a miracle, to be sure."

****

Maria Sabella opened the front door, a broad smile on her face. "*Buongiorno*, Liza. *Buongiorno*, Claire. Come in, come in. I get granita for you."

Liza returned the older woman's smile. "Good morning, Maria. I brought the cooler. You just sit. It's too hot to move too much. I'll go into the kitchen and get the granita." She looked innocently at Claire. "Sit with Maria for a minute and tell her who you met last night. I'll be right back." As Liza moved toward the kitchen, she looked back and saw Claire helping Maria into her rocker as she took a seat near her. *Oh, luv, you are going to make her day!*

****

Maria settled herself in her rocker and reached for Claire's hand. "Okay, my sweet girl, tell me who you met last night." She frowned. "You go out last night, after dinner? You have to watch. This is big city. You shouldn't go out by yourself."

Claire smiled shyly. She liked the feel of the aged hand holding hers. Growing up, she always missed not having grandparents. Her father's parents died when he was quite young, and both her mother's parents died when Claire was just a little girl.

She marveled that there was something in the touch of the old woman's hand that reminded her of Tony, the warmth, the peace. "Oh, I didn't go out last night, Mrs. Sabella. I wasn't ready for bed, and it was such a lovely evening, I asked Aunt Liza if I could go up to the roof."

The old lady studied the lovely girl seated next to her. The girl's hand lay so trustingly in hers. Once again, she could sense that she had been hurt, but was trying valiantly to hide the pain. So much like her Antonio, so much like her treasured grandson. She came back from her musings when she heard the words "...up to the roof." *The roof? Claire was on the roof last night? She met someone?*

Maria's eyes opened wide. "You met my Antonio last night? On the roof, you met my Antonio?" The look on Claire's face answered Maria's question. *Dio 'e buono! God is good.*

Chapter Twenty-Eight

Pete and Joe were re-attaching the hoses on the trucks used to battle the warehouse fire the night before when Tony sauntered into the station, humming softly. The two firemen exchanged puzzled looks. *Tony's humming?*

Tony walked over to the time clock and punched in. "Morning, Pete, morning, Joe. How's it going, guys? How's Katie doing, Pete?"

Pete raised his eyebrows. "Kate's fine. And before you ask, Skipper's fine, too. Cutting some teeth, so he's cranky. My mom and dad are fine; my sister and her family are fine; I'm fine. Everything's fine. I can't speak for Joe here, but he looks okay. Now that we've checked up on everybody, let's talk about you."

Tony busied himself at his locker then put his lunchbox in the refrigerator. "Me? I'm great." He glanced outside. "Man, another hot one, huh? I'll get the stuff ready to give the trucks a good wash. Lots of soot and ash from last night."

Joe stood holding the heavy fire hose, gawking at his friend. "What's gotten into you, Antonio? You on something? You been drinking?"

"I'm just high on life, Joe. Just high on life. Man, another hot one, huh? I'll get the wash stuff."

Joe Raimy and Pete Callahan watched their friend walk out the back door and head for the storage shed.

When Tony was out of sight, Joe gave Pete a worried look. "Whaddya think that was about?"

Pete shook his head. "Man, I don't know. Do you think he's taking something? Smoking something? Maybe it's LSD. I didn't smell anything on him when he came in, so I don't think he's drinking. You got any thoughts?"

Joe shook his head. "His eyes looked clear; in fact, he hasn't looked that good since before he went to Nam."

As soon as the words were out of his mouth, Joe and Pete looked at each other, eyes wide. "You don't think? You thinking what I'm thinking?" Simultaneously, they dropped the heavy fire hose, tripping over themselves getting to the storage shed.

Just as they reached the out-building, the door opened, and Tony, still humming, started to walk out. Joe was a step ahead of Pete and put his hand on Tony's chest, gently pushing him back into the small room, Pete right behind him, closing the door.

Tony gave them a puzzled look. "What's going on, guys?"

Joe stood nose-to-nose with his friend. "Uh-uh, no way, fella. You're not fooling us. We're not leaving this furnace 'til you tell us what's going on with you."

Tony shook his head and smiled. "Nothing is going on. It's all good."

Pete leaned against the door, arms crossed over his chest, legs crossed at the ankles. "No dice, man. We know you. We've been buddies since we were five years old. If it's *all good*, it's because something happened last night, after the fire. Where did you go after you left us? And don't tell us you went to your grandmother's."

"Okay, I won't tell you that, but that's exactly where I did go. You wanna call Nonna and ask her?" Tony turned his back, resuming his humming as he began straightening the tools lying on the table.

Pete looked at Joe and shrugged his shoulders in frustration.

Joe shook his head, indicating he wasn't buying any of it. "So, you went to your grandmother's. Then what? You stop at a bar, pick somebody up?"

"No, from my nonna's, I went up to the roof of her building to look at the stars. I just needed some peace, you know? If you recall, it was a tough night, losing those two guys. I just needed a quiet place to think."

Joe frowned in dismay. "You got a hooker, didn't you? Man, Tonio, that's risky. What would your nonna say? I mean, I know you want to meet a girl, but a hooker? That isn't like you at all."

Tony turned to face them and leaned against the work table. He kept his hands busy polishing a wrench with a dry cloth. Laughing, he shook his head. "I did not pick up a hooker. I can't believe you could even think that. Jeez, Raimy, get real."

"Okay, pal. Here's how we see it." Pete sighed in frustration. "You haven't been the same Tony since coming back from Nam. You know it, we know it. You haven't had a date since God knows when. You come to work every day looking sad, not angry, just sad. And it kills us to see you like this.

"The fire last night was tough on all of us; it's never easy losing victims. This morning, you walk in here humming, asking how we are, commenting—twice—on the weather, and you expect us to believe this change is just because you visited with your grandmother and then went up on the roof and did some star-gazing?"

Tony continued polishing the heavy metal wrench. "That was it, fellas, honest to God." He hesitated and then spoke in a hushed voice. "Did I mention meeting an angel up on the roof?"

Joe rolled his eyes and shook his head. "Hey, we're just trying to help out here, pal. We don't need any wisecracks about star-gazing and visions of angels."

Tony finally made eye contact with his friends. Pete and Joe were astonished by the look of peace and happiness on their friend's face. "Oh, but I did meet an angel, guys, and her name is Claire. Claire O'Brien."

Pete Callahan pushed himself away from the door, sweat pouring down his face. He shook his head, exasperated. "Fine. That's the story you're giving us—fine."

Tony raised his eyebrows and shrugged. "What? I told you the truth."

Joe stepped away from his childhood friend and glared at him. He rolled his tongue back and forth inside his cheeks as he did a slow burn. "That's it. I'm done. Hey, Pete. Our buddy here met an angel last night—with a last name, to boot. What's not to believe?" He turned his back in annoyance. "Come on. I guess we know where we stand now." With a final furious look at Tony, the two firemen stalked from the shed.

****

The morning wore on as the men busied themselves with the daily minutiae of operating a fire station. The only sound was the constant humming signaling Tony's newly-found good mood. Finally, at midmorning break, Tony attempted reconciliation.

"Hey, guys, how 'bout I go around the corner and get us milkshakes? Pete? Sound good? Joe, what'll it be?" His offer was met with silence. He waited a moment longer, and shrugging his shoulders, he headed out. "Okay, I'll surprise you."

Minutes after Tony rounded the corner out of sight, Liza Brady walked through the wide entrance of the station. "Hi, fellas, remember me?"

Pete Callahan, rubbed his moist hands on his thighs as he smiled and offered his hand. "Sure do, Mrs. Brady, how you been? I haven't seen you since the Sabellas' picnic last month. How's Mr. Brady?"

Liza smiled and shook his hand. "He's well, thank you, Pete." She turned as Joe Raimy appeared from behind one of the fire engines. "Hi, Joe. Heavens, you look hot. It's sweltering out there. Thank goodness for the fans you have going in here—at least it keeps the air moving."

Joe grinned down at the attractive woman, a friend of Tony's parents. "Sorry you missed Tony, Mrs. Brady. He just left to pick up some milkshakes."

"Oh, that's a shame. We're here on an errand for his grandmother."

Joe craned his neck to look beyond Liza. "We?"

Liza turned to look over her shoulder. "Claire? Claire, where did you go?"

Joe and Pete quickly exchanged shocked looks. *Claire?*

Just then, the tall, lithe form of Claire O'Brien entered the station, carrying a small cooler. She wore a sleeveless, light cotton navy blue polka dot shirtwaist dress with a broad red patent leather belt cinching her tiny waist. The dress came about two inches above her knees, the matching red patent leather flats accentuating her long legs. Her gleaming ebony hair was pulled back from her brow by a red hairband and hung in a soft flip at her shoulders.

"Pete, Joe, this is Claire O'Brien, from Ireland." Liza noticed the men staring at her and moved closer to Claire. "Claire, this is Pete Callahan and Joe Raimy, friends of Maria's grandson, Tony."

So like her mother's, Claire's smile lit up the already bright room. As she raised her lovely violet eyes and began to speak, the men stood gawking at their visitor.

"Good day to ye, gentlemen. We surely don't mean to be disturbing ye, but Mrs. Sabella thought you might like to cool yourselves with a bit of...of...I'm sorry. What did she call it, Aunt Liza?"

Liza laughed. "Maria called it lemon granita."

"Yes, that's it—granita." She laughed softly and lowered her voice to a whisper. "We just call it ice in Teaghlach. Could one of ye be so kind as to put it in the icebox? We wouldn't want it to melt after all Mrs. Sabella's efforts."

Liza struggled to keep from laughing as Joe elbowed his friend out of the way and retrieved the small cooler from Claire's outstretched hand.

"Thank ye both. Ye are very kind. Well, we best be off. Please tell Tony I was very sorry to have missed him. I'm sure I'll be seeing him at his grandmother's. Good day to ye, gentlemen." Claire nodded and walked out of the building.

Liza watched Tony's friends staring after Claire.

"Yes, thanks so much for freezing that." She hesitated and then couldn't resist her last remark as she followed Claire from the station. "I hope it cools you off a bit, gentlemen. Bye now."

****

Tony trudged back a block and a half, carrying a cardboard tray containing three milkshakes melting in the oppressive heat. As he entered the station, he hurried over to the table. "Quick, get some napkins. This stuff is melting all over the place." His attention was on the whipped cream dripping down the sides of the plastic cups, so he didn't notice Pete and Joe lounging on chairs by the fan. "Guys, take these before it's just watery milk." He lifted the tray to offer the melting mass when he noticed that his friends were already eating something in cereal bowls.

Disappointed, he lowered the cardboard carrier and looked closer. "What are you eating? Wait, is that Nonna's lemon granita?"

Joe ignored him for a moment and then spoke. "Yes, Antonio, this is your nonna's delicious lemon granita. She made it especially for you and your dear friends."

"I missed Nonna? How did she get here? She couldn't have walked here in all this heat. Did Frankie bring it?"

Pete was licking his bowl as well as his lips. "No, man, it was your neighbor, Mrs. Brady. She's a nice lady. Pretty, too, don't you think, Joe?"

"Oh yeah, for an older woman, she's quite attractive, but…"

"Raimy, don't be gross. She's almost old enough to be your mother. Have some respect. Sheesh!" Tony shook his head in disgust.

Joe continued. "Let me finish, please, before you scold me, Pops. I was going to say that yes, Mrs. Brady is quite attractive, but man, oh man, she doesn't hold a candle to Claire. You know, Tony—Claire O'Brien?"

Tony stood gaping at his friends. His head began to swivel as he scanned the room. He ran to the front of the station house then back to the kitchen area, his eyes darting everywhere. "Claire was here? Where'd she go? How long ago did she leave? Damn! I was only gone for a few minutes."

Pete stood up and slapped Tony on the back. "Well, in those few minutes, Joe and I were practically brought to our knees regretting that we didn't believe you about your *angel.*" He shook his head. "Jeez, Tony, you were right—she is an angel."

Joe stood and slowly walked over to his friends. "I don't know. I beg to differ with you, Pete."

"What? You don't think Claire O'Brien looked like she was sent straight from heaven?"

"Well, I don't think she's an angel." Joe pushed out his lower lip and furrowed his brow. "Actually, after seeing her—and listening to that Irish lilt—I'm thinking she...is...a...*goddess!* Sweet lord, Antonio. Sit your butt down and tell us everything."

****

Tony sat between his two best friends, looking into the distance, a secret smile on his face. "Nothing much to tell, guys. I was up on the roof, looking at the stars— just like I told you—and then I saw her standing there. We introduced ourselves, and we shook hands and...and...and it was like...I don't know. I can't describe it."

Pete and Joe sat, watching their best friend as he talked about Claire. When Tony hesitated, Joe urged him on, his voice a low whisper. "Try, buddy. What was it like?"

Tony slowly shook his head as he continued to stare into space. "Don't laugh, guys, but it was like something touched me right here."

Pete Callahan grinned as Tony put his hand to his heart.

"It was like I felt hope again. Hope that things are going to be okay. Does that make sense?"

Pete patted Tony's shoulder and spoke quietly. "Yeah, buddy. It makes sense. It's called falling in love."

Tony smiled as he looked at Pete. "I think you're right, Pete. I think I'm in love. I feel like I've been away for a long time, and now, I'm home."

Joe Raimy swallowed hard as he wrapped his muscular arm around his friend's shoulders. "Welcome home, pal. We've missed you."

Chapter Twenty-Nine

Liza and Claire finished shopping and began their walk home in silence. Finally, Claire spoke.

"Aunt Liza, I think I could care for Tony. I know it sounds silly to admit after only just meeting him, but it's something I feel deep in my very soul. It seems so right, but…"

Liza placed her hand on Claire's arm, giving it a gentle squeeze. "There's a small park up ahead. Why don't we sit for a while before going home?"

Claire nodded in silent assent and let Liza guide her to a solitary park bench. "I need your thinking on this, Aunt Liza. I need your sense."

Smiling tenderly, Liza reached for Claire's hand. "Well, luv, I do have some thoughts on what you've just told me. I confess I noticed something this morning. I can't tell you that love at first sight isn't real. I think I loved Thomas from the moment I met him. Your mum told me long ago that she loved your father when she was six years old. However, you're not six, nor are you a young maid of sixteen. And neither your mum nor I were recovering from a shattering attack on our psyche.

"You met Tony Sabella just last night. It was a starry night, you were feeling blue, and all of a sudden, this man, and a very handsome man I might add, came out of the shadows and was kind to you. Claire, you must be completely honest with yourself right now. Is it possible that you think you care for him because he made you feel comfortable? Made you feel safe? Is it possible you want to hold on to that person, that feeling because you think it might be the only time you'll feel that way and don't want to gamble on losing it?" Liza glanced at the young woman next to her. Claire sat with her head down, silent tears dripping on her polka dot dress. *O, God, give me the wisdom she needs right now.*

"I hear what you're saying, Aunt Liza, I do. And they're the same words that have been rolling around in my head all day.

"I didn't tell ye the other day 'cause it's so hard to talk about, but I told Mum and Da before I left that I didn't think I could be with a man—that way—ever again. Even yesterday, when Bridget said something about boys being interested in me, my stomach flipped, and I almost threw up."

"Bridget shouldn't have said that to you."

Claire smiled through her tears. "Bridget was trying to say something nice to me. She has no way of knowing what's happened. But I did have that reaction. That's one of the reasons I went to the roof last night. I guess I was feeling lonely about maybe never feeling like I did when my boyfriend, Rory, kissed me.

"I truly liked being kissed and held. I'm not saying I was an angel, but Rory and I knew when to stop. I wanted the moment I gave myself to someone completely to be the most special thing in my life. I didn't want any shame in it. Now, that's all gone, so I have to salvage what I can and move on."

"Of course, I've never experienced what you have, Claire, but in my years of counseling girls who suffered abuse as you have, I can tell you that many of them have confessed an inability to consider ever being intimate with a man again. I'm sure several of them overcame their fear—their aversion, if you will—and have led normal lives of sexual activity. There are no studies on this, so I can't give you absolute facts; however, I do know some girls, who have kept in touch with me over the years, are happily married and have children. And, yes, some girls have never recovered from their trauma." Both women's thoughts automatically turned to Minnie.

"I can't explain it, Aunt Liza, but when Tony appeared out of the darkness, a voice inside my head said just one word—*trust*. And when he took my hand last night when we introduced ourselves, I can't describe it as anything but magic. I know this all sounds crazy and desperate, but I feel something in here."

Liza watched Claire touch her heart. She sat in wonderment at the love that radiated from Claire's beautiful face. Could it happen that fast? Liza thought. *Perhaps.* But even if Claire did, indeed, love Tony Sabella, there were other issues involved here.

"Claire, you know that if Tony has the same feelings for you, you must tell him everything before this goes any further. Are you prepared to do that?"

"Well, prepared or not, I know I have to. I would never go into a relationship, feeling as I do, without being completely honest with Tony."

Liza took in a deep breath and exhaled. Was it her place? She pondered. *I must.*

"Luv, there's one more thing. Tony just returned from Vietnam last year. He's not the same man today as he was when he left. I don't know the whole story, but he was injured over there and sent home. His wounds healed—his external wounds, that is. But he's still suffering, I think, from what he saw over there—friends dying, civilians dying. We see it on the news every day, but he was there and witnessed these horrors.

"I've known Tony since he was a little boy. He's gentle and kind. I think what he saw over there has wounded him emotionally. He's going to need a lot of understanding and love to heal the trauma to his soul. Just as Tony should know your pain, you should be aware of his. It will be very telling if he keeps this part of himself from you."

She smiled at her best friend's child, who she was quickly growing to love as one of her own. "So, Claire, dear, I will give you my last thoughts on this. You will probably see him very soon—possibly as early as tonight, I would suspect. Try to get to know him. Talk about everything. Then, if you think this is going somewhere, tell him what happened to you. If you open up to him, hopefully, he will reciprocate.

"If he is open with you, let it happen. But if he isn't as honest with you as you are with him, I would advise you to go no further. For your sake and his, go no further. Does that sound reasonable to you?"

Claire wrapped her arms around Liza and hugged her tightly. "Thank you, Aunt Liza. I know that's just what my mum would be saying to me now. Yes, it sounds reasonable; it sounds right." She smiled as she wiped her eyes and gently blew her nose. "Who knows? This might all be for nothing."

Liza shared her smile and rose from the bench. She knew that this conversation took place at a most opportune time. The two women linked arms and strolled through the park, each lost in thought.

Chapter Thirty

The clock struck four when Bridget entered the kitchen. "Hey, Mom. When's dinner? I only had some fries for lunch—I might die of starvation before we eat."

Liza smiled indulgently at her teenage daughter. "I doubt very much you'll expire before we eat, Bridget. Want to have a cup of tea with your old mum? We could chat for a while, catch up, as they say."

"Mom, no one says that unless they're old ladies who haven't seen each other for a long time. I saw you this morning. Where's Claire? Maybe she could sit with us while we *catch up, as they say.*"

"I'm not feeling the love, Bridget. Isn't that something your generation says now?" Liza chuckled. "Claire's in her room. Why don't you go up and ask her to join us? Dad has a meeting, and Sean is heaven knows where."

Bridget nodded. "Be right back." She took the stairs two at a time and knocked on Claire's door. "Hey, Claire. Mom and I are having a cup of tea together. Come join us. I want to show you this cheer we learned today." Bridget waited a moment, but there was no response. "Claire?" She knocked again and slowly opened the door.

Claire was lying on her side, her back to the door. Bridget tiptoed across the room and stood by the bed.

"Claire, are you sleeping? Are you okay?" Again, no response. Bridget noticed that her dress was lying on the chair, her shoes tossed carelessly in the corner. She crept back out of the room and hurried downstairs.

"Mom, I don't think Claire is feeling well. She's just lying on the bed with her robe thrown over her. The shades are down, too. Do you think that long plane ride caught up with her? Should I try to wake her up?"

Liza felt a pang of worry but tried to mask the concern in her face. "No, just let her rest. We had a rather long walk down to the fire station today. All the heat must have gotten to her."

"Why'd you go to the fire station?"

"Maria Sabella asked us to take some lemon ice to Tony and his friends, that's all."

Bridget grinned. "Ooooh. Did Claire meet the hunk? I mean, Frankie's cute, but oh my gosh, his brother is really something. I wish I were older—that's a fact."

"Bridget, don't call Tony a hunk. Honestly, it sounds like he's a piece of meat."

"Well…"

"That's vulgar, Bridget. And as a matter of fact, Claire did meet Tony—last night."

"She did? Tell me!" Bridget exclaimed excitedly.

"There's nothing to tell. Claire met him by chance on the roof last night. They introduced themselves, and that was it."

"That was it? Didn't she say anything else? Mom, he's such a hu…he's gorgeous, and so is she. They would make gorgeous babies."

"Bridget! Stop talking like that. Honestly, is that how nice young ladies talk?" The teenager shrugged nonchalantly.

"You make the tea. I'll see how Claire is. I'm sure she was just done in by the heat." Liza tried to act casual as she hurried from the kitchen. Claire was very quiet after their talk in the park. Liza worried that she had been too forthright with her.

****

As she approached the bedroom door, she heard the unmistakable sound of weeping. "Claire? It's me, Liza. May I come in?" A moment passed, and then she heard a quiet "Yes." She opened the door and entered the darkened room. "Luv, what is it?"

Claire's shoulders heaved in stifled sobs. "Oh, Aunt Liza. How can I tell him about me—about what happened to me? I'm not a *nice* girl anymore; I'm sullied and used. How could I think he would want to be with me after I tell him. But I know I do have to tell him. It wouldn't be right to hide something like that."

Liza sat down on the edge of the bed and drew Claire into her arms, stroking her hair. "Claire. Why are you thinking the worst? What about the 'magic' you felt when he took your hand? Don't you think he felt it, too? Don't you think there might be more to Tony than a quick judgment of you?"

"But, Aunt Liza. He's a nice man. Ye said so, yourself. Would a nice man want to be with someone like me? And I started thinking about...ye know...being with him, and I don't know. Even if he wanted me, could I ever forget the first time? It was so horrible. I start thinking about a man touching me, and my stomach turns, and that's God's truth."

Liza gently grasped the young woman's shoulder and pushed her away so she could look into her eyes.

"Claire, look at me." Claire obediently raised her eyes. "Luv, I want to say something to you, and then I want you to think before you answer. I want you to be completely honest in your answer. Don't say what you think you should say or what I want you to say. Just the truth. Will you do that?"

Claire took in a shaky sob and nodded.

"Sweetheart, close your eyes and reverse all of this. For a moment, pretend that Tony has a secret; some horrible secret he has no blame for, but he hasn't told anyone. It's so painful for him; he's hidden it from the world. Now suppose you two meet, just like you did. And suppose the simple touch of your hand was like a miraculous balm to his shattered soul. It made him remember, if only for a moment, that there was still love and beauty in the world. He felt a glimmer of hope because you touched him deeply. He felt a glimmer of hope that some of that love, some of that beauty, could be his.

"Imagine he wants to come to you and tell you this horrible, painful secret he's been hiding. He wants to share his grief with you because he sees a chance for happiness with you. But he's afraid of what you'll think of him. Would you reject him, Claire? Would you turn your back on someone blameless? Someone hurting? Someone who only wanted to love and be loved in return? What would you do?"

Claire sat with her eyes closed and listened carefully. She smiled sadly. "I would hope, Aunt Liza, that he would trust me enough to tell me everything. How could I not love him for trusting me to understand? And if I didn't understand, then I was never worthy of his love or trust to begin with."

Liza reached up and gently brushed Claire's hair away from her face. "There you go, luv. You have your answer. And one more thing. "I truly believe that your fear of intimacy is just temporary. I believe that with time, love, and trust, you will overcome that fear. With love and trust, you will learn the joy and beauty of the physical part of a relationship—with love and trust."

Chapter Thirty-One

Tony had been flying high all day. He awakened feeling happier than he had in months, and it was all because of the angel he met last night. He marveled that the simple touch of Claire's hand could bring light to his darkened soul.

When his friends told him he just missed her visit to the fire station today, his momentary disappointment gave way to a thrill he couldn't explain. He counted the minutes until the workday was over. He called his grandmother when he got home from work. She hadn't even bothered to think up a pretense to get him over there.

"Hi, Nonna. Thanks for the granita. Hit the spot today."

"*Bene*, Antonio, *bene*. You met my Claire up on the roof last night? *Bella ragazza,* beautiful girl, Antonio. You come back tonight."

Tony chucked. "*Your* Claire? How did she become your Claire, Nonna?"

"When I first see her, I say, *there's the girl for my Antonio*. And I right, no?"

He swallowed hard and answered her, his voice tight with emotion. "Maybe, Nonna. Maybe that's the girl for me. I'll see you later. *Ti voglio bene*, Nonna."

"*Ti amo anch'io, il mio tesoro.*"

****

The cold shower felt good after the sweltering heat. Tony had a perfect day. He even went for a couple of beers with the guys, just like the old days—well, not quite.

Tony let the spray gently pelt his face as he raised his head to the water. His mind replayed every precious moment of meeting Claire O'Brien. He suddenly recalled that she was crying. How could he have forgotten that? He'd been so taken with her unexpected appearance, somehow, he forgot that she seemed upset. And then when their hands touched, all rational thought was gone from his mind.

But now he recalled that she had been crying. What kind of unfeeling jerk was he to ignore the fact that she was upset about something? She didn't appear to be physically hurt; maybe she was homesick for her parents, for Ireland.

Unease slithered into his mind. Maybe Claire was missing someone, a guy someone. *Oh man, I never even considered that. A girl as beautiful as she is, she must have a boyfriend back there. She didn't say anything; she didn't act like there was someone else. But we didn't really talk that long.*

The longer he stood under the cooling water, conjuring up various scenarios about the reason for her crying, a familiar feeling of despair crept back into his heart. The more he dwelled on those thoughts, the delicate flicker of hope that began with the touch of Claire's hand threatened to die out, leaving him in hopeless darkness once again.

He finished the shower, quickly dried off, and walked into his bedroom. He lay on the bed in the darkened room. *Even if there isn't another guy, what can I offer her? What was I thinking? Why should I start something I can't possibly finish?* The VA doctors told him that his 'condition' was most likely temporary. *Great! Temporary. What exactly did temporary mean? Months? Years? What was the point? What was the point of any of it?*

He quickly sat up. *I can't do this. I can't lie here wanting something I'll never have. That part of my life is gone; it's over. Stop feeling sorry for yourself. Go to Nonna's. She means well. I don't have to drag her down with me. Just smile, Tony. Hide it with a smile. You've been doing that for a while now.*

He dressed quickly and left his apartment. Nonna would be waiting for him.

****

Maria sat in her rocker, her ever-present knitting on her lap. As soon as she heard the door open, her heart leaped, and she smiled—Antonio was here. Maria had several grandchildren from her two daughters and her son, Enzo, but Antonio held a special place in her heart. When he went to Vietnam, Maria fervently prayed that he would return unharmed. Well, God answered part of her prayer; Antonio returned, but he wasn't unharmed. He suffered some physical injuries, but they healed quickly. It was the injury to his soul that concerned her. Maria was sure that all he needed to heal completely was the love of a good woman. She was also confident that Claire O'Brien was that woman.

Her keen insight into human nature never failed her in her long life, and she knew it wouldn't fail her now. From the moment she watched Claire step out of the taxi, she knew this *bella ragazza*, this beautiful girl from Ireland, would be the one to heal her Antonio. Just like she knew Antonio would be the one to heal the hurt inside of Claire.

Tony crossed the room, kissed his grandmother, and then took a seat on the divan, close to her rocker. "Hi, Nonna. How are you handling the heat? Are the fans cooling it off enough for you? Maybe I should get you an air conditioner."

"Antonio, stop. I'm fine. Stop worrying about me, about everything. You're young. You should have other things on your mind—maybe one special person?"

Tony laughed. "Nonna, Nonna, don't you ever give up?"

"No, I never give up till I see you smile again."

"I smile all the time. Look, I'm smiling now." He pointed his finger toward his mouth and grinned."

Maria cocked her head and looked intently at her grandson as she touched her hand to his heart. She spoke softly. "I not give up till you smile here, Antonio." Her heart clenched as she saw pain flicker across his face. "Tonio, what is it?"

Tony chided himself for dropping his guard. He forced a smile for his grandmother, knowing he wasn't fooling her for a moment. He took her hand and kissed it. "It's nothing, Nonna. Just another long day."

"You go up to the roof now. I think God wants to talk to you again."

He laughed at her blatant lie. "Nonna, I don't think God has time to talk to me. He's got more important things to do."

"More important than helping *tesoro mio,* my treasure? No. You go. Now. You come back tomorrow."

Tony heaved a deep sigh. "Okay, Nonna. I will go

talk to God, for you."

"You talk to Him up on the roof. He's closer up there."

"Yeah, Nonna, I know. I know." He kissed Maria's wrinkled cheek and walked quietly out the door.

Maria closed her eyes and bowed her head. *Please, Dio, please ease his pain.*

Chapter Thirty-Two

Tony saw her as soon as he opened the rooftop door. Claire was standing in the same spot she was the first time he saw her. Just like last night, the starlight was shimmering on her hair. Just like last night, she turned when she heard him. Just like last night, he was astonished by her beauty. Just like last night, she had been crying.

"Hi, Claire. I'm sorry I missed you today at the station. Thanks for bringing the granita down for my grandmother. That was nice of you."

"You're welcome. I'm sorry I missed ye, too. Your friends were nice."

Her voice was hoarse from crying. Tony wouldn't make the same mistake again tonight. "Are you all right? I want to apologize for last night, by the way."

Claire gave him a curious look. "Why, what did ye do?"

He shook his head. "You were crying last night. I didn't even bother to ask you if you were okay. It was just that you looked so..." He swallowed. "You looked so beautiful standing there. I thought you were an angel, and I just forgot about everything else."

"You're very kind to apologize, but there's no need, truly." She laughed softly. "And thank ye for saying ye thought I was an angel. You're a kind man, Tony."

He couldn't help himself as he walked toward her, inexorably drawn to her as if an invisible rope were pulling him closer. Would he feel that same peace and contentment if they touched again? He had to know. He was frightened earlier tonight in his apartment when he felt that coldness returning to his heart along with the dreaded hopelessness. Could the mere touch of her hand make all the pain go away? He had to know. Before he lost all hope, he had to know.

"You were crying again just now. Can I ask you why? I don't mean to pry; it's just that…well, it's just that if you're crying because you left someone back home in Ireland—someone special—I have to know."

Claire's breath caught in her throat. She could only manage a whisper. "No, Tony, I wasn't crying because there's anyone special—in Ireland, that is."

"Oh. Is there someone special here, then?"

"Well, I guess I don't know yet," she whispered again, breathless.

He slowly reached out and offered his hand to her, speaking her name so quietly, so reverently, it was almost like a prayer. "Claire."

As their fingers touched, he drew her to him slowly, gently, their faces inches apart. His eyes closed as an overwhelming feeling of contentment filled his heart. He opened his eyes and looked searchingly into hers. Raising his hand, he traced his fingers slowly down her face and across her beautiful mouth. He felt her tremble.

****

Once again, Claire felt the magic of his touch, and her heart opened. As he came closer, she closed her eyes, savoring the tender touch of his fingers on her face, her mouth. She quivered in anticipation. She wanted nothing more than to feel his lips on hers, but could she begin a relationship without being completely honest with him? She struggled with what she knew to be the only answer. She opened her eyes and put her hand on his chest. "Tony, we have to talk."

"Now?" he asked pleadingly.

"Yes, it has to be now. Before...before..."

Tony raised her hand to his lips and kissed each finger, one by one. "Okay. But can we pick up right where we left off when we finish talking?"

She smiled sadly and hung her head as she clung to his hand. "Tony, I think what we have—what's beginning for us is something that I feel in my heart could last forever. But it's only going to last forever if I can be completely honest with ye."

****

Tony felt the icy fingers of doubt creeping toward his heart. "I agree. What we feel is going to last forever—as long as we hold on to each other." Again, he raised her hands to his lips.

Claire inhaled a shaky breath. Tony felt her tremble, not in desire but fear. "Claire, what is it, angel? You can tell me anything."

"That's just it, Tony. I'm not an angel."

Tony put his fingers to her lips. "Claire, we aren't kids. We've both had lives before meeting one another. I would never judge you for anything that happened before this moment. Please trust me when I say the past doesn't matter. Now matters, Claire. Now and forever. "

Claire's eyes filled with tears, her heart swelling with love for this man whom she knew so little about, who knew so little about her. "But I have to tell ye so ye understand. If I can't…if I can't love ye the way I should, ye will understand the why of it."

Still holding her hand, he raised his free hand and lifted her chin to look into her tear-filled eyes. "Claire, there is nothing you can tell me that will make me love you any less. You fill me with hope when I thought all hope was lost; you fill me with light when I've been in darkness for so long. I know it sounds crazy. Just one moment, one touch, and I knew it was you, forever and always."

She raised her hand and touched his face. "Oh, Tony, how do I begin to tell ye?" She heaved her chest and averted her eyes. "I was working at a restaurant in Teaghlach. I recently graduated from nursing school and was working there to keep myself busy until I found a nursing job. I was hoping to work at a hospital in Belfast. I was in the restaurant's storage room, just straightening things up a bit. I was alone when…when a man came in." Claire closed her eyes, as though trying to put the memory from her mind.

Tony's heart quickened as his stomach clenched. *Oh, God, no, no, no.* He held her hand tighter as she continued.

"He raped me, Tony. He raped me, and he hurt me. I had never been with a man, in that way. Now, ye see, I'm ruined. I'm ruined for ye. I always wanted my first time to be with my husband in our marriage bed—not on the dirty floor of a restaurant storeroom."

Tony stood, shaking his head. "My poor angel. I'm so sorry. I'm sorry you had to suffer that, but you're not ruined, Claire. What that monster did to you was horrible. But you're not ruined. It doesn't change who you are; it doesn't change what you mean to me. Is that what you're afraid of? That I would think less of you?"

The tears that she'd been struggling to keep inside now flowed freely, tracing a path down her flushed cheeks. "Tony, there's a fear inside me that I could never give myself to ye properly, as your wife, ye see. Ye had to know all of it before this, whatever this is, goes any further. I don't know if I could ever be your wife the way I should be. "

Too full of emotion to speak, Tony pulled Claire to him in a desperate embrace. He buried his head in her silky hair, inhaling her scent. Light was still aflame in his heart; hope was still alive in his soul.

"You shame me, and at the same time, you give me courage, angel," he said, his voice husky with emotion. "You trusted me with your pain, and you've shown me what a coward I've been. But just holding your hands gives me the courage to face my pain and share my pain."

He tightened his arms around her, drawing strength from her nearness. "I saw terrible things in Nam, Claire; things I still can't talk about, maybe I'll never be able to talk about them. And because those things haunt me, I didn't think I could ever love or be with a woman again. And then, there you were in the starlight, like an angel sent from heaven, and I knew, just by the touch of your hand, that I loved you. It was just the touch of your hand in mine, and I knew."

He finally pulled away from her to look into her eyes. "Claire, since you were honest with me, I have to be honest with you. "I don't know if I can ever be with you as I want to be. Even with all the feelings I have for you, I can't say for sure that I could love you the way you should be loved, physically.

"I don't know where that leaves us, sweetheart; I really don't. I just know that you brought me back into the light, and I don't want to go back to those dark places ever again."

Claire cupped his face with her hand. "Tony, we don't have to decide anything right now, do we? Why don't we just see where this takes us? At the very least, we shared our burdens, so we don't have to feel alone anymore. Even if we find that neither one of us can overcome our nightmares, can't we be thankful that we found one another? As long as we hold on to one another, Tony, we'll never be alone. Maybe that's enough."

Tony smiled into her beautiful face, marveling that she had come into his life. In his heart, he felt as though he'd known her a lifetime. "Just promise me one thing, Claire."

"I will if I can," she whispered.

"Never let go. Promise me you'll never let go."

She stepped willingly into his embrace and lifted her lips to his, sealing the promise with a kiss.

The kiss wasn't passionate, nor did it stir any primal desire inside either of them. Tony and Claire were still too raw from the emotional traumas each suffered. But for Claire, it was an enormous step toward trusting another person; for Tony, it was the first step in believing that all of his humanity hadn't been destroyed in Vietnam.

Although the kiss ended, their embrace did not. Again, there was no passion in the embrace; each seemed to draw strength and comfort from the other's nearness. It was enough; for now, it was enough.

****

Claire slid easily into a daily routine. She would spend her days with Liza, helping with daily housekeeping chores or exploring the neighborhood shopping haunts. If Claire was going to begin her new life here, she wanted to learn the ins and outs of everyday life in America. She decided to wait until September before applying for a nursing position in one of the hospitals nearby.

Bridget was happy to introduce Claire to the city's rapid transit system. Between Liza and Bridget, Claire visited the posh stores of Fifth Avenue and the shops in Greenwich Village, the Metropolitan Museum of Modern Art in Manhattan, and the Cloisters in Harlem. Every day, Claire enjoyed discovering life in New York City.

Tony filled her nights with long walks through the neighborhood, visits to local coffee shops where they would talk for hours, getting to know one another, and bistros where Tony proudly introduced her to his life-long friends. Claire was also introduced to life with a large Italian family in Brooklyn.

The Sabella family consisted of the matriarch, Maria Sabella, the eldest son, Enzo, who was married to Angelina, Tony's parents. Enzo and Angie had three children in addition to Tony; Angela, married with two children; Sophia, married with one child; and Frankie, seventeen. Maria Sabella also had two daughters; Lucia and Gina, both married with children and grandchildren. Altogether, the Sabellas totaled thirty immediate family members.

Because they were close-knit, they all saw the change in Tony since he came home, and they all shared the sadness that this once-gregarious man returned from the war solitary and broken. Word spread quickly throughout the family that Antonio had maybe, just maybe, found someone at last. It only took two Sunday dinners for the entire family to see the change in their son, brother, uncle, nephew, and cousin. And it was apparent to all that the reason for this change, or rather, this return of the Antonio they all knew and loved, was a beautiful girl with an Irish lilt.

Chapter Thirty-Three

Liza heard the old stairs creak as Claire descended from the second floor and walked slowly into the kitchen. She smiled as she turned to greet the young woman, but her smile quickly disappeared as she took in Claire's appearance. "My God, Claire, what is it? Are you sick, luv?"

Claire's usually creamy skin had a green tinge to it; her eyes were bloodshot and cloudy. She spoke in a whisper, swallowing hard as if struggling not to gag. "Oh, Aunt Liza, I feel so ill. I just made it to the loo before I threw up. I'm so dizzy, I barely made it down the stairs. I just came down for some tea, but after smelling the breakfast ye made for Uncle Tom, my stomach's turning again. I guess I'll go back to bed."

"Oh, Claire, dear, I'm sorry. Let me see if you have a temperature." She quickly approached Claire and felt her brow.

"No, darlin. You've no temperature, but you do feel a bit clammy. Maybe the heat is too much for you. It's been so dreadfully hot. You go back to bed, and I'll bring you a cool cloth. We've no plans today, so you just stay in bed." Liza put her hands on Claire's shoulders, turned her around, and pointed her toward the stairs. "Shall I help you?"

"No, thank ye. I just feel so tired, so nauseous, and dizzy. I just need to lie down a bit longer. I'll be fine,

Aunt Liza."

"You go along, luv. I'll be right up." Liza watched Claire drag herself up the stairs, a heavy feeling beginning to fill her heart. She had borne two children. She knew first-hand the symptoms of morning sickness.

****

The soft knocking on the door roused Claire. "Come in, Aunt Liza. I'm awake."

Liza entered with a small tray in hand. "Brought you some tea, along with some water and soda crackers. They help to settle the stomach. How are you doing, luv?" She sat on the edge of the bed and stroked Claire's brow.

Claire heaved a deep breath. "It's all right, Aunt Liza. I'm fine. We both know I'm not sick. Ye forget, I just graduated from nursing school. I know the whys and wherefores of my illness—or what we all call morning sickness."

"Oh, God, Claire. I was afraid that's what it might be. Are you sure?"

Claire lifted her downcast eyes to look at Liza. "Yes, I'm sure, Aunt Liza. I thought missing my time was because of all that's happened, and then traveling here. But now, with how I feel this morning, I'm sure. I'm pregnant, Aunt Liza, I'm pregnant, and I don't know what I'm going to do." She breathed deeply and then burst into sobs.

"I took your advice. I told Tony everything. I trusted him, and he didn't disappoint me; I love him, Aunt Liza, and I know he loves me. He told me what happened to me didn't change me. But now, I am changed, aren't I? I'm not the same Claire. I've got a life growing inside me, and I'm changed forever."

Gathering Claire in her arms, Liza attempted to sooth her troubled mind. "We'll figure it out, luv. We'll figure it out. You're not alone; remember that. I'm here, and we'll face this together. I promise you. We'll face this together." Liza held Claire until her tears were spent. Memories of holding Minnie in her arms all those years ago slowly unfolded in Liza's mind. Her heart ached for Claire as it had for Minnie.

But, thank God, this was different. It would be difficult, but Claire would have a choice about what she would do. It was 1966, not 1946. Minnie had no choice then. She had to bow to the will of a crazed nun who ruled with an iron heart and an iron fist. There would be no taking of Claire's child against her will; she would decide her own path and that of the child. Liza knew from Claire's breathing that she'd fallen asleep. She lay her down and crept from the room.

Painful memories of Liza's years in the convent now returned. How many girls like Minnie wasted away in the Convent of the Guardians of the Penitents? How many girls had their babies stolen from them? Too few had devoted sisters like Arlis O'Brien, who could not, would not, allow her sister to suffer in that horrid place. And not only did Arlis save Minnie, but she also saved Liza. She would owe Claire's mother a debt of thanks for the rest of her life. Every time she looked at her husband and their children, Liza uttered a prayer of thanksgiving for Arlis O'Brien.

And now, here was her friend's only child suffering as Minnie had. To think that this was happening again to someone in the same family overwhelmed Liza's senses. All those years ago, the only way she could help Minnie was to make a phone call. She closed her eyes and prayed for guidance. Slowly, a face began to emerge in her mind; a kind face, a strong face, a face of someone who might just love Claire enough to be the answer to Liza's prayers.

She crept downstairs, picked up the telephone and dialed. She cleared her throat and breathed deeply.

"Station 250, Raimy speaking."

She smiled, hoping it would somehow transfer into her voice. "Hello, Joe. It's Liza Brady. Would Tony happen to be available?"

"Sure, Mrs. Brady. He's around here someplace. Hold on." Covering the mouthpiece, Joe Raimy looked toward the station entrance. "Hey, Tony. Telephone for you."

Tony rounded the corner. "What's up?"

"It's Mrs. Brady."

****

Tony reached for the phone. "Hi, Mrs. Brady. Is everything okay? Is my grandmother all right?"

"Hi, Tony. Yes, Maria is fine. Are you coming by to visit Claire this evening?"

Although she struggled to sound casual, Tony noted the strain in the woman's voice. "I was planning on it. Is Claire all right?"

"Could you give me a few minutes before you see Claire? I want to talk to you alone. I can meet you in the park, by the fountain."

"Yes, of course, Mrs. Brady. Is seven o'clock okay?"

"Thank you, Tony. I'll see you at seven. Goodbye."

"Bye." Tony continued to stand with the phone to his ear a few minutes after he heard a click as Liza disconnected. Maybe she didn't know that Claire told him about the assault. Maybe she wanted to prepare Tony for what Claire already told him.

Since their revelations to one another almost two weeks ago, Tony thought of little else. Whenever he imagined the terror and pain Claire endured at the hands of some fiend, his heart ached for her. After they kissed that night—after their painful revelations—he wrapped her in his arms and held her tightly. There might not have been passion in their kiss, but there was the confirmation that neither of them was damaged beyond repair. There was the confirmation that both were capable—and deserving—of loving and being loved.

From the sound of Liza Brady's voice, Tony knew something was wrong. Whatever it was, Tony would fix it. He promised himself that, no matter what, he would not let the light leave him ever again. And Claire promised him that she would never let go.

Tony checked the time. It would be a long day.

Chapter Thirty-Four

Tony arrived at the fountain precisely at seven o'clock to find Liza sitting on a park bench, elbows on thighs, eyes closed, forehead resting on clasped hands. The sounds of summer whispered through the trees.

"Mrs. Brady?"

Liza lifted her head and opened her eyes. "Hello, Tony. Thank you for meeting me before you see Claire." She smiled and gestured for him to sit beside her.

"Yes, ma'am." He sat at the opposite end of the bench, his body language tense. "Please, Mrs. Brady. Please tell me what's wrong. Is Claire all right?"

"Tony, I'm not going to mince words with you. I know Claire has told you about the assault. She told me how kind and understanding you were, and I'm so relieved. Spending time with you and your family these past two weeks has helped Claire adjust to being away from her parents, her home, and is helping her heal from her ordeal. But this morning, we—that is, Claire—discovered something else, something more."

Tony looked at her questioningly.

"Tony, Claire is pregnant."

He closed his eyes and slowly shook his head. "My God, Mrs. Brady. I've got to go to her now; I've got to see her." He started to rise when Liza caught his arm.

"Tony, she doesn't know I'm here, telling you this.

I can't tell you what to say to her or even how to feel. I know it's only been a matter of weeks, but I know she has deep feelings for you and you for her. I wanted you to know just in case…well, just in case."

"Thank you, Mrs. Brady. Thank you for telling me. I'll take care of her. She won't go through this alone." He stood. "She's home now?"

Liza nodded. "She's on the roof."

Tony leaned down and gave Liza a gentle hug. "Thank you, Mrs. Brady. Thanks for being Claire's friend. I'll take care of her. I promise."

****

"Hallo? Hallo? Antonio? Is that you?"

Claire had been on her way to the roof when she heard the old woman's voice. She turned and leaned over the railing as Maria Sabella looked out her door. "No, Mrs. Sabella. Tony's not here yet. It's just me, Claire. Do ye need something?"

"Ah, *bene, bene.* You sit with me until Antonio comes, yes?"

Claire blinked back tears and swallowed hard. "Of course, I'll sit with ye." She turned and walked quickly down the steps. As she got to the bottom of the staircase, she raised her chin and forced a smile on her face. "How nice of ye to invite me in, Mrs. Sabella. Ye are very kind."

Maria beamed as she enveloped Claire in a warm embrace. *"Bella ragazza!* You come. I give you something to cool you. So hot. So hot."

After she gave Claire a glass of lemonade, she settled herself in her chair, wasting no time with chitchat. "So, you like my Antonio? He nice boy. He needs nice girl, like you. I try. I bring girls here to meet him, but he not interested. Then I see you come, and I say, 'Yes. That's the girl for my Antonio.' "

Claire smiled again, struggling to keep her emotions in check. "I agree with ye, Mrs. Sabella. Your grandson is a nice man." Her voice trembled. "I...I don't know if I'm the right girl for Tony, but you're very kind to say so."

"No, I right. I always right about people." Maria put her finger close to the corner of her eye. "I see inside people. I know. I know Antonio hurts—here." She placed her hand on her heart, and then she stunned Claire with her next words. "You hurt here, too. I see. But you don't see—Antonio don't see—that God has brought you together, to help each other not hurt anymore."

She paused as she studied Claire's stricken face. *The girl is in pain and fear. Mio Dio, my God, help them.* Maria pushed herself out of her rocker and walked over to Claire. Pulling her up, she hugged her tightly, her head resting on Claire's chest. Maria felt Claire relax in her arms. Her head lay against Claire's breast, and she heard the beat of the young woman's heart. Maria stiffened for a moment then pulled Claire closer, her own heart beating faster.

****

Tony wanted to rush up to the roof, but years of conditioning would not allow him to pass his nonna's door without a quick kiss and hello. As he entered his grandmother's home, he was taken aback by the scene that greeted him; the two people he loved most in the world locked in a tender embrace.

"Nonna?"

Maria smiled lovingly at her grandson as she

released Claire. "Antonio, look who's here." She continued smiling as Claire turned to Tony.

Claire smiled nervously. "I was on my way to the roof when your grandmother invited me in for a cool drink. Shall I get ye a glass of lemonade? Would that be all right, Mrs. Sabella?"

Maria shook her head. "No, you go to the roof. Wait for the stars." She reached up and cupped Claire's cheek in her wrinkled hand. "Thank you for visiting an old woman. You come back soon, yes?"

"Oh, I'd like that very much. Thank ye, Mrs. Sabella. Good night."

Tony hugged his grandmother. "Are you sure, Nonna? We can stay for a while."

"No, go now. Wait for the stars." She walked them toward the door. As she pushed them out, she whispered, "Things look better under the stars."

Chapter Thirty-Five

As it was from the first moment, Claire felt enveloped in a cocoon of safety and quiet happiness in Tony's touch. For Tony, Claire's touch dispelled all his doubts and fears, all his pain and sadness. Hand in hand, they walked up the stairs to the rooftop, under the shelter of twilight.

Tony opened the door, and they began to walk to the edge of the roof. But instead, Tony steered Claire around the corner of the storage shed. Claire was surprised to see a loveseat positioned against the wall of the shed. She looked questioningly at Tony.

He shrugged. "I thought we spent so much time up here, we might as well be comfortable. My mom wanted to get rid of it, so I took it off her hands." He raised Claire's hand to his lips and tenderly kissed each finger as he gazed into her eyes. Although she attempted a bright smile, Tony could see the pain in her violet eyes. He gently pulled her down beside him as he sat on the small couch. Never letting go of her hand, Tony slid his other arm around her shoulders, guiding her head to rest against his chest. He gently stroked her hair as she wrapped her arm around his waist. No words were needed as they sat holding one another, each feeling the intense love flowing from one to the other. Finally, Tony spoke.

"Sweetheart, I know it's only been two weeks, but

I don't think either of us has any doubt about how we feel. I also know that we both have a lot of baggage we're carrying with us. I can't guarantee that both, or either of us, will ever be completely rid of that baggage, but I do know, without a doubt, that I love you, and I have to have you in my life now and forever." Here, he paused and shifted his body so that she could see his face and look into his eyes.

"I know it's asking a lot because you're young and you have your whole life in front of you, and it should be a life that includes everything you want. But, honey, I'm going to be selfish right now because I can't imagine my life without you."

Without letting go of Claire's hand, he slid off the loveseat and knelt before her on one knee. "Claire O'Brien, my Irish angel, will you marry me?"

Claire struggled in vain to stop the tears. He saw the sadness in her eyes. As she opened her mouth to speak, Tony gently placed his fingers on her lips.

He smiled and gently squeezed her hand. "Wait, angel, I'm not finished. I know about the baby."

Claire's eyes widened in shock as she stood abruptly. She began to sob. "Oh, God, no, no, no. Ye were never to know; ye were never to know. I'm so ashamed, Tony. I'm so sorry I can't marry ye." She hung her head in utter despair as she wept.

Tony continued to hold tightly to her hand. He stood and placed his fingers under her chin, gently forcing her to look at him. "Claire, listen to me. I'm not a particularly religious guy. I go to church, sure— mostly because I don't want to disappoint my grandmother. But, sweetheart, don't you think this is meant to be? You came to me in the darkest time of my life; you came to me and brought light and hope back into my soul—just by holding my hand. I know you felt it, too. I know you were hurting and kind of lost, too. But we found each other, Claire—two people who, if not broken, are certainly damaged a bit, found each other. And now we have a chance at real happiness." Tony swallowed hard and fought to choke back tears of his own.

"Honey, I had given up all hope of having a wife and children. Then God sent me you. And now, I can have all of it—a wife, a child, all of it. Please, Claire. Please say yes. Say yes to marrying me. I promise I will make you happy. With you by my side, I know I have a real chance at getting rid of all this stuff in my head that's keeping me from being everything I can be. I know that together, our love will heal us. I love you, Claire. Please marry me."

****

Claire saw the unbridled love in Tony's eyes. She heard the sincerity in his words, but could she allow him to be a father to another man's child? A child conceived in violence—in rape? Could she let this wonderful man marry her and give her child a name, a home? She did, indeed, love Tony. And if she brought him light and hope, as he said, with the simple touch of her hand, she, too, had begun to heal—her heart, her mind, her soul—when he held her hand in his. Could she let him go?

Suddenly, she recalled the Sunday she attended Mass in Kilkenny when she decided to come to America. It was then that she felt so strongly that God had a plan for her and that her future would be in America. *Is this what God wanted for me? Did He send*

*me to America to meet Tony so that he would love me
and care for my baby? I do love him so much. I promise
you, O Lord, I will heal him. I will make him whole—
not for my sake, but his.*

Tony squeezed her hand and looked hopefully into
her eyes.

Claire returned the pressure and smiled. Her voice
trembled as she spoke. "I love ye, Tony. Ye are the
music of my heart. Yes, I will marry ye, and we'll be a
family." She released his hand and walked into his
waiting arms. Their lips met, the purity of their love
exploding in an aura of light that challenged even the
brightest star.

Chapter Thirty-Six

Liza busied herself in the kitchen, nervously wiping the counter for the tenth time when she heard the water rushing through the pipes, signaling that Claire had awakened.

She knew that Claire was meeting Tony on the roof last night. Liza's heart broke for the young couple; there were so many obstacles, so many painful truths to face. But Liza knew that facing those truths was the only way they would ever have a chance at happiness. With the unexpected news of Claire's pregnancy, hard decisions would have to be made and made very soon.

Could Tony accept another man's child? It would take an extraordinary person to come to terms with something of that magnitude. Was Tony that strong? Did he love Claire enough to claim this child as his own?

And Claire? What would she do? What could she do? Abortion was illegal, but if Claire were desperate enough, would she go that far? No, Liza couldn't imagine Arlis's daughter even considering that. The only recourse left to her would be to go to a home for unwed mothers and give the baby up for adoption.

Adoption! A lump formed in Liza's throat as she recalled that day all those years ago when Sister Assumpta came into the nursery and took Minnie's son from his crib and handed him to the American couple.

The sly old witch waited until Minnie nursed and settled him. The memory was as vivid as if it occurred just yesterday.

****

Minnie's child's birth was fraught with complications; her labor started two weeks early and was intense from the start. Perhaps it was because she was so young and her body not yet fully developed.

As the novice Elizabeth, Liza was present for numerous births within the confines of the Convent of the Guardians of the Penitents. She witnessed the agony these young women were forced to endure when denied any kind of medication to ease their labor. Most of these girls were ignorant of the birthing process, being almost babies themselves.

Liza herself knew nothing of labor and delivery when she arrived at the convent. Still, since that was her *obedience* as dictated by Sister Assumpta, she was forced to assist with deliveries during the four years of her confinement. Thankfully, Liza had an instinct for nursing and provided a modicum of comfort and proper care to the new mothers and their babies.

Seventy-five-year-old Sister Gertrude was the resident midwife. She and Sister Assumpta were of like mind, believing that the pain the girls suffered during labor and delivery was God's punishment for their transgression. And if a girl bled to death or suffered a stroke on the table, it was God's will. Not the slightest attempt was made to lessen the pain.

Minnie was in labor for more than twenty hours with no steady progression except for the intensity of the contractions. Her only source of comfort was in the touch of the novice Elizabeth, who never let go of her hand nor ceased to offer words of encouragement.

As the contractions increased in intensity, so did the bleeding. Finally, Minnie fainted. Elizabeth wasn't sure if it was because of the pain or the loss of blood, or both. Not being able to stand the girl's suffering anymore, the novice gathered her courage. "Sister Gertrude, forgive my impertinence, but I don't think Minerva's pelvis is allowing the child to come through the birth canal. Perhaps we should take her to hospital."

The old nun sneered at the novice. "I've seen this before, girl. The babe's not in the right position, tis all. I'm going to turn it a tad. That should do the trick."

The novice watched in horror as the midwife reached her hands inside Minerva's body and manually turned the infant. As she retracted her blood-soaked arms, miraculously, the baby's head crowned. Sister Gertrude then gently turned the baby's shoulders and guided them through Minerva's narrow pelvis. The rest of the tiny body quickly followed, and baby boy 1947-37 came into the world. Liza was thankful that Minnie was unconscious through the final stage of her ordeal. She was quite aware that any concern the old midwife demonstrated was not out of compassion for the young mother; she just didn't want to risk harming this latest addition to the convent's *inventory.*

When Minnie regained consciousness, the child was brought to her. Again, there was no intentional kindness in this, but instead, it was a purely pragmatic gesture. It was believed that a child began to flourish quickly if nurtured on its mother's milk shortly after birth.

Although weak from the arduous labor and extreme loss of blood, Minnie quickly took to nursing her son, whom she immediately named Brian. For a girl of fifteen, she seemed to have a highly-developed maternal instinct. From the moment Minnie held Brian, all memory of his conception and birth were buried deep in her young mind. She was overwhelmed with the knowledge that this child belonged to her, and the love she felt for this tiny little being surpassed anything she ever felt before.

It was standard procedure at the convent for new mothers to nurse their babies for six to eight months, and then the adoptions would take place. In Minnie's case, however, the adopting parents were working under time constraints. Elizabeth overheard Sister Assumpta telling Sister Gertrude that a couple was adopting an infant to fulfill a legal requirement; if the gentleman could not produce a male heir before his grandfather died, his entire inheritance would be forfeit. The couple had to return to America with an heir before the old man's death. The grandfather's health was deteriorating quickly, so the couple invented a story that the woman delivered a baby boy while traveling abroad. The adopting couple knew they were risking the infant's life by undertaking a trans-Atlantic trip so soon after the child's birth, but the money involved far outweighed the value of human life. Seven days after Minnie gave birth to her son, the child was on his way to America.

Chapter Thirty-Seven

Liza sat at the table, wiping her eyes as she tucked the painful memories away. After all these years, she still felt enormous guilt for not being able to save Brian. She would talk with Tom tonight. She knew he would agree that Claire would not have to give up her child. They would take care of her; they would support her. Nothing she could do to help Claire would ever begin to repay the debt Liza and her husband owed to Arlis and Jamie O'Brien. She rose from the table to pour herself another cup of coffee when the telephone rang.

"Hello?"

"Liza, this is Maria. You come over for coffee today? I want to talk to you."

"Good morning, Maria. Yes, I can stop by. Is anything wrong?"

"You come as soon as you can. I make coffee."

The phone call ended abruptly, leaving a leaden feeling deep in Liza's stomach. Claire still had not appeared, so Liza put her coffee cup in the sink, took a quick look in the mirror then headed out the door.

Liza just raised her hand to rap on the dense wood, when Maria Sabella opened the door. She turned and waved Liza into her home, a home filled with the scents and sights of family.

"Come into the kitchen. I'm making bread, but it's rising, so we have time to talk."

The feeling of dread continued in the pit of Liza's stomach. *Something's happened. She couldn't know about Claire; how could she?*

Liza struggled to keep the nervousness out of her voice. She smiled brightly at the older woman. "Oh, the bread smells wonderful, Maria. All these years we've known each other, and you've never taught me how to make bread. I'm going to put that on my 'to-do list'. " She eased herself onto a kitchen chair, waiting for Maria to join her.

Maria bustled about the kitchen, checking the rising dough as she poured the strong Italian coffee, placing a steaming mug in front of her guest. She took a chair next to Liza.

"Claire visited me last night—before she went up to the roof. We had nice visit. Liza, I know things. I know things about people, sometimes even before they know. I know from the minute I see Claire when you bring her from airport; I know she's the one for my treasure—my Antonio. I pray, and I pray, and then Claire comes here, and I know. Even though my Antonio is still hurting from war, I see a light in his eyes again, a peace. And I know that the light comes from Claire. I know Claire is hurting, too. But when she is with Antonio, I feel her pain not so much. I think, 'Thank you, God. Thank you for bringing them together.' But then, last night…"

Maria reached for Liza's hand and grasped it tightly. "Liza, you tell me now. You tell me the truth. Is Claire going to have a bambino?"

Liza couldn't mask the apparent shock on her face. She knew it was futile to lie to her friend. She inhaled deeply and looked steadily into Maria's eyes. "Yes,

Maria. Claire is pregnant." She took a long sip of coffee, debating how much to tell Tony's grandmother. She had no way of knowing what transpired between Claire and Tony last night, but somehow, Maria suspected the truth. Whatever happened between the young couple, the pregnancy would be evident soon enough. She watched Maria's reaction to the news.

The old woman closed her eyes and bowed her head, nodding sadly. "I know it last night. Does she have husband in Ireland? If she is having bambino, why is she here?"

Liza squeezed Maria's wrinkled hand. "Maria, it isn't my place to tell Claire's story, but I think it would be too painful for her to tell you." Liza took another shaky breath, straightened her shoulders, and raised her chin. "And, I suppose, before I tell you Claire's story, I have to tell you mine."

Maria placed her other hand atop Liza's and squeezed gently. "You tell me. I listen."

Liza had difficulty swallowing, her mouth suddenly dry, the muscles constricting in her throat. Her voice was thick with emotion as she began to speak. "It was such a long time ago, a lifetime, actually."

Liza began to weep as she told Maria about her life in Ireland: her arranged marriage, the lengths to which she went to break up the arrangement, and her father's revenge.

She recounted her life in the convent and how she came to know a fifteen-year-old rape victim and through her, how she came to know Arlis O'Brien. Liza told Maria of Arlis's bravery the day she rescued Minnie and herself, as well. She explained that, from the time she arrived in America, she and Arlis worked hand-in-hand to help other girls escape a similar fate to the one Minnie O'Shea suffered. The hardest part of the story to recount was Claire's assault and newly-discovered pregnancy.

****

Maria Sabella sat motionless on the kitchen chair, her mind reeling, her heart aching. *So much pain, so much hurt, Mio Dio, Mio Dio.* She rose slowly and stood before Liza. She placed both her hands on either side of the woman's face and placed a gentle kiss on Liza's forehead.

****

As Maria kissed her, Liza wrapped her arms tightly around the old woman's rotund form. Maria pulled the seated woman to her chest and stroked her hair. At that moment, Liza realized how she, herself, missed the loving touch of a woman—a mother figure—to hold her in understanding and compassion. Several minutes passed in this silent embrace.

Finally, Liza released her arms and wiped her eyes. "Maria, I want you to know that I told Tony about the baby. As with you, I knew it would be too painful for Claire to tell him. I haven't seen her yet this morning, so I don't know if Tony told her he knew everything. I think it's obvious to everyone how they feel about each other, so I sincerely hope they will remain good friends. Tom and I will keep Claire with us. It's 1966 America. And there is no way in hell I will let Claire give up her child."

****

Maria padded to the kitchen window and looked out upon the busy street. Her mind was full of what Liza just told her as well as her own thoughts about all the people involved in these three distinct tragedies.

Liza looked at her quizzically. "Maria, one thing I don't understand. How did you know Claire was pregnant?"

Maria turned back to her. Her voice came out in a hushed whisper. "I felt new life in her."

Liza nodded, obviously confused by Maria's revelation. "I see. Well, as I said, I hope Tony and Claire will remain good friends."

A small smile played at the corners of Maria's mouth. She turned her gaze back to the window. "You don't know my treasure."

Chapter Thirty-Eight

Liza returned home, unsettled by her discussion with Maria Sabella. Still, she felt a certain comfort, too, knowing that she confided intimate details of her early life to her neighbor, and Maria offered her support, not recriminations.

How could Maria have possibly known Claire was pregnant? Liza dismissed Maria's comment about feeling *new life*, chalking it up to an old woman's superstitious beliefs—and yet, how else could she have known?

Liza was hesitant about telling Tony's grandmother all that happened in Ireland. Still, she disclosed everything so that, hopefully, Maria could understand what Claire had gone through—and what she was going through now. Maria thought that either Claire was married, or she was promiscuous. Liza knew how Maria adored Tony. Of course, she would do everything she could to protect her grandson from any more emotional pain. He, indeed, had suffered severe emotional damage from the war; finding out the woman he recently fell in love with was pregnant might be his breaking point.

Liza's heart was heavy from the memories she raked up this morning of Minnie's labor and delivery all those years ago. Reliving her own horrors, as well as Minnie's and Claire's, left her feeling incredibly sad. She wanted to call Tom. Liza needed to hear her husband's quiet voice. She needed him to tell her everything would be all right. As she had most of her life, Liza needed him. He always was her strength.

She shuddered to think of what her life would be like if Tom hadn't loved her enough to pursue her; if her mother hadn't contacted him; if he hadn't reached out to Arlis. Would Liza have turned into a cold-hearted, cruel, lonely old woman like Sister Assumpta? Tom risked everything—his job, his very life—to rescue her from her convent prison. Liza loved him for all these things, but she loved him mostly because she knew the depth of his love for her. Just thinking about him and their life together lightened her heart. She wouldn't bother him at work. She would pour out her heart to him later—as he held her tenderly in the quiet of the night.

A soft cough interrupted her thoughts. She turned to see Claire enter the kitchen, looking wan but peaceful.

"Good morning, Aunt Liza. Ye seemed so deep in thought; I didn't want to disturb ye. Are ye all right?"

Liza smiled at the young woman, looking so much like her mother. "I'm fine. Thank you for asking. More importantly, dear, how are you?"

Claire sighed and took a seat at the kitchen table. She smiled sadly. "I guess I have ye to thank for telling Tony about the baby."

Liza closed her eyes and nodded slowly. "Yes, dear, I told Tony about the baby. I knew it would be too painful for you to tell him. I hope you're not angry with me, Claire. I just can't bear for you to deal with anything more. You're not to worry about going away to have the baby. This isn't Ireland; this is America.

You have the right to choose what you want to do and how you want to live your life. You will stay with us, have the child, and we'll figure it out as we go along. I've told you before, Claire. I owe your parents my life—my children's lives, come to that. Whatever you want to do, I'm here for you—we're all here for you."

Claire's voice was barely a whisper. "Tony asked me to marry him last night, Aunt Liza. He asked me to marry him—baby and all—and I said yes."

Liza gently pulled Claire into her arms. "Oh, Claire. I am so happy for you. I'm so happy for both of you."

Just then, Bridget stomped into the kitchen, her ginger curls bouncing with each step. "Mom, would you please tell Sean to get off the phone. I have to call Pam. We're supposed to go to the movies tonight, and I—hey, what's going on?" Her eyes widened. "Did you and Tony break up, Claire? I heard he used to do that a lot with girls. I'm sorry. Guys are such jerks. He's gorgeous, but still—what a jerk. I'm going to tell Frankie that, too."

Liza pulled away from Claire as both women shared a quiet laugh. "Calm yourself, Bridget. Claire has some news."

"What? You're not going back to Ireland, are you? I know you've been very homesick, but you can't go back there. Please don't tell me you're leaving."

"Bridget. Stop talking for a minute and just listen. Go ahead, Claire."

A light blush crept over Claire's face, hiding her morning paleness. "Well, Bridget, I am leaving, but I won't be going far, at least I don't think it's that far. I—"

"You're getting your own place? Cool! Can I come and stay with you sometime? We could have a real blast. Maybe—"

"Bridget! Stop! Just listen to what Claire is telling you, please."

Claire giggled at the teenager's impatience. "Tony asked me to marry him, Bridget, and I said yes."

"Married? You're getting married to Tony, to that hu—" Bridget caught the disapproving look on her mother's face. "I mean, to that gorgeous man? Oh...my....gosh. It's so romantic, just like in the movies—like love at first sight." Bridget crossed the room in seconds and wrapped her arms tightly around Claire. "Oh, Claire, I'm so happy for you. You were really bummed when you came here, but since you met Tony, you don't look sad anymore. I have to tell Pam."

Claire spoke quickly. "Bridget, would ye wait a bit on that? Tony just asked me last night, and we want to tell his grandmother and his parents tonight."

Liza nodded. "Yes, Bridget, let's let this be our secret—just us three girls—until Claire and Tony tell his parents and Maria."

"Oh, cool. Yes, that makes it even more romantic. Mrs. Sabella is going to be so happy. I see the way she smiles whenever she sees you, Claire. She likes you a lot. And Frankie told me how she's been trying to find a 'nice girl' for Tony. This is so, so totally cool. I promise—I won't say anything to anybody until you say it's okay."

Bridget was so excited, she actually skipped from the room. Liza shook her head as she heard her daughter repeat one phrase over and over again as she climbed the stairs to her room, her phone call to Pam forgotten. "Rad, this is so totally rad!"

Claire smiled as her eyes followed Bridget from the kitchen. "I don't think Bridget has any idea how right she is, Aunt Liza. It was love at first sight for us, or rather, love at first touch. I want ye to know—it's important that ye know—I'm not marrying Tony for the baby; I'm marrying him because I've loved him from the first time I held his hand. It was like magic, Aunt Liza, truly, like magic. And I have to say it again. I've had this feeling for a while now that God has a plan for me. There's something I'm supposed to do; something I'm a part of—and Tony's a part of it, too. I know it in my heart, Aunt Liza. I know it in my heart."

Liza watched Claire closely as she was speaking. The young woman was radiant. Liza thought back to Maria's comment about feeling new life within Claire's. Now she listened as Claire talked about a divine plan in all this. *Perhaps there's truth in what Claire believes. Who am I to discount the power of God? Didn't I witness His power when Minnie and I escaped the hell we were living in? And today, when Claire told me Tony was going to marry her, even though she was carrying another man's child. A divine plan? Yes, I have to agree with Claire. Something extraordinary is happening here, something divine.*

Chapter Thirty-Nine

"Mama, what time is Anthony stopping by?" Enzo Sabella sat directly in front of the fan, trying to stop the sweat from trickling down his chest as he sipped his beer. "Who else is coming? Can I take off my tie, please? I'm dying here."

Maria frowned at her eldest child. "You sound like a little boy, Enzo. Stop whining. Yes, take off your tie." The old lady took pity on her son. "You can roll up your sleeves, too." Maria Sabella was not happy. She was used to feeding her family, but Tony called and insisted that she not go to the trouble of making dinner. Well, she complied—no dinner—but he hadn't said anything about dessert. Maria had prepared Tony's favorite dessert—panna cotta with fresh raspberries.

Angie sat, fanning herself as she settled in a chair opposite her husband. "En, I agree with Mama. Stop whining. I know you want to get home where it's cooler, but Tony said he wanted to see us tonight, and it's easier to come here than to get Mama to our house." Angie pursed her lips. "Do you think he got a promotion at work?"

"To what? Fire chief? He's too young for that, Angie. Naw. Maybe he just wants to visit, like he used to. Since he met Claire, he's like his old self, don't you think? He seems calmer, not so uptight all the time. That little girl's been good for him." Enzo directed his

227

comments to his mother. "What do you think, Mama?"

Maria smiled an enigmatic smile and shrugged her shoulders.

Angie watched her mother-in-law closely. She squinted her eyes and cocked her head. "Mama, you know something, don't you? You always have feelings, and they're always right on the nose. What are you feeling about tonight?"

Before Maria could feign ignorance, they heard one short rap on the door as Tony entered the apartment—hand-in-hand with Claire.

He immediately walked over to Maria and kissed her cheek. "Hi, Nonna." After Maria, Tony greeted his mother and then his father, each with a kiss. "Hi, Mom, Pop."

Claire followed close behind Tony, greeting Maria with a soft kiss. "Good evening, Mrs. Sabella." As she approached Tony's parents, she bent to kiss Tony's mother as she smiled at his father. Angie smiled warmly, and Enzo stood and returned Claire's smile. "Good evening, Mrs. Sabella, Mr. Sabella."

"Claire, dear, it's nice to see you again. How are you bearing this heat? If it bothers you, you certainly don't show it. You look so fresh and cool."

"Thank ye, Mrs. Sabella. I cheated a bit and took a cold shower just before Tony came by."

"Well, whatever you do, you look beautiful. You and Tony sit down. What would you like to drink? Tony, do you want a beer?"

"Thanks, Mom. I'm good. Sweetheart, how about I get you some lemonade?"

Enzo and Angie exchanged looks.

"No, thank ye, Tony. I'm grand."

Maria was silent, carefully watching the interaction between the young couple.

Enzo had just raised his glass of beer to his lips when Tony began to speak.

"Thanks for coming over to Nonna's tonight. Claire and I have something to tell all of you. I don't think it will come as much of a surprise. I've asked Claire to marry me, and she said yes."

Angie raised her hands to her face and covered her mouth, her eyes wide with surprise. Enzo smiled broadly and uttered a quiet "I'll be damned."

Only a second passed before Angie was on her feet, pulling Claire into a warm embrace while Enzo hugged his son, his grin so wide, he looked like a little boy on Christmas morning.

"Congratulations, son. That's terrific news, terrific news. Now, may I kiss the bride-to-be?"

Angie released Claire only to grab her son and hold him tightly. Her throat constricted with emotion. "Oh, honey, I'm so happy for you. God bless you both."

Enzo carefully wrapped his arms around Claire and gently kissed her cheek. "Welcome to the family, Claire, dear. We couldn't be happier for you and Anthony."

Maria remained seated in her rocker; she closed her eyes and bowed her head, her lips moving silently.

Tony was surprised that his grandmother hadn't acknowledged his announcement. A niggle of dread settled in the pit of his stomach. "Nonna? Nonna, are you all right?"

Claire stepped beside Tony and slipped her hand in his as they walked toward Maria's rocker. She knelt before the old woman. "Mrs. Sabella? I love your

229

grandson very much. I promise ye I will make him happy; I'll always be a good wife to him, and I'll always take care of him. He's the music of my heart, ye see."

Maria slowly rose from her rocker as Claire followed suit. Her ancient eyes glistened with tears as she opened her arms to embrace her grandson and then Claire. As she hugged Claire, she gently pulled her head down toward her and whispered in her ear. "And you are the music of mine."

Claire placed another soft kiss on the aged cheek. "Thank ye, Nonna."

Angie was sharing an embrace with Enzo. She pulled away quickly, her excitement palpable. "Come sit down, you two. We have plans to make. Have you set a date already? Maybe Christmas? That would be a lovely time to get married—everything all decorated. Of course, it might be hard to find a hall. And then, of course, there's the caterer; they're always so busy that time of year and then…"

"Mom? Mom, hold up a minute. Claire and I were thinking a bit sooner than Christmas."

"Oh, honey, I'm sorry. I'm just so excited. How much sooner? Thanksgiving? That's a lovely time, too—either way, the whole family will be together. Oh, Claire, will your parents be coming over for the wedding? They are most welcome to stay with us."

"Angie! Give the kids a chance to talk. Sheesh. We've waited so long for Tony to settle down, let's savor the moment." He softened his chastisement with a gentle kiss. "Go on, Anthony."

Tony's mother blushed. "I'm sorry, Claire, Anthony. As your dad said, we've waited so long to hear those words from you." She beamed at the young couple standing before them, hands still clasped. "I'll be quiet—I promise."

"Thanks, Mom. I'm glad you're happy for us. Claire and I were thinking…"

"Now. You get married now."

Four pairs of eyes stared in shocked silence at Maria Sabella, who was standing next to Claire, holding her hand.

Enzo was the first to speak. "Mama, what do you mean *now*? They just can't up and marry now. We have to make arrangements, decisions, plans."

"What arrangements? They already make decision to get married, so they get married at St. Paul's, on my birthday. Enzo, you know you don't make plans for marriage—God does."

Maria shook her head in bewilderment. "You never listen to me. I tell you over and over, God has His own plans for you, for all of us. And besides, that's what I want for my birthday." She made a decisive nod and sat back down in her rocker, like a queen issuing a royal decree.

"Mama…" Enzo was silenced as Maria looked at him with one raised eyebrow.

Tony bent low and kissed his beloved grandmother's cheek. "Thank you, Nonna." Turning to his parents, he began to speak—his voice so full of emotion that he struggled with every word. "Mom, Pop, you know—we all know—that I came back from Nam a different guy.

"Things happened over there I don't think I will ever be able to talk about. I thought any chance of a normal life was gone. And then just a few weeks ago, I met Claire up on the roof. She's brought light back into my heart. I don't want to spend one more minute without her in my life—completely and forever." He looked lovingly at Claire as he raised her hands to his lips.

Angelina Sabella stood looking at her son, weeping tears of sadness—and joy. She knew he returned from the war broken and sad. But to hear him put his loneliness into words—and such beautiful words— touched her heart more deeply than she had ever been touched before.

Enzo sniffed loudly and cleared his throat. "Well then, I guess Mama's going to get a birthday present none of us will ever forget."

Angie frowned as a thought entered into her mind. "Oh, wait. What about the banns? Don't they have to be read before you can get married?"

"Three weeks before wedding. I know. I call Father Calabrese tomorrow. Banns will be posted on Sunday and then two more. Enough time. Angelina, you're as bad as Enzo. I told you—I told all of you—God's plans. Have faith."

Claire was standing quietly as the Sabella family discussed her wedding, but she didn't mind. Her heart was full of love for this man who was willing to marry her while carrying another man's child. She was as shocked as everyone else that Tony's grandmother was insisting they get married immediately.

She and Tony fretted that the marriage would appear rushed, but Maria's edict was not to be questioned. Once again, the feeling of being part of something beyond her understanding filled her. Claire felt the hand of God in all of this. Perhaps the end result would never be revealed to her, but she was comfortable with that. She felt blessed that she'd been allowed to be a participant in this—whatever *this* was.

"Claire, will your parents be able to make arrangements to come so soon?"

"Unfortunately, Mrs. Sabella. I don't think my parents will be coming. My mum has to care for Aunt Minnie. And from what I read in her last letter, my da was just promoted to chief constable at home, so they couldn't come even if they didn't have Aunt Minnie."

"Sweetheart, I've got a surprise for you."

Claire looked questioningly at Tony.

"I figured your parents wouldn't be able to come here for the wedding, so as my gift to you, angel, we are going to honeymoon in Ireland—Teaghlach, to be exact."

Claire's breath caught in her throat as she wrapped her arms around the man who captivated her heart with just the touch of his hand.

Chapter Forty

Claire and Tony spent the Friday before their wedding day settling her into Tony's apartment. They hadn't bothered to enlist anyone's help; only a few of Claire's suitcases had to be moved from the Brady's brownstone to the little four-room apartment a few miles away. Tony was careful not to let Claire lift anything. She was touched by his concern, even though she thought he was being a bit too cautious.

"Darlin, stop. I can hang up my own clothes. What do ye think women with two or three bairns do when they're expecting?"

"I don't know what other people do, sweetheart, but my wife will take it easy. Now put those dresses on the bed, and kiss me...please."

"Are ye getting bossy, husband-to-be? You'll learn soon enough that will never fly with me. Wait till ye meet my mum." Claire wrapped her arms around Tony's neck and willingly shared a kiss, followed by a long embrace.

Unwittingly, they had slipped into a comfortable relationship, talking openly about Claire's pregnancy, as if it were their child, together—but they were careful to do it only when they were alone. They decided that, except for Liza Brady and Claire's parents, no one would ever know that the child Claire was carrying wasn't Tony's.

From the very beginning, Tony put the *third party* out of his mind. The baby that grew within Claire was his child—without reservations. Claire and this child had, indeed, been the answer to his most profound hopes and dreams.

A light rap on the door caused a reluctant end to their embrace. "It's gotta be my mom. She called earlier before you came. She has something for us." Tony clasped Claire's hand as they answered the door together.

Angelina Sabella stood unseen behind an enormous box beautifully wrapped in wedding paper. "Hi, you two. Tony, please take this. I barely made it up the stairs."

"Mom, why didn't you come up and get me? Honestly, what is it with these women in my life who don't trust my Superman strength?" Tony quickly took the unwieldy package from his mother. "Whoa, what's in here?"

"Well, open it and see, dear. Just wait till I sit down and catch my breath." She kissed Claire on the cheek before sitting on the sofa and kicking off her shoes. "This heat hasn't let up since June. Honestly, I hope Father Calabrese has those fans going tomorrow. The church is going to be an oven. I might faint."

Claire sat down next to Angie and smiled. "Thank ye for the gift, Mrs. Sabella. That's very kind of ye." She watched as Tony tore at the paper, noting his excitement. *Just like a little boy at Christmas.*

Angie returned her smile. "Just so you know, dear, 'Mr. and Mrs. Sabella' is fine for today, but tomorrow after the wedding, I will expect 'Mom and Dad' from you. Legally, you might just be an in-law, but our children's spouses become our children in our hearts and minds. Enzo and I have always believed it doesn't matter who made you; it matters who loves you. And, Claire dear, Enzo and I couldn't love you more if you were our own flesh and blood. So remember—tomorrow, it's 'Mom and Dad,' okay?"

Tony stopped unwrapping the gift to watch Claire closely as his mother spoke. Angie would never know how much her sentiments meant to both of them. Claire met Tony's eyes as they shared a private smile. He returned his attention to the enormous box. "Okay, wrapping is off. Sweetheart, do you want to open the box?"

"No, darlin. You're having too much fun. Ye go on and finish what ye started."

"Yesss! I hear and obey."

Angie turned to Claire and patted her hand. "Good start, dear. The training should begin right away. It takes a lifetime."

Tony grinned at his mother as he opened the box and removed the gift.

Claire's eyes lit up with happiness. "Oh, Mrs. Sabel...Mom." She smiled as she stumbled on the word, stressing the American pronunciation. "Mom, it's beautiful."

"What is it?" Tony asked.

"It's bedding, darlin. A bedspread, pillows, sheets, a blanket, bedding."

"But I have sheets—pillows, too. Maybe I don't have a bedspread like that, but..."

"Well, I'm glad you appreciate them, Claire, dear. Men can be obtuse sometimes. And I made sure to wash everything, so they're ready to be put on the bed."

Angie turned to her son.

"Tony, every bride should have all new linens for the marriage bed—especially when the couple moves into the husband's old apartment." She made a cursory look around Tony's apartment. "Well, at least it's clean, but it needs a woman's touch."

Tony scowled. "Of course, it's clean. Do you remember who raised me? Between you and Nonna, there isn't a chance in hell I wouldn't have a clean apartment."

"Well, you still have some work to do with your language, but we'll leave that for another time—baby steps." Angie rose from the couch and slid into her shoes. "I have to be off.

"I know it's an Italian tradition for the female relatives to make up the marriage bed for the bride and groom, but I think there's something so romantic about a couple making up their marriage bed together, so I leave you to it." With a quick hug for Claire and a loving pat on her son's cheek, Angie walked out the door.

Now it was Claire's turn to watch Tony closely as his mother exited the apartment. She noted the pain in his eyes, and her heart tightened with compassion and love. She wrapped her arms around his waist and listened to his heartbeat as he began to speak, somehow the pain he was feeling sounded in his voice.

"Claire? Sweetheart, am I being selfish in marrying you? You could easily find someone who would love you—physically, I mean—the way you should be loved. It's not too late to stop this, you know. You…"

Claire stopped his words with her lips. She poured all the love she felt for him into that kiss, as she ran her fingers through his thick, wavy hair.

Tony's response to her mouth was immediate as he pulled her tight against his body. It was the longest kiss they had shared, and it left them both breathless.

"I'm not for breaking promises, Mr. Sabella. I promised ye I would never let go, and I never will." Claire looked deeply into his eyes as she ran her fingers over his handsome face. "Now, if that's your way of getting out of making the bed, I guess I know what to expect for the next fifty years."

He caught her hand in his and raised it to his lips and whispered. "You found me out, my Irish angel." He tossed Claire the pillows as he grabbed the new sheets and bedspread. "Only fifty years? I was thinking at least seventy-five."

She cocked her head and looked at him straight-faced. "Well, darlin, I guess that will depend on how well ye make the bed."

Chapter Forty-One

Tony and Claire climbed the two flights of stairs and stood before the door to their apartment. They left the birthday party/wedding reception amid cheers and good wishes from all their friends and family members, along with several good-natured winks, nods, and nudges from Tony's many male friends.

Standing at the doorway, Tony pulled her to him and kissed her deeply. "I love you, Mrs. Sabella, my beautiful Irish angel."

Claire's smile was radiant as she gazed into his eyes. "And I love you, Anthony, the music of my heart."

His heart surged with joy as he unlocked the door. Lifting her in his arms, he carried her across the threshold. Reluctant to put her down, Tony took Claire to the bedroom and collapsed onto the bed with her still in his arms. They reclined together, wrapped in each other's embrace. They lay side by side, enjoying the exquisite feeling of oneness.

Claire spoke first, softly, haltingly. "I've never done this before, Tony. I've never laid on a bed with a man before. I'm feeling strange. But then I think— you're my husband, so it's allowed."

Tony worried he'd been too forward with her. He shifted away from her and raised himself on one elbow to look at her. "I'm sorry, sweetheart. Too much, too soon?"

"Oh no, darlin. I like it. I like lying next to ye. It will just take some getting used to, is all."

"I think I'm dreaming; I still can't believe you're my wife." He gently traced his fingers along her brow, her eyes, her nose, down her cheeks, outlining her full lips. His fingers lingered there, and then he continued to her neck, fluttering his fingers down her arm. He wanted to keep exploring her body, but fear overcame his desire.

****

Claire studied his face as he followed his fingers gliding across her silken skin. She watched as a myriad of emotions flickered in his eyes; of course, his love for her was ever-present, but Claire also saw longing—and fear.

She was astonished that she, herself, felt no fear as he touched her. These were not the cold, violent gropings of an animal; they were the loving caresses of her husband, and she trusted him completely. At that moment, glowing embers of desire began to burn deep inside. She would bury these longings until she could share them fully and completely with this man she adored.

And that moment would come—Claire believed it with all her heart. Her love would heal Tony and would make him whole again.

"Darlin, ye must be burning up in that suit. Why don't ye take it off and put on some shorts and a shirt? I'd like nothing more than to shed this dress and do the same."

****

Tony smiled, grateful that he would have an excuse

to stand up. Lying beside her was torture for him, wanting to touch her but not sure where it would lead— or rather, fearing it would lead to a dead end.

"Thank you. I was wondering how long I would have to wear this thing. I'll go take a shower, and then we can go through some of the wedding gifts." As he started to roll off the bed, he turned back to Claire for one more kiss.

****

A contented smile played on her mouth as he lifted his lips from hers. "Go take a shower. I'll still be here when you're finished."

Claire closed her eyes and mentally followed Tony's soft padding across the room to the bathroom. She heard him turn the shower on. It dawned on her that she never saw him without a shirt on. She saw his legs, or rather part of his legs when he wore shorts. She saw his bare arms in short-sleeved shirts, and she admired his physique when he wore T-shirts. Suddenly, Claire was struck with an overwhelming curiosity to see his body. She felt her cheeks heat with embarrassment, and she giggled softly to herself. *You're daft, girl.* Again, she was astonished that she felt no fear of intimacy with Tony. She knew that when they finally did make love, it would be the natural culmination of the love they shared.

Still laughing to herself, she rose slowly from the bed, unzipped her dress, and stepped out of it, carefully hanging it in the closet. She lay back down on the bed, feeling much cooler just wearing her slip. She closed her eyes again, and immediately, visions of her husband, shirtless, came into her mind. Sleep took her as these pleasant thoughts brought her peace.

****

Tony stood under the pelting shower, his mind filled with visions of the day—their wedding day. He saw Claire gliding down the aisle of St. Paul's on the arm of Tom Brady, her eyes locked on Tony's, a shy smile on her face. Sunbeams slanted through the stained-glass windows, casting a golden aura around her as she walked toward him. There was no doubt that she was the answer to his prayers, his Irish angel. His heart tightened as he recalled her soft voice, pledging her love to him before God and everyone. The look of complete love, complete trust, in her beautiful violet eyes left him in awe.

His thoughts drifted to his new wife, now lying on the bed—their bed—in the next room. His fingers still tingled as he re-lived their journey through her luxuriant hair, down her face, her mouth, her arms. He braced his arms against the shower wall and bowed his head, his heart beating faster, his breath quickening as the shower sprayed icy drops on his back and down his legs. But the frigid water did nothing to quell the heat deep inside. He wanted her so badly; he wanted to touch her, feel her, love her. He wanted…He wanted…

He raised his face to accept the cold spray. It helped to clear his head, to bring him out of his despair. He wouldn't let these negative thoughts ruin this day. Some day, he and Claire would consummate their marriage. Until then, he would be satisfied to hold her, wake up with her beside him every morning, and come home to her every night. As long as Claire held on, Tony knew he would be all right. His body finally shivered. He turned off the water and stepped from the shower, wrapping a towel around his waist.

It was then that he realized he hadn't brought any clothes with him into the bathroom. He was so used to drying off, shedding the towel and walking, naked, into the bedroom to dress. *Have to rethink this from now on, man, at least for a while. Maybe she's in the living room, looking at the gifts.*

Tony slowly opened the bathroom door and peeked into the dimly-lit bedroom. The scene before him made his heart trip; Claire was lying on the bed, clad only in a white slip. One arm was gracefully resting above her head; the other lay across her stomach. Her hair splayed out on either side of her face, framing her exquisite features. Her naturally-pink mouth was turned up in a secret smile, as though she was having a very pleasant dream. Her long, bare legs were crossed at the ankles. Tony smiled as he noted the deep pink-polished nails that decorated her slender feet. The gentle rise and fall of her chest spoke of total peace. The entire scene reminded him of the Sleeping Beauty fairytale; only true love's kiss could awaken the sleeping princess.

He certainly wanted to kiss her, but he didn't want to wake her, not just yet. He wanted to continue watching her sleep. He crept silently across the room and knelt by the side of the bed.

In awe of her beauty, he marveled at so many things right now—her beauty, her sweetness, her love for him. He marveled at the depth of his love for her; he marveled at the realization that Claire was his wife, for time and all eternity. She knew of his issues, and she loved him anyway. She loved him.

Tony reached his hand to her hair. He gently stroked the silken strands and lifted them to his face to take in the fragrance that was uniquely Claire. He closed his eyes and inhaled deeply, becoming undone by her scent. He groaned softly as he leaned closer and gently kissed her parted lips.

****

Claire had sensed Tony's presence as she lingered in a half-dream state. The sound of water had lulled her into a light sleep with thoughts of him standing in the shower, beads of water running in rivulets down his muscular body. She heard his whispered movements as he knelt beside her. She enjoyed the feeling of his eyes taking in all of her. Claire wasn't frightened by his nearness, but rather, she reveled in the love that now surrounded them. She remained still, hoping that he would kiss her, lie next to her. She felt his fingers glide through her hair, and she felt him lift her tresses to his face. Her heart quickened in anticipation as she heard his soft murmur of desire.

When his lips touched hers, she slowly opened her eyes and met his heated gaze.

****

Tony saw the desire in Claire's eyes. He felt the heat course through his body as she silently conveyed her permission. He slid onto the bed and took her in his arms as he placed a soft kiss on her lips.

****

Tiny shocks nipped at Claire's fingertips as she ran her hands over Tony's shoulders and down his back. She never felt his bare skin before, and she enjoyed how it heated under her touch. She pressed her nails lightly on his back and felt the increased pressure of his kiss. She answered, her nails biting deeper, and she instinctively arched her body to meet his. Suddenly, she felt Tony's body begin to pull away as he lifted his lips from hers. She watched him as he hovered above her.

Tony smiled down at her and spoke low, his voice so full of emotion, he whispered his words. "I love you, Claire, my Irish angel. You are the light in my heart, the hope in my soul. I will love you forever." He lowered his mouth and savored her lips as he slid his hand gently down her side.

Claire didn't close her eyes as Tony brushed his lips over hers. She delighted in the smoldering passion in his eyes; she reveled in his heated touch. She had never felt so cherished, so loved.

Their lovemaking wasn't just the joining of two bodies. It was the joining of two hearts, two souls, the transcendence of a unique love borne out of compassion, understanding, trust, forgiveness, and faith.

Chapter Forty-Two

Teaghlach, Ireland

Arlis and Minnie sat at the kitchen table, sipping tea as the clock ticked away the minutes. For what seemed the hundredth time, Minnie's voice interrupted Arlis's thoughts.

"Arlis, what time did Jamie say Claire would be here?"

"Luv, they'll be here as soon as they can. Why don't ye take Brian on the front porch and wait for them."

Minnie smiled brightly. "Oh, yes, that's a grand idea." Securing the raggedy doll in her arms, she walked from the room.

Arlis's stomach roiled as she fought back nausea. She sighed deeply; she needed solitude right now. She needed to gather her thoughts. Claire was married—and pregnant. So much like Minnie's experience, yet different. Claire was right about her feelings that her future lay in America. If she had stayed in Ireland, she would never have been allowed to keep her baby. The social stigma would have been intolerable for her and the child.

When she and Jamie received a call from Claire telling them that she was pregnant, their worst fears were realized. Claire was strong and brave, but could she raise a child alone in America? They hoped that she would be able to put the horrors of her assault behind her and get on with her new life. Now, with a child growing in her womb, would she ever be free of the nightmare?

It was only days later that Claire called again to tell them she was getting married. She sounded so happy when she told her parents about this young man who appeared out of the shadows one night and touched her soul. The sound of Minnie's squeal roused Arlis back to the present. What kind of man was Tony Sabella? Well, she was about to find out.

She took another deep breath to settle her stomach. There was something else she was dealing with, something she didn't want to tell Jamie yet. Her health issues would have to be faced, but not yet. Not until she knew for sure. She thought back to her mother's death and shuddered. She was experiencing all the same symptoms her mum had; cancer of the brain was such an ugly way to die. How would Jamie cope? How would Minnie survive? Arlis couldn't bring herself to confide in Jamie. He was so devastated by Claire's attack and subsequent move to America, how could she burden him with yet another crisis?

The episodes started a few weeks after Claire left for America—severe nausea, dizziness, and fatigue. Her appointment with the doctor was scheduled for tomorrow. She planned to cancel it until after Claire's visit, but the episodes were happening more often. She would tell Jamie tonight.

She smiled as she heard Minnie squeal again. Her sister's innocence always made her smile. She walked from the kitchen as she heard the clamor at the front door.

"Arlis, Arlis! Claire's here...with a friend. Come and see!" Minnie rushed up to her sister and grabbed her hand, tugging her impatiently.

Claire bounded up the steps and through the door into her mother's open arms. "Mum, oh, Mum. It's so good to see ye. I've missed ye so."

Arlis hugged her daughter tightly, never wanting to let go. She inhaled Claire's scent and was immediately transported back to when Claire was a baby. She would often pick her daughter up from the cradle and bury her face close to the baby's neck and inhale deeply. Just the scent of her child calmed Arlis during those dark days of Minnie's imprisonment in the convent. All these years later, nothing was different. As she held her daughter now, peace filled her heart, sure that all would be well.

She broke their embrace and studied her daughter's radiant face. "Oh, luv, it's so good to have you home." As Claire beamed at her mother, Arlis noticed the man standing behind her, Jamie's hand resting on his shoulder.

"Darlin, this is Tony. Tony, this is Claire's mum."

From his open body language, Arlis immediately knew that Jamie approved of Claire's husband. She smiled brightly and approached Tony with open arms. "Tony, it's wonderful to meet ye. Welcome to our family. Come in, come in, and sit down. Ye must be tired from your journey. Would ye like to rest, or can we visit for a bit?"

Tony returned her embrace. "Thank you, Mrs. O'Brien. We both slept on the plane, so we're fine. Claire has told me so much about all of you. It's good to meet you."

Claire slid her hand into Tony's as they settled themselves on the sofa. She patted the seat next to her. "Auntie, come sit beside me. I've missed ye so much."

Minnie was hanging back, studying the interaction going on among the group. She smiled shyly and took her place next to Claire. She spoke to Claire in a whisper. "Is he your boyfriend, Claire?"

Claire smiled as she wrapped her arm around Minnie's thin shoulder. "No, Auntie, Tony is my husband." She offered her left hand to Minnie and wiggled her fingers. "See my ring? I'm married, Min."

Minnie's eyes grew wide. "Oh, Claire, that's grand, truly." Her voice lowered even more. "He's handsome, isn't he?"

"Yes, I think he's handsome, too." Claire laughed. "And he's very nice, Minnie. Why don't ye talk to him?"

Minnie's face heated in shyness. "Maybe tomorrow, Claire. Maybe tomorrow. Will we see him tomorrow? Is he staying for a while?"

Arlis walked over and placed her hands on Minnie's shoulders. "Of course he's staying, luv. He's Claire's husband, remember? They're both staying for a while. Maybe ye can help Claire show him around the county. Won't that be grand?"

"Yes, Arlis. That'll be grand. Can I go out on the swing now with Brian? He likes to watch the birds."

Arlis nodded quietly. "Yes, luv, ye take Brian for a swing. See how many different kinds of birds ye see and then tell me later."

Four pairs of eyes watched Minnie exit the house, a raggedy doll clutched close to her heart.

Arlis caught the look on Tony's face as he watched the woman-child walk out of the room. She was taken with the apparent compassion in his eyes, deeply touched by his concern.

Tony cleared his throat and softly squeezed Claire's hand. "Mrs. O'Brien, Claire has told me about all that Minnie has gone through over the years. I can't begin to imagine your pain, as well. Claire has also told me of all the work you and Chief Constable O'Brien have done to help girls escape similar fates today. I think it's wonderful that you work with Mrs. Brady in America."

"Thank ye for your kind words, Tony. And please, call me Arlis." She smiled and gestured toward her husband. "And call the Chief Constable over there Jamie, if ye please. We don't want him getting too big for his britches now, do we?"

The gentle teasing cut through the pall that had settled on the small group. "Now then, you two, let's talk, shall we?"

Jamie nodded in agreement. "First off, Tony, I know I speak for me dear wife here when I say how glad we are that ye and Claire are husband and wife. I'll be honest with ye, son, I wasn't keen on our girl going to America. Truth be told, I was afraid she would find an American fella and marry him and never come back home. Well, my first fear came to pass, and here ye are. But that's the thing, ye see? Here ye are. Ye took the trouble to bring our Claire back to us if even for a little while and for that, we will be forever thankful to ye."

Jamie's voice trembled as he continued. "The Lord saw fit to give us only one child; of course, He saw fit to give us the best child in all of His creation, so we're not complaining. That being said, I want ye to know, from what I've seen and from what Claire has told us, I'm proud to call ye son. Ye must be something truly special for our Claire to love ye like she does."

Tony smiled. "Thank you, Chief...I mean, Jamie. Your words are very kind, but I don't deserve them. You know how special Claire is, but I want you both to know that from the moment I took her hand, I knew that she was the only woman I will ever love, in this life as well as the next."

Arlis smiled tenderly. "Thank ye, Tony. We both know ye love our Claire as she loves ye, but like anyone who knows me will tell ye, I don't dance around a situation. I face it head-on, even if it means hurting someone's feelings. Now, I have to bring up a subject we've been dancing around—the child Claire's carrying."

Claire hung her head, unwilling to look at her parents or her husband.

Tony glanced at Claire. He gently lifted her head and held her gaze as he kissed her tenderly.

She smiled tremulously, breathing deeply and straightening her shoulders. She kept her head raised as her eyes focused on Tony.

He nodded and began to speak. "Arlis, Jamie, the child my wife is carrying is my child. Perhaps it doesn't carry my blood, but it is my child. What happened to Claire has absolutely nothing to do with our lives now. We've put all that behind us, and as I understand from what Claire has told me, you've done so, as well."

Tony directed his comments to Jamie. "Sir, a minute ago, you called me 'son.' Why? I suppose it's because your daughter loves me, so it follows that you would love me, too. When we told my parents we were getting married, my mother explained to Claire that once we wed, they would consider Claire their daughter—not their daughter-in-law, their daughter. My mom told us that she and my dad always felt that it doesn't matter who the biological parents are; it only matters who loves that person and why. They genuinely love Claire as their own because I love Claire. I repeat—the child Claire is carrying is my child, without reservation."

Arlis nodded in understanding. "Thank ye, Tony. May I ask ye, do your parents know of the child?"

"No, my parents don't know Claire is pregnant. We decided that, other than you two and Mrs. Brady, no one will ever know that our child is not biologically mine. First of all, it isn't anyone's business, and secondly, what purpose would it serve to reveal the child's paternity? Our child will be baby boy or baby girl Sabella. Now, I hope that answers your questions and your concerns."

Jamie stood quickly. "Well, it sure as hell answers mine. If ye ladies will excuse us, I'm taking my new son down to the pub and show the fellas what an American fireman looks like. Come on, Tony."

"You don't mind, sweetheart?"

"No, darlin. Ye go along with Da. I'm going to help Mum get tea."

Arlis stood and walked over to Tony as he rose from his seat on the couch. "Thank ye, Tony, for your honesty. There are very few men who would do what ye are doing, and I admire ye greatly. I do have one final question, though."

Jamie rolled his eyes and shook his head. "Darlin,

what other question could ye possibly have?"

"Hush, Jamie. It's an important one that I'm asking." She looked from Claire to Tony. "Ye both are intelligent young people. In the name of heaven, couldn't ye come up with any better names than baby boy or baby girl Sabella?"

Seconds past as the ridiculousness of the question settled in. Claire giggled, Tony laughed as he stepped into Arlis's outstretched arms, and Jamie just stood and shook his head. "Darlin, there are no words. Come on, Tony. The pub awaits."

Chapter Forty-Three

Claire lay nestled in Tony's arms, his fingers feathering down her arm. She smiled as she recalled their initial visit with her parents. "I told ye me mum was something."

Tony snuggled closer, trying hard to mimic her lilt. "To be sure, darlin. The woman is not to be trifled with. I think the only person who might be a match for her is Nonna."

Claire giggled. "Yes, oh, yes! That would make for quite an evening." She raised her head and sought his mouth. "I love you, Tony."

"I love you, too, my Irish angel. You must be exhausted, sweetheart. Anything planned for tomorrow? Maybe you should just rest."

"Mum asked if we could take Minnie with us tomorrow to tour the county. She and Da have an appointment, and she doesn't like to leave Auntie alone. By the way, what did ye think of Min?"

"Truthfully? She broke my heart, Claire. When I recall the story you told me, I feel sick. How could anyone be so cruel? And to think those nuns were entrusted with the care of those poor girls. I just can't get my head around it. My God, Minnie was just a baby herself. I see what you meant about her doll. And she still holds out hope she'll find him someday, huh?"

"She does, truly. She asked me if you knew Brian

since you live in America. She might ask you about him tomorrow."

Tony could feel the tension growing within Claire, knowing that thoughts of Minnie's child brought back the horror of her own attack. "Sweetheart, don't." He pulled her closer and whispered low. "I've got you, honey. I've got you. Just hold on to me, and don't let go."

"Never, darlin. I'll never let go." Claire sighed deeply and closed her eyes, her head resting on Tony's bare chest. Sleep captured her as she listened to the beat of his heart.

****

Jamie spooned his large frame around Arlis. "How long have ye been feeling this way, darlin?"

"Don't get mad, Jamie. It's been a while now— shortly after Claire left for America."

He struggled to keep the frustration out of his voice. "And you're just telling me now?"

"I asked ye not to get mad. I didn't tell ye because there was nothing to tell. I sometimes would feel sick, and then I would get a bit dizzy. I didn't think much of it until the past week or so. Maybe it's just the flu, or maybe it's something else."

"Somethin else like what?"

"I don't know. Maybe I'm hitting the change."

"Don't be daft, woman. You're only forty-two. That's too young for the change."

"Jamie? What if it's like my mum?" She felt his body stiffen.

He heard the fear in her voice and pulled her closer. "Don't say that, darlin. Don't even think that. The doc will figure it out tomorrow. Now put it out of your head, and get some sleep. I love ye, Arlis."

"I love you, too, Jamie. Thank ye for being such a good husband to me." She closed her eyes and drifted off.

Jamie would spend a sleepless night, holding his wife—his life—in his arms.

****

Arlis woke to an empty bed. She heard the tea kettle whistling in the kitchen and knew that Jamie must have awakened with the chickens. *Ah, my husband, I do love ye so.* Swinging her legs over the side of the bed, a sudden wave of nausea swept over her. The room became a violent eddy as she staggered toward the bathroom. The attempt was in vain. Blackness enveloped her as her legs crumbled beneath her.

Jamie heard the thud, and his heart tightened. He rushed from the kitchen and took the stairs two at a time, arriving at the bedroom door as Claire was opening the door to their room. She panicked when she saw the look of fear on her father's handsome face.

"Da? What is it? What fell? Where's Mum?"

Jamie threw open the door and ran to where his wife lay in a heap on the floor beside the bed. Kneeling before her, he whispered urgently. "Claire, call Emergency."

Claire had entered the room with Tony. She turned to call an ambulance as Tony rushed toward his mother-in-law. Together, he and Jamie lifted Arlis onto the bed. Having had extensive first aid training, Tony immediately sought a pulse and gently raised her closed eyelids.

Trying to ease his father-in-law's fears, he spoke

quickly. "Her pulse is strong, Jamie. I think she fainted. Let's get a couple of pillows under her feet." Tony glanced up to see Minnie standing in the doorway, staring wide-eyed and slack-jawed. He spoke gently. "Aunt Minnie, why don't you go and get a cool cloth for her forehead. That would be a big help."

Minnie nodded absently and ran from the room. She was back in minutes with a small damp facecloth, which she had carefully wrung out and folded. She approached her sister, gently laying the cloth on Arlis's forehead as she picked up her sister's limp hand. "I'll take care of ye, Arlis. I'll always take care of ye."

Jamie knelt at the other side of the bed and took Arlis's other hand. "Arlis? Wake up." He choked back a sob. "You're scaring me, darlin."

Claire returned to the room and stood at her father's side. She patted his shoulder. "They're on their way, Da."

Tony came up behind Claire, and she leaned into him as he wrapped his arms around her waist and held her to him.

Although it seemed like a lifetime, only minutes passed before Arlis's eyelids fluttered open. Looking confused, she glanced around the room. "What in the name of God are ye all doing here looking at me?"

Jamie closed his eyes and dropped his forehead to the bed. "Sweet Jesus, darlin, ye scared the wits out of me."

As she made to rise, Tony spoke. "Arlis, just lie back. The ambulance should be here any minute."

"Ambulance? Holy Mary! I don't need an ambulance, Jamie. I just got dizzy and fell, is all. I'm fine. Now, let me up, if ye please."

Jamie placed his large hand on her shoulder and eased her back down. "You're staying put, for now. And don't give me any sass. You're waiting for them to check ye out." As his wife opened her mouth to protest, Jamie quelled her comments with a dark look. "Arlis, do ye want to make a bad impression on Claire's new husband? Tony will be going back to America with tales of how difficult his mother-in-law is. We know that to be God's truth here in Ireland, but do ye want all of America to know it, as well?"

Arlis glared at her husband as Minnie giggled at Jamie's chastisement, joining Claire and Tony in quiet laughter. A sharp rap at the door signaled the arrival of the ambulance. Tony patted Claire's arm and walked quickly from the room.

****

Tony offered to stay back with Minnie while Jamie and Claire drove to the hospital in Jamie's car. "Aunt Minnie and I are going to look at picture albums while you're gone. We'll be fine. Right, Aunt Minnie?"

Minnie looked unsure about staying behind with this man she just met yesterday. She hung her head and spoke softly. "Just us?"

Claire shared a worried look with Tony. He smiled. "How about we take a walk outside? We could take Brian with us, too."

The woman-child visibly brightened. "Brian would like that." She turned to Claire. "That's okay, isn't it, Claire?"

Claire smiled gratefully at Tony, then looked at Minnie. "Oh, Auntie, I think that would be grand. You can show Tony all the places ye like to take Brian." Minnie nodded happily. Claire hugged her husband in gratitude and love. "Thank ye, Tony. You always know what to say."

Tony wrapped his arms around his wife and kissed her. He released her as he stroked her face. "We'll be fine. You and Jamie go with your mom. Give her our love. And, sweetheart, it'll be fine."

Jamie was anxiously waiting by the door. "Okay, all the kisses are done, Minnie's set. Let's go, Claire." He was halfway through the doorway when he abruptly turned back to Tony. "Thank ye, son. You're a good man."

Tony acknowledged the comment with a wave of his hand. "No problem, Jamie. Go!"

Chapter Forty-Four

When Jamie and Claire arrived at the hospital, a young nurse met them. She smiled, appearing professional, yet compassionate. "Mr. O'Brien, Doctor Madden has asked that ye take a seat in the waiting room. He's ordered several tests for Mrs. O'Brien so it might take a while. Would ye like some tea while you're waiting?"

Jamie shook his head absently as though he couldn't comprehend what the nurse was saying. "No. No, thank ye."

Claire smiled at the girl. "Thank ye, miss. We're fine. Do ye know what kind of tests the doctor ordered?"

"Nothing out of the ordinary, ma'am: bloodwork, urinalysis, EKG. The doctor is quite thorough. He'll send for ye when he has the results."

"Thank ye again, miss. Would you take this bag to Mrs. O'Brien? It's got her clothes in it."

The nurse nodded in reply.

Claire walked over to sit next to her father. She put her arm around his broad shoulders and sighed deeply.

Jamie sat with his forearms resting on his thighs, his fingers entwined, his hands supporting his chin. His eyes looked vacant as he stared into space. "We had a doctor's appointment today. That's why your mum asked ye to take Minnie for a ride. She wanted to keep all of ye busy so you wouldn't ask about the appointment."

Claire looked questioningly at her father. "Has Mum been sick, Da? She never said, but I did think she looked a bit tired yesterday. I just chalked it up to her overdoing it, getting the house ready for our visit. Was it too much for her, do ye think?"

"No, luv, no. Your mum told me last night she hasn't been feeling well for a while now. She should have told me sooner. She should have seen Doc Madden sooner." Jamie closed his eyes and hung his head. "I didn't know she wasn't doing well. I just didn't see it." His voice trembled as tears welled in his eyes. "She's afraid she's got cancer, like her mum. She told me last night the symptoms were the same."

His words came out haltingly now. "She's a firecracker, that one, make no mistake. You should have seen her the day we took Minnie from that hellhole. I can still see it, plain as if it were yesterday. Her hair like fire in the sunshine, those blue eyes shooting sparks; that Irish temper of hers was up that day. Why, she got up in the old nun's face and made that old woman turn to jelly. She was something that day, Claire. You should have seen her. But then, truth be told, she's something every day." He released a sob, his voice a harsh whisper. "I can't lose her, Claire. I can't lose her. She's life to me…she's life to me."

Claire laid her head on her father's shoulder as she shared his fears. "I know, Da, I know."

Two hours later, the bright young nurse called out Jamie's name. "Mr. O'Brien, the doctor would like to see you now." She hesitated and looked from Jamie to Claire. "Ah, he asked that ye come alone, sir."

Jamie and Claire nodded in understanding. He wrapped his daughter in a firm embrace.

Claire returned his hug. "It'll be okay, Da. I feel it in my heart. It'll be okay."

He nodded sadly as he followed the nurse down the sterile-looking corridor.

****

Jamie entered Arlis's hospital room and heaved a sigh of relief when he saw his wife sitting on the edge of the bed, fully clothed. "They're not keeping ye, then, darlin?"

Arlis had been ready to chastise her husband for going to such dramatic lengths by calling an ambulance, but when she saw the terror in his eyes, her heart melted.

"Jamie, I told ye it was just a spell. I'll be fine." She smiled tenderly and held out her hand. "Well, I'll be fine just as long as you're standing beside me."

Jamie grasped her hand and bent down, taking her mouth in a deep kiss. A soft cough alerted them they were no longer alone. Jamie quickly stepped back and smiled sheepishly.

"Good day to ye, Doc. I'd say it's good to see ye, but then I'd be lying."

Doc Madden had been Jamie and Arlis's GP forever. Now in his late sixties, he was still practicing medicine with the same dedication he always did. He was the beloved physician for almost the entire county. The serious look on his face did nothing to allay their worst fears.

"Chief Constable, have a seat next to Arlis while we go over her test results."

Arlis scooched over and patted the space next to

her on the hospital bed. Jamie sat and immediately took her hand in a firm grasp. He breathed deeply. They both looked steadily at the older man.

The doctor pulled up a chair and faced the couple. "All righty, then. Let's see what we have." He studied the papers before him. "Well, your EKG looks good, your blood pressure is fine, your urinalysis was quite revealing, as was your blood work—but we'll get to that in a minute." He shifted in his chair. "How long have ye been having these spells, dear?"

She shrugged her shoulders. "I'm not sure; a couple of months, I guess." She noted Jamie's reaction out of the corner of her eye as he shook his head slowly. She ignored him and looked at the doctor.

"I see. Well, I'll relieve your worries straightaway by telling ye there's no cancer inside ye. I know ye were worried ye were like your mum, but I assure ye, dear, ye are nothing like your mum."

Jamie let out the breath he'd been holding and pulled Arlis into a hug, feeling the tension slowly ebb from her body. He heard the doctor begin to speak, and his heart tightened again.

"Now that being said, I've got to tell ye, something is going on in there." The doctor gestured with his head and his hand.

"I'm confused, Doc. Whadda mean? I thought ye said Arlis didn't have cancer."

"She doesn't have cancer; she's pregnant."

The word hung in the air, surrounded by silence.

"Come again?"

"I said, son, Arlis is pregnant. That's why she's been nauseous and dizzy and tired—all the symptoms of pregnancy."

Arlis struggled to speak, shock paralyzing her. "I can't be pregnant, Doc. You're wrong."

"Am I? Okay, let me ask ye a few pertinent questions. First off, are ye still having your monthlies? Maybe missed one or two?"

She nodded absently.

"Wonderful. Second question. Are ye keeping your husband here happy?"

Jamie blushed a deep red.

"Well, by the color of Jamie's face, I'd say that's a 'yes'—a very definite 'yes'. "

It was obvious the doctor was genuinely enjoying this.

"Final question. And this is a tough one. Do ye both understand how to make babies?"

Jamie and Arlis nodded dumbly, still in apparent shock.

"Do either one of ye have any questions then?"

Arlis whispered one word. "How?"

"Well, I thought we just covered that, unless ye were lying, and ye don't know how to make babies."

She cocked her head and sighed deeply. "Doc, I know how to make babies. It's just that all those years ago, ye told me that even though there was no medical reason, Claire would probably be our only child."

"That's true, dear, but think about what you, or rather, I said. *There was no medical reason.*" He stood and took Arlis's hand in his. "Dear, sometimes there are no whys or wherefores in life; we just have to look at something like this and see it for what it is—a miracle, an unexpected gift from the Lord above." He smiled at them tenderly.

"I hope ye both are happy about this; I think it's

wonderful. As I said, a miracle—an honest-to-goodness miracle."

He laughed at the dumbfounded look that remained on Jamie's face. "Maybe I should treat Jamie here for shock." He shook his head as he continued to chuckle. "Now, I'll have the nurse bring Claire in. I won't spoil the surprise, I promise." He stepped forward and hugged Arlis as he grinned at Jamie. "Let me be the first to congratulate you, Chief Constable. Arlis, dear, make sure ye call the office tomorrow for an appointment." He squeezed Jamie's shoulder in affection and left the room.

Jamie and Arlis remained as they were, sitting on the edge of the hospital bed, staring blankly into space; both struggling to comprehend what the doctor just told them. Claire found them like that when she entered the hospital room.

Her stomach rose in her throat at first glance at her parents. From the looks on both their faces, it was clear they had just received shocking news. She couldn't imagine life without her mother. Even if they were an ocean apart, Arlis was—and always would be—a significant presence in Claire's life. How would her father ever survive without her? And Minnie? Oh, God! Minnie.

"Mum? Da? What did the doctor say?"

The sound of their daughter's voice brought them out of their shock-induced fog. They slowly turned their heads to look at each other. At once, they burst into tears as Arlis fell into Jamie's arms.

Claire rushed to her mother's side and grasped her hand. "Oh, Mum, tell me, please." It was then Claire noticed the sound of laughter. *Holy Mary! They're both hysterical.* She looked from one to the other, totally confused by their behavior.

Jamie, keeping one arm around Arlis, raised his other arm to embrace his daughter. A broad grin spread across his face as Arlis began to speak.

"Claire, luv, what you've got seems to be catchy."

"What I've got? I'm not sick, Mum, I'm pregnant. Ye can't catch…" Comprehension dawned. Her eyes bulged in shock as she looked from her mother to her father. From the mile-wide grin on her father's face and the look of utter joy on her mother's, Claire knew it to be true.

"You're pregnant?" she squealed. "You're pregnant? How?" Quickly realizing the question just asked, she blushed. "Forget I asked that. "Mum, oh, Mum, I'm so happy for ye, for both of ye." She gathered her mother in her arms and kissed her cheek as Jamie embraced both his women—a tangle of limbs, a shower of kisses, and a deluge of laughter.

****

Claire and Arlis shared a tearful goodbye at the airport. "Mum, take care of yourself. Don't overdo and tire yourself out. I wish I could stay and help ye."

"Listen to yourself. Luv, ye make sure ye heed your own advice. I'm fine. I've done this before—tho' I will admit it's been an age." She shook her head. "How many mums and their daughters compare pregnancy notes like we'll be doing?"

Claire matched her mother's radiant smile. "It's wonderful, Mum. I'll call ye every week, I promise." A final hug and she turned to Jamie.

"Da, are ye ever going to lose that grin on your face?"

Indeed, Jamie hadn't stopped smiling since they were told of Arlis's pregnancy a week before. He'd spent the last seven days in a state of euphoria, and his face mirrored his joy. But in the privacy of their bedroom, Jamie would lay holding Arlis as they wept with profound joy at the miracle God had granted them.

"Why shouldn't I be smiling? I'm going to have a child and a grandchild within weeks of each other. Could a man be any more blessed? I ask ye."

Tony grinned at his in-laws as he stood next to Minnie. Since being left in his care last week when Jamie and Claire accompanied Arlis to the hospital, Minnie hardly left Tony's side.

In all the years that she lived with her sister, Minnie never spent time with any man except her brother-in-law. Even when Claire had boyfriends over, Minnie would hide in her room and wait until they left. Since her brutal attack, she never felt comfortable around the opposite sex—that is, until she got to know Tony. Perhaps it was his deep comprehension of what it was like to live with ever-present nightmares of the past. Like Claire, Tony understood Minnie's suffering, and Minnie responded to his gentle kindness; in Tony, Minnie found a trusted friend.

As the boarding sign flashed for their flight, Claire shared one last hug with her parents. "Mum, Da. I love ye both so much. I'll call ye next week."

Turning to Minnie, Claire opened her arms and drew her aunt into a warm embrace. "Auntie, ye be sure to tend to Mum now. I know how much she'll be depending on ye."

Minnie returned Claire's smile. "I'll take care of Arlis, Claire. I promise." She stood on tiptoes to whisper in her niece's ear. "Can I ask ye something, Claire? Will ye do something for me when ye get to America?"

Her aunt's gentle whisper moved Claire. "Of course, Auntie. Would ye like me to buy ye something in America?"

"No, there's only one thing I need from there." Minnie hesitated, her child-like persona vanishing briefly. Claire noted the deep breath she took before she continued. "Claire, will ye look for Brian for me? Will ye and Tony find my son?"

Fighting back tears, Claire held her aunt in her arms. Suddenly, questions began to flood her mind. *Is this what I'm supposed to do? Is this why I went to America? Not only for myself and Tony, but for Aunt Minnie, too? Am I supposed to find her child?*

Slowly, she released Minnie and held her at arms' length, looking steadily into her periwinkle blue eyes, which now held complete child-like trust. She smiled through her tears. "I promise ye, Aunt Minnie. I promise ye I will do everything I can to find Brian. It might take a while, so you've got to be patient. But I promise ye, Auntie, I will try very hard to find him."

Minnie nodded and smiled sweetly. "Just try. That's all I ask. Just try."

Chapter Forty-Five

The warm autumn air wafted through the open bedroom window, softly caressing Claire's skin as she lay on the bed. Her eyelids had grown heavy as she concentrated on the project in her hand, so she decided to set it aside and close her eyes for a few minutes. Tomorrow was Tuesday, and every Tuesday, she spent all day with Tony's grandmother, who was teaching her to crochet. Ever since she and Tony returned from their honeymoon, Claire had made it a point to spend at least one day a week with Maria. She was eager to show Tony's grandmother the progress she was making on the afghan she was crocheting, and so, she worked on it every day throughout the week.

She now nestled on her side, placing one arm across the small bump. She smiled as she closed her eyes. Thoughts of the life growing within her filled her mind with wonder. Her thoughts turned to her husband, and her smile broadened as she drifted off to sleep.

****

Tony heard the radio playing as he entered the apartment. He smiled and followed the sound of the music into the bedroom. He found Claire asleep on the bed, looking much like she did on their wedding day, except now, her tummy was a tiny mound. His heart quickened with joy. He wanted to shout that joy from the rooftops, but they decided to wait until

Thanksgiving to announce the impending birth of their first child. In Tony's mind and heart, this was *his* child. He ached with love for Claire—the answer to his prayers, the fulfillment of his dreams.

He slipped off his shoes and slid into bed, spooning into position behind her. He rested his hand on her stomach, closed his eyes, and savored the fragrance of her hair and the feel of her body close to his. He felt total contentment in the stillness of their bodies.

Suddenly, his breath caught in his throat as his eyes flew open. *Was that...?* He applied light pressure to Claire's belly and waited. *Again!* Tony lay utterly still, all his concentration on his hand lying on Claire's stomach. Two more flutters followed. In the stillness of the moment, deep within his soul, he knew the child was communicating to him alone.

Claire continued to sleep, seemingly unaware of the baby's movement. These flutters were for Tony. It was as though the child were saying *I'm here, Daddy, I'm here. Feel me. I'm alive.* The love that he felt for this child and its mother overwhelmed him. He snuggled closer to Claire, unwilling to remove his hand from her stomach. He had seen the sonogram, he had watched the gradual growth of Claire's stomach, and with each day, his joy increased. But this! To actually feel the new life growing within her sent his heart soaring with a happiness he'd never known.

Claire stirred in Tony's arms. As she came fully awake, she felt the comforting presence of his body next to hers. Turning to face him, Claire wrapped her arm around his waist and placed her other hand on his heart. She smiled, silently asking him to kiss her. He willingly complied. As the kiss ended, she looked into his eyes. "Darlin, are ye all right? Ye look...different. It's something in your eyes. Tell me."

Tony brushed her lips with his. "I just met someone."

"Ye met someone? Who? Where?"

"Well, Mrs. Sabella, actually I met him, or her—don't know which yet—right here in this room, right here in this bed." He placed a hand on her tummy. "Right here in this belly."

Claire beamed. "Ye felt the baby? While I was sleeping?" She watched Tony return her radiant smile. "Oh, Tony, I'm so glad. I've been feeling her for a while, but I didn't want to say anything until you could feel her."

"Her? Do you know it's a girl?" Tony asked, looking amazed.

Claire laughed. "No, darlin, of course not. I've just gotten used to calling it *her*, that's all. Now that we've both felt her—it—moving, I guess it makes it more real, doesn't it?"

Suddenly, Tony looked at Claire in wonder. "Sweetheart, we're going to be parents. I'm going to be a father!" He added quickly. "I want to be a good father, Claire. I want to be the best daddy in the world. I want...I want..."

She placed her hand on his cheek and stroked his mouth with her thumb. She whispered, her eyes peering deeply into his. "Tony Sabella, ye are the best man that the Good Lord ever created, and you will be the best daddy He ever made. The Lord created you to be this baby's daddy. I believe that with all my heart. I don't know what the Lord has in store for us, but I do know He's got a plan, and we're a big part of it. That's why

He sent ye to me, and I'm so thankful every day that He did. Now kiss me, and tell me what she said."

Tony smiled as the light of love burned brightly in his soul.

Chapter Forty-Six

June 2009

Claire shut down her computer, making a mental note to take home the three case files that sat on her desk. It had been a long week. Unfortunately, the rape crisis clinic where she volunteered as a counselor always experienced an increase in assaults as the weather warmed.

A distant rumble of thunder warned her to take her umbrella for her walk home. Absently, she slid the files into her briefcase and grabbed the umbrella. Her eyes scanned the office as she clicked off the lights, closed the door, and walked down the silent hall and out into the rain.

The pelting drops on her umbrella awakened memories of walking in the rain with Tony. When most people sought shelter during a storm, Tony and Claire would don their jackets, bundle up the kids, and take long walks, enjoying the fresh scent in the air, the silence in the park. To this day, all three of their children and their grandchildren loved walking in the rain.

Claire sighed as she crossed the empty street. Memories. That's all she had now—memories of Tony. Like hundreds of other families, the horrific attack on September Eleventh took a beloved spouse, a devoted parent, and a doting grandfather. Tony kissed her goodbye that beautiful, sunny September morning, and that was the last time she saw him alive.

As the rain fell, she continued to reminisce about her life with Tony. He was euphoric at the birth of each of their children; every day, he was thankful for all God's blessings. Often when he lay beside Claire at night, he would recall the dark days before meeting her, and he would marvel at the miracle of her presence in his life.

Although she was devastated by his death, her children and grandchildren—Tony's legacy—showed their mettle and brought her through the darkness of despair. His absence in her life left an ever-present void; her heart ached to see him one more time, to feel his arms around her, to hear his laughter in the day and his whispers in the night. Claire still believed that she and Tony were a small part of a much larger plan. This belief, and her family's love, filled her life with peace and purpose.

She turned onto the familiar street, and, as always, her heart warmed as her home came into sight. Emma would be waiting for her with a cup of tea and a smile. Her granddaughter filled the loneliness with endless chatter and laughter; the young girl filled the house with new life. When Claire's daughter, Ann Marie, suggested that Emma live with Claire during the summer months, she was grateful for the company.

Probably more than anyone, Ann Marie understood her mother's loss. She and her father were always close. Tony adored her because he adored Claire. He would often tell his daughter that she was the miracle that saved his life. If Claire was Tony's queen, then Ann

Marie was most certainly his princess, and he treated her that way. Yes, indeed, Ann Marie felt Tony's loss as keenly as her mother. That's why it was so difficult for Claire to come to the decision she had.

Shortly after her university classes ended for the summer, Emma informed Claire that she participated in a DNA study in her genetics class before she left school. She was excited at the possibility of finding some long-lost relatives in Italy and Ireland.

Claire became aware of the importance of DNA after 9-11. For many, DNA tests were the only way to identify victims. At the time, she expected that the authorities would ask for a DNA sample to identify Tony. Thankfully, they were able to recover her husband's body from the rubble of the second tower of the World Trade Center, so no testing was needed.

With Emma having her DNA tested, Claire realized that now she would have to tell her daughter and granddaughter the truth about Ann Marie's paternity. All those years ago, how could she and Tony have foreseen the miracle of genetic tracing? Claire couldn't allow her daughter or her granddaughter to be caught unawares by the inevitable results of the test— there was no Italian blood in them. She decided to tell them the truth tonight before the test results came back.

She mounted the steps to the porch. Before she could turn the key in the lock, Emma opened the door. "Hi, Nana. Tea's brewing." The girl's radiant smile was a welcome light after a gloomy day.

Claire was always astonished at the resemblance between her mother, and her daughter, Ann Marie. Although all three women shared similar features, Claire had inherited her father's dark hair and eyes;

Ann Marie was the image of Arlis with her dark auburn hair and sparkling blue eyes. Emma, Claire's granddaughter, was the image of Aunt Minnie—or rather, what Aunt Minnie would have looked like had she lived a normal life. Unlike Minnie, Emma's eyes were always full of life and happiness; her demeanor one of anticipation and natural curiosity.

"Nana? Are you all right? You look sad."

Claire smiled at Emma and stroked the girl's long silky hair. "I'm fine, Emmie. But I do need to talk to you and your mum. Why don't you ring her up and see if she can join us this evening?"

Emma gave her grandmother a quizzical look. "Okay, Nana. I'll call her right now."

Claire nodded. "I'm going up to change. I'll be back down in a jiffy." She turned and walked up the stairs, suddenly emotionally drained at the thought of what faced her. She whispered one word—*Tony.*

Chapter Forty-Seven

The hour-plus ride from Long Island to Claire's home in Brooklyn gave Ann Marie time to quiet her nerves. The rain had stopped, so the traffic on the parkway was light. The concern in Emma's voice was evident when she called. "Mom? Nana just came home, and she told me to call you to come over. She wants to tell us something. Do you think she's sick, Mom? Could Nana be sick?"

Could her mother be ill? Claire appeared to be a vibrant, healthy sixty-two-year-old woman. She was active; her job, though stressful, seemed to fill a need she had to help people in crisis. Ann Marie knew that her grandmother in Ireland, worked closely with Liza Brady in Brooklyn for many years, helping victims of abuse. Since Liza's death from cancer in 2000, Claire had picked up the gauntlet and continued to help girls in need of emotional support.

Mom can't be sick; I can't lose her, too. Ann Marie turned off the parkway and drove the last three blocks to her mother's house. *Please, God, don't let Mom be sick.*

****

Ann Marie found Emma and Claire seated at the kitchen table, the aroma of Irish tea wafting from the delicate teacups in front of them. She quickly hung her jacket on the back of a chair and patted Emma's shoulder as she approached her mother. Placing a kiss on Claire's cheek, she spoke.

"Hi, Mom, Emmie. The tea smells wonderful. Perfect, considering the weather." A glance to Emma elicited a slight shrug of her daughter's shoulders. She sighed deeply.

"I'm not going to beat around the bush, Mom." Her voice dropped to a whisper. "You're scaring Emma, and you're scaring me. What's going on? Are you sick, Mom? Is that it?"

Claire patted her daughter's hand. "I'm sorry, Annie. I didn't mean to scare you. If anyone's scared, it's me."

"Why, Nana? Why are you scared?"

"Oh, darlin. Where do I start?" Claire looked from Ann Marie to Emma, noting the fear in their eyes. "Oh, my girls. I'm sorry. First off, I'm not dying, if that's what's worrying you. I'm fit as a fiddle at a *ceilidh*, make no mistake. The only thing wrong with me right now is that my stomach is turning inside out with fear."

Claire opened her arms, offering her hands to her daughter and granddaughter. Ann Marie and Emma quickly entwined their fingers in hers.

"Annie, I thought maybe I should just be discussing this with you, but then I thought, no, Emma has a right to know. So I hope you'll both forgive me if I shock you or embarrass you."

"It's okay, Mom. We love you, and you couldn't possibly have done anything that will shock or embarrass us." Ann Marie gently squeezed her hand and waited. "Whenever you're ready, Mom. Take your time."

Claire closed her eyes and hung her head as she

began to speak. "It was a lifetime ago. I was twenty years old and had just graduated from nursing school. I was working part-time at a restaurant in Teaghlach— something to keep me busy until I got a job at one of the hospitals in Dublin. I had just closed the place for the night and was straightening the storage room where we kept all the pots and pans."

She raised her head, and Ann Marie noted the faraway look in her eyes, as though she was looking far into the past. Her voice trembled as she recounted her attack.

****

Ann Marie and Emma sat in stunned silence.

"Mom, why didn't you ever tell me? How could you think this was something I had to forgive you for? None of it was your fault. You were a victim. I'm not telling you anything you don't tell your clients every day. Rape is a crime against you! You're the victim."

"I know, darlin, and I thank you for saying it. But that was just the beginning of my story." Claire took a sip of tea to steel herself.

"My parents allowed me to decide for myself what I wanted to do—after. I took a couple of days to think everything over. I remember we went to Mass that Sunday in Kilkenny—me, Mum, Da, and Aunt Minnie. During Mass, I felt this overwhelming peace come over me; it was like the Lord spoke to me, telling me to go to America, that my future was in America. I felt as though I was a small part of something big the Lord was planning. Maybe I was just trying to justify what happened; I don't know. But I told my parents that perhaps something positive would come from what happened to me.

"Well, the next week, I arrived in America. Mum had arranged for me to live with her good friend, Liza Brady." Claire's whole demeanor brightened immediately. "The next day, I met your father, and my life changed forever. I swear to you, it was just my hand in his, and my hurting soul was healed."

"That's a beautiful ending to a sad story, Nana. But why haven't you told us this before?"

"Well, that's not the end, Emmie." Claire increased the pressure on their hands, gaining strength from their touch.

"We saw each other every day for two weeks. I told your dad right off what happened in Ireland. He was dealing with some significant issues of his own after coming back from the war in Vietnam. We talked honestly, holding nothing back. We knew we shared a love that doesn't happen to everyone. Even with all of our baggage, we loved truly and deeply.

"Then, one morning, I woke up, and I felt very sick. I knew right away what it was." Claire felt her daughter's hand begin to tremble. "I confided in Liza; she was a wonderful stand-in for my mum. Well, she knew what I was thinking. In those days, society wasn't as accepting as it is today. Of course, there was never any thought of abortion, so my only recourse was to give the baby up for adoption. The thought sickened me. All I could think about was Aunt Minnie and how she never knew her child.

"Liza took it upon herself to tell Tony about my situation." Claire's voice rasped with unshed tears. "He proposed to me that very day. He told me that this was the answer to his prayers. You see, your father experienced terrible trauma in Vietnam; trauma so bad, he didn't think he would ever be able to father a child. He told me all about it when I told him about the attack. His *condition* didn't matter to me. I truly believed that if we loved each other enough, if we trusted each other and believed in each other, we could heal each other.

"We decided that no one need ever know that the child I was carrying was not biologically his. We were protecting each other, I suppose. When you were born, Annie, everyone assumed you were premature."

She sighed and smiled sadly. "I remember the first time your father felt you moving inside me. I was napping, and he came home from work and laid next to me. He put his arm around me, and his hand was lying on my belly. When I woke up, he told me that he felt you and that you had talked to him from inside me. He said that you wanted him to know you were there and you called him *Daddy*. I swear he glowed with love for you from that moment until the day he died."

Where there had been heavy silence before, now there was quiet weeping. Claire released their hands, covered her face, and wept. Emma laid her head on the table and cried. She cried for the horror her grandmother endured all those years ago, she cried for the pain and confusion her mother must be going through now, and she cried for her beloved Papa. Not tears of sadness, tears of love and admiration for a man who suffered much but still saw beyond his pain and opened his heart to love a woman and her unborn child.

Ann Marie stood and walked to the window, a strange numbness moving through her. She wasn't sure how to feel…angry that she'd been kept in the dark all these years? Sad that the man she adored, the man she thought was her biological father, was just her mother's husband and had no genetic tie to her? Dirty because she was the result of rape? How should she feel?

As she stood staring out the window, she saw her reflection in the glass. She startled as an image emerged in the reflection. It was her father, her dad, Tony Sabella. He was standing behind her, smiling. She felt the light pressure of his hand on her shoulder as he leaned in and whispered in her ear. *I loved you by choice, not chance. Marrying your mom and being your dad saved me. Always remember that, princess.*

Ann Marie smiled through her tears. She reached up and placed her hand on her shoulder, where she felt her father's touch. Turning from the window, she approached Claire, knelt, and laid her head in her mother's lap. Without opening her eyes, Claire reached down and began caressing her daughter's hair. No words were necessary.

Emma raised her head from the table and dried her eyes. She looked lovingly at the scene before her, the two women she loved and admired most in the world sharing their pain, each finding strength and comfort in the other's touch.

After a time, Ann Marie lifted her head to look at her mother. She saw the fear and uncertainty in her eyes. She smiled. "Mom, it's okay. I understand why you and Daddy never told me. And I don't need his blood in my veins to confirm he was my father. He was always there for me—always. Everything I am, everything I've done, I owe to you and Daddy. It's not the physical act that makes a father; it's the teaching and the loving and the example. That's what I tell my students at school every day. And I learned that, firsthand, from you and Daddy." She kissed Claire's hands as they lay in her lap. "Everything's going to be all right, Mom. But I do have one question. What prompted you to tell us all this now."

Emma's eyes bulged. "It's the DNA testing, isn't it, Nana?"

"Yes, luv. When you told me about having your DNA tested, I knew there wouldn't be any Italian genes showing up. I knew I should tell you before you found out that way. I have to say, I'm feeling so much lighter, having told you. Thank you for being so understanding, Annie. You're an angel."

"Mom, don't say that. Of course, I understand. I admit when what you were saying sank in, I was shocked. But I know you, and I knew Daddy. It just makes me love you both more."

Ann Marie sat down and pulled her chair closer to her mother. "Mom, I know I said just one question, but things keep popping into my head. If you want to stop talking about it, that's fine."

"No, go ahead and ask your questions. I've kept this hidden for so long, it's like it happened to someone else, and I was just a bystander."

"Did you know the man?"

"Yes, that I did."

"Why didn't you tell your father—or report the fiend to the police?"

Claire looked past her daughter, remembering every moment of the attack. "Because he threatened me. He told me that if I said anything, he would tell my da I flirted with him, seduced him. I knew Da would never have believed that, but I also knew that Da would kill him—and that's not just a figure of speech. I knew my da would kill him; then, he would be in gaol and

Mum would have to suffer twice, not to mention the shame of it all.

"Mum told me right off that nothing was going to change what happened; that I had to learn to forgive and then let it go. I saw how the same kind of attack took Aunt Minnie's mind; of course, that's because they took her boy from her. But even if she was able to keep Brian, I don't think she would ever have been right in the head again. I was blessed to have my mum and da. They stood by me and gave me love and understanding. No one ever had finer parents."

Ann Marie smiled and squeezed Claire's hand. "Well, I think I would take issue with that, seeing as I had the best parents."

"Thank you, Annie."

Emma cocked her head and spoke hesitantly. "Nana, you knew the man, then? He wasn't a stranger?"

"No, Emmie. He wasn't a stranger. He was well-known in town. My da knew him quite well. He was married and had grown children."

"And you never told anyone his name?"

"No. I didn't even tell your father, Annie. What was the point? I never wanted his name to come from my lips. He didn't deserve to have his name spoken by decent folk." Claire sighed.

"But now, with this DNA testing, I suppose someone will know his name. I'll be curious to see what comes of it. How does it work exactly?"

Emmie left the room and quickly returned with a textbook, eager to explain the concept to her captive audience.

"Wait. Before Emmie goes into the explanation of the wonders of DNA, I think we need some more tea.

Mom, you sure you're not too tired? I know this has been a lot for you tonight."

"No, Annie. I'm fine. As I said, it's been so long, I feel like I'm remembering a scary movie."

"It's all in here, Nana. I'll make it as simple as possible."

Chapter Forty-Eight

Middleton, Connecticut

Dr. Susan Brightman opened her office door and turned on the lights. She headed for the window and opened it wide, allowing the fresh morning air to permeate the stale room. Classes had been over for three weeks, but the head of the genetics department of Wentworth University emailed her last night, asking her to meet him this morning on a matter of utmost urgency, as he put it. She smiled to herself and slowly shook her head. *What could be so urgent on a beautiful summer morning? Mark probably wants to know what wine to bring for dinner tomorrow night.* She had just settled herself at her desk when she heard a light rap on the door. "*Entre*, Dr. Gable."

Dr. Mark Gable, department head of the Sheeran School of Genetics Studies, strolled into her office, a cup of coffee in each hand, and a slim manila folder tucked under his arm. "Hey, Suzie. I brought you coffee, my peace offering for asking you to come in this morning."

"This better be—how did you put it in your email? Oh yes, 'a matter of the utmost urgency.' What's up?"

"I think you will concur, learned colleague and friend, when I show you what I have here." Mark sat opposite his friend and slid the folder across the desk.

"The test results from your freshman genetics class."

Susan's stomach fluttered, and her heart thrummed as she reached for the folder. "Another match?"

"Yes, ma'am. But there's more. Take a gander."

The geneticist studied the papers before her. She furrowed her brow in confusion. "Are you sure about these results? No chance something got screwed up in the lab; vials got mixed?"

"No, Suzie. After I got the results, I had my doubts, so I re-ran the test myself. One of your students shares a definite DNA link to Jim's father *and* mother."

Susan swallowed hard, hesitant to allow herself to hope. "A mitochondrial match? Mark, could this be true? After twelve long years, could we have found her?"

"Well, I don't know if we've found *her*, but DNA doesn't lie; we sure as hell have found an extremely close relative. After all these years, this is the first time we have any hits for Jim's mother. We've had numerous links to his father from other DNA labs, but this one—and it's one of our very own students. I can't believe it. She's right here. How do you think we should handle it?"

Susan chewed her lip as her mind raced. "Well, I know one thing for sure. I'm not telling Jim anything until we are 99.9 percent sure." Her chin quivered as she looked at her friend and colleague. "I'm not going to get his hopes up for nothing. Finding his mother is all he thinks about, Mark. At our age, he knows she's probably dead, and he's accepted that; but he just wants to know who she was and why she gave him away. He wants—no, he needs—answers."

Mark Gable nodded in understanding. "I know,

Suzie. I went ahead and pulled the student's file. Here's her email address. She lives on Long Island with her parents."

"Long Island? Hmm…Interested in attending a conference on genetics in Manhattan on Monday?"

"There's a conference on Monday? I didn't get any information on it."

"That's because I just organized it—a conference of two. I need to tell Jim something if I'm going out of town for a day or so. I hate leaving him out of the loop, but we have to check this thoroughly before I tell him anything. What do you say? Will you be my accomplice in this innocent deception?"

"If it means bringing my best friend one tiny step closer to finding his mother, need you ask? You know I'd go through hell for him."

"Thanks, Mark. I'm going to email this girl right now. What's her name?"

"Emma Bateman."

Chapter Forty-Nine

The BelAire was one of the trendiest restaurants in Brooklyn. When her genetics professor emailed suggesting lunch with Emma and her parents, the first restaurant that came to Emma's mind was the BelAire. Now, as she looked around the room, she cringed inwardly, thinking that she should have picked a restaurant that wasn't so upscale, so pricy.

"Emma, stop fidgeting with that spoon." Ann Marie gently reprimanded her daughter. "You're making me nervous. Now, before Dr. Brightman arrives, tell us again what she said in her email."

Emma took a steadying breath and carefully replaced the fork to its rightful place. "Dr. Brightman said that she received the results of my DNA test and that she and Dr. Gable found some *interesting* markers. They wanted to talk with you and Daddy, to clarify some things, as Dr. Brightman put it."

She noted the thoughtful look on Claire's face. "I'm so glad you came, Nana." Her voice dropped in sadness. "Do you think this has to do with what happened to you in Ireland?"

"Yes, darlin, I think this meeting has everything to do with that." She smiled at her granddaughter. "Luv, it's nothing to worry about. I told you. It happened a very long time ago. I'm glad I told you and your mum everything when I did. I know it was hard for both of

289

you to hear, but now there'll be no surprises, unless they tell us your dad is an alien. Maybe it has nothing to do with me. What do you think, Dave?"

David Bateman grinned at his mother-in-law, relieved that she could bring a bit of levity into this rather uncomfortable situation. Initially, he had been piqued that Emma hadn't consulted him before having her DNA tested. He understood Ann Marie's shock after learning that Tony was not her biological father. Dave felt they should just let sleeping dogs lie, but now that Emma had opened up a Pandora's Box, they would have to live with the consequences. However, there was no way he was going to subject his wife or his mother-in-law to any needless suffering. He was here today to support them emotionally and protect them legally.

Interestingly, Claire was intrigued by the possibility that this had something to do with Minnie's long-lost child. Well, they were about to find out. Dave tapped Ann Marie's hand and gestured toward the entrance. All eyes turned to the stylish woman who was walking toward them. Her face was open and friendly, fine lines crinkled around her green eyes as she smiled broadly. Her grayish-blond hair was pulled back in a simple short ponytail at the nape of her neck. Her companion was rather nondescript. There was little doubt as to his profession; he had the unmistakable look of an academician—longish hair, goatee, and wire-rimmed glasses.

Dave rose from his seat as the couple neared. He extended his hand in greeting. "Hello. I'm David Bateman, Emma's father. May I introduce my wife, Ann Marie, and my mother-in-law, Claire Sabella. Of course, you know Emma."

Susan Brightman acknowledged everyone with a nod as she shook Dave's hand. "How do you do? I'm Dr. Susan Brightman, and this is my colleague and department head, Dr. Mark Gable. Thank you all for agreeing to meet with us."

Mark Gable shook hands with David and nodded to the women. "Hello, everyone. As Susan said, thanks so much for meeting with us."

Susan and Mark took the remaining two chairs at the table. Susan spoke first. "I'm sure you're curious about my email to Emma. Shall we order lunch first?"

Ann Marie nodded. "Yes, let's have lunch, and then we'll talk."

****

Lunch passed with amiable conversation about the weather, world events, and Emma's classes at Wentworth. Once the server removed the dishes and poured coffee, Claire wasted no time focusing on the purpose of their meeting.

"Dr. Brightman, do you mind telling us exactly what you saw in Emmie's test results? I don't understand the workings of this DNA, so I'd like you to tell us what the test showed."

Dave nodded in agreement. "Yes, we certainly don't mean to appear rude, but since Emma told us about your somewhat cryptic email, we've been anxious about the results. What exactly is so *rare* about her DNA?"

Susan Brightman noted the older woman's Irish lilt, and her heart quickened with excitement. She nodded her head and began to speak. "Of course. I do apologize for being so mysterious. I was just surprised by the results, that's all." Susan took a sip of coffee, her fingers absently erasing the light lipstick smear on the rim of the cup. She inhaled deeply. "Perhaps I should let Mark give you some background." She squeezed Mark's forearm, silently asking for his assistance.

"I suppose I should begin at the beginning." Gable shifted in his seat. "When I was a boy, my parents sent me to a military boarding school in a little town called Manlius, not far from Syracuse. I was only nine years old—and very homesick. My first night at school, another boy, a bit older than myself, saw my distress and helped me through that first night, and many nights after that. He became a sort of big brother to me, and we've remained close friends ever since. I look back on those years at boarding school, and I know, without a doubt, that I could never have survived the loneliness, the fear, if he hadn't been by my side, supporting me, just being my friend. I always told him that if there was anything I could ever do for him, all he had to do was ask.

"Well, about twelve years ago, he came to me with a request." The scientist's face took on a faraway look as he recalled the memory. "All those years we were at school together, I never knew—but then, I guess I never asked—about his family. All I knew was that he came from money, a lot of money. He was an only child, and not a very happy one. I guess that's why we hit it off so well; we were kindred spirits, I suppose.

"An au pair pretty much raised my friend; his mother never expressed much interest in him, and his father was too busy making his millions to care about his son. That's why he was at boarding school." Gable frowned. "As I said, we were kindred spirits." He paused as a look of sadness again flitted across his face." Gable raised his eyes to his hosts.

"Forgive me for being so long-winded." He looked directly at Ann Marie. "Mrs. Bateman, after reviewing Emma's DNA test results, it appears her DNA, and that of my friend are linked. Now on the face of it, that might not appear odd—except that the link appears twice in her DNA; that is to say, Emma shares a DNA link to my friend through the nuclear DNA which is inherited from the father and the mother. Interestingly, Emma is also linked to my friend's birth mother through her mitochondrial DNA, which passes only through the mother."

Ann Marie spoke first. "Dr. Gable, I know next to nothing about DNA, but wouldn't it be logical to assume that your friend's ancestors and my ancestors shared a twig in an enormous Irish family tree on my mother's side that was planted hundreds of years ago? I don't understand why you consider this so rare."

David Bateman nodded as his wife spoke. "I agree with my wife, Dr. Gable. Why all the uproar over this link? Yes, my wife's heritage is Irish, but we know that over thirty million Americans can claim Irish descent; that's about ten percent of our population. And you consider Emma's DNA match rare?"

Mark Gable smiled. "You are both correct in what you say; ten percent of our country is of Irish descent." He looked closely at everyone in the group, wondering if he had, perhaps, over-reacted to the test results. Before he could continue, Emma spoke up.

"Excuse me, Dr. Gable, but I have a question."

"Of course, Emma. What is it?"

She was sitting between her grandmother and Susan Brightman, listening carefully to the conversation. The answer to her question seemed rather obvious, but she decided to ask it anyway. "Dr. Gable, why didn't you just ask your friend's mother, or his family, about their Irish roots?"

"That's precisely what I want to do, dear. But that's easier said than done."

"Why?"

"Because, Emma, my friend doesn't know who his birth parents were; my friend was adopted."

Chapter Fifty

Mark and Susan watched each person's reaction at the table. David Bateman closed his eyes and shook his head slowly; Emma's eyes grew wide in surprise; Ann Marie observed her mother as she grasped her hand; Claire had gone ghostly white. She squeezed her daughter's hand as she closed her eyes and hung her head.

David cleared his throat, trying to keep the irritation out of his voice. He spoke quietly. "Dr. Brightman, Dr. Gable, we're getting into an area here that I consider quite intrusive. I'm not saying we don't want to cooperate, but we would like some time to digest this information."

Susan Brightman spoke in a rush. "Of course, we understand. Mrs. Sabella, Mrs. Bateman, we apologize if we've caused you any distress. That was certainly not our intention."

She smiled sadly as her voice wavered. "I will be perfectly honest with you. The 'friend' of whom Mark speaks is my husband, and he's been searching for his birth mother for a very long time. When I saw a common link in Emma's test, I suppose I got a little too excited and overstepped the bounds of proper decorum. I do sincerely apologize."

For a moment, no one spoke. Finally, Claire's quiet voice broke the silence. "Dr. Brightman, does your husband know about this genetic link?"

"No, Mrs. Sabella, he does not. As I mentioned earlier, for several years, Jim, my husband, has been on a quest to find his birth mother. He submitted his DNA years ago. Since testing is becoming more common, he's had several matches to his father's DNA, but Emma's was the first match to his mother's. Before I tell my husband of this latest match, Mark and I wanted to make absolutely sure that through this DNA match, we could trace the link back to Jim's birth mother. And let me add, this was the first—and only—match to his father *and* his mother. That's what's so intriguing."

Claire nodded and gave a tired smile. "Thank you, Dr. Brightman. You need to know that I understand what your husband is going through, and that's the truth of it. But as Dave said, I think we all need some time to digest what you've told us. Would you mind if we got back to you this evening?"

A flicker of hope appeared in Susan's eyes. "That's most generous of you, most generous of all of you." She reached into her purse and produced a business card which she handed to Claire. "Here's my card with my mobile phone number on it. I'll wait for your call. Again, thank you so very much."

After the scientists left the restaurant, Ann Marie reached across the table, offering her hand to Claire. "Mom, are you okay?"

Dave quickly hailed the server and ordered three glasses of wine. When they were delivered, Ann Marie picked up Claire's wine glass. "Here, Mom, take a sip. You looked like you were going to faint. I know how much all of this has upset you."

"I'm not upset. I guess I find myself afraid to

believe it could be so simple."

Emma looked quizzically at Claire. "What could be so simple, Nana?"

"After all these years, after all the searching and praying and hoping, could it be as simple as you taking a test, and just like that, we might have found Aunt Minnie's boy?"

"But, Mom, what do you make of Emmie's DNA indicating a link to both parents in this man's DNA?"

Claire sighed deeply. "Annie, it's always been there, in the back of my mind, all these years. At first, that thought kept niggling at me. Then, as time passed, I buried it, along with the memory of that night. I buried it because there was nothing to be done. It happened, and now it was over."

Emma's eyes grew wide with realization. She spoke hesitantly. "Mom, I think I know what Nana means." She looked at Claire. "Nana, you believe the same man who attacked your aunt also attacked you—twenty years later, right?"

Ann Marie gasped. "What? Mom, is that true? Is that what you think?"

"Yes, luv. With what Emmie's test revealed, I know I was right all those years ago. There were so many similarities between our attacks; both happened after work, we both worked at the same restaurant, Minnie vehemently denied knowing her attacker, as I did. Although Auntie never spoke about it, my mum told me that she thought Minnie knew her rapist, and he threatened her to keep quiet.

"I think my mum saw the similarities, too, but because I never told her who attacked me, she couldn't connect the two. I couldn't tell anyone his name. He threatened me with shaming my parents, but as I told you, that wasn't why I kept my mouth shut. I kept quiet because I knew my da would kill him."

Claire's voice choked with emotion. "I remember like it was yesterday the pain in my da's face after my mum told him what happened. He blamed himself for it. And that's not the only thing I saw on his face, in his eyes. No, I saw pure, burning hatred. If I told him who raped me, there would have been no stopping him. He would have killed him. But, thankfully, Da listened to Mum—we both did—and we went on with our lives.

"Now, my thoughts keep going back to the feeling that overwhelmed me right before I came to America, that feeling that this was, somehow, all part of God's plan. Now I know what His plan was, and how I figured into it."

Ann Marie shook her head. "I'm sorry, Mom, I don't follow you."

Emma's eyes welled with tears as she whispered. "Don't you see, Mom? If Nana and Papa hadn't met, she would have had to give you up for adoption. It would have been almost impossible to find Minnie's son, Brian. But because Nana and Papa did meet and did get married, we can find Aunt Minnie's baby."

Emma jumped up and hugged her mother. "Mom, it's you. You're the key to this whole mystery. Dr. Brightman's husband knows who his father is through DNA matches with people in Ireland. This same man assaulted both Nana and Minnie, so you and he share the same ancestry on the paternal side. But because Nana and Aunt Minnie are related, our mitochondrial DNA shows a link to this man's mitochondrial DNA."

Ann Marie stared at her daughter, trying to make

sense of the tangled web of DNA of which she was a part. She turned toward Claire and saw the tears in her eyes. "Mom? Oh, Mom. I'm so sorry you had to relive such a horrible time in your life. Emmie shouldn't have opened this can of worms."

"No, darlin, no," Claire whispered. "Ye don't understand my tears. I always knew God sent your dad to me. Emma's right. If we hadn't married, we wouldn't be sitting here right now. But because we did, and because we are, I believe we're on the brink of making Min's dream come true—we're going to bring Brian home."

Chapter Fifty-One

Mark and Susan sat in the lounge of the St. Regis, sipping Bloody Mary's, each lost in their own thoughts. Finally, Susan spoke.

"We probably could have handled it better, don't you think?"

Mark shrugged. "I don't know how else we could have done it, Suzie. Let's take this from the top, okay?" He looked to her for a response, but mentally, his best friend's wife was miles away. He smiled in understanding.

"From the top, then—Emma's mother's name is Ann Marie. She might have adopted Emma, which would mean that none of them, except Emma, is connected to this. But I don't think that's the case. Ann Marie is definitely the daughter of the older woman, Claire Sabella; she looks just like her, except her coloring is different. We must have hit on something painful because the grandmother was visibly shaken when you mentioned Jim was looking for his birth mother, and from her accent, there's no mistaking her country of birth. By the way, were you surprised that the *grandmother* is about our age?"

"Absolutely. I thought Claire Sabella would be older. When I looked at the report, I thought she might be Jim's mother."

"Yeah, me too. None of this makes any sense, but

DNA doesn't lie, Suzie. There are definitely close family genetics in the mitochondrial DNA. Hopefully, Emma's family will agree to talk with us further. We just turned their world upside down, so we have to understand their hesitation."

"I know. I'm so glad Jim doesn't know anything about this. He's hit so many brick walls over the years. It's hard to believe we could be so close now. I want to tell him, but could he take another disappointment?"

"Suzie, I don't think I could take another disappointment—and it isn't even my mother."

Susan startled at the sound of the ringing phone.

"Hi, Dr. Brightman, it's Emma Bateman. Thanks for lunch this afternoon." Emma took a deep breath before continuing. "After you and Dr. Gable left the restaurant, my parents, my grandmother, and I talked about everything, and my dad suggested that my mom have her DNA tested. Our family history is rather complicated, so we think it best to wait and see what Mom's test shows before making any decisions about going any further with this."

Susan closed her eyes and expelled a breath. "I concur. I think that's very wise, Emma, and please tell your parents and grandmother how much I appreciate their cooperation. I'll make arrangements with a lab in Manhattan and will email you the contact details. When shall I tell them to expect your mother?"

"She's available Monday afternoon if that's all right."

"I'll give the lab a heads up, and I'll tell them to put a rush on the test. We should have the results midweek."

"Thanks, Dr. Brightman." Before she ended the

call, Emma uttered one last thought. "Who knew a class in genetics would open up a whole new world?" She sighed. "Good night, Dr. Brightman."

Susan stood, holding the now-disconnected receiver. "Indeed, a whole new world."

Chapter Fifty-Two

It had been three days since Ann Marie submitted a DNA sample. Three days of interminable waiting for Ann Marie and Claire, as well as Susan Brightman and Mark Gable. Finally, late Thursday evening, Susan called the Bateman home.

Since meeting Emma's genetics professors, Claire was staying at her daughter's home—for her daughter's solace as well as her own. Ann Marie was just beginning to come to terms with the shocking news that her father, Tony Sabella, was not her biological father. Dr. Brightman had compounded the surprise by informing her that a donor's DNA was closely linked to Emma—what the geneticist described as an extremely rare match. On hearing this, Claire's long-buried and unspoken suspicion proved to be accurate; she and Aunt Minnie were raped by the same man—twenty years apart.

The sound of the ringing phone relieved their tension, yet heightened their anticipation.

"Hello? Oh, hi, Dr. Brightman. My mom is right here. Just a moment, please." Emma brought the phone over to her mother.

Ann Marie sat on the sofa, her mother's hand clasped tightly in hers. "Hello, Dr. Brightman. We've been anxiously awaiting your call."

"Good evening, Mrs. Bateman, and please, call me Susan. The testing took longer than usual because we ran the DNA several times." She paused. "Mrs. Bateman, the results are conclusive. It's rather difficult to explain over the phone. You and your family have been so cooperative thus far. I hesitate to ask, but would it be possible to meet with you again? I could come to your home tomorrow evening. I think it would be much easier to understand if you saw the results in graphic form."

"You'd like to stop by tomorrow evening to go over the test results?" Ann Marie raised her eyebrows, silently asking her family for their opinion. Claire, Dave, and Emma all nodded enthusiastically. "Yes, Dr. Brightman, I mean, Susan. We can do that. Shall we say seven o'clock?"

The hesitation in Susan's voice was unmistakable. "I, ah...I know this is an enormous request on my part, Mrs. Bateman, but would you permit me to bring my husband with me tomorrow?" Her request met with total silence. "Mrs. Bateman?"

Ann Marie's heart began to race. She met her mother's eyes. "That will be fine, Susan, and you must call me Ann Marie. We'll see you tomorrow at seven."

Susan released a breath she'd been holding. "That's wonderful, Ann Marie. Thank you; thank you so much. We'll see you tomorrow then. Good night."

Dave took the receiver that now dangled absently in Ann Marie's hand. "Well, hon, what did she say?"

A myriad of emotions raced through Ann Marie's mind, trepidation, excitement, and hope, to name a few. She looked at Claire. "Mom, Susan Brightman said that the test was conclusive." She took a deep breath to calm her racing heart. "And she asked if she could bring her husband with her tomorrow. I said yes. Mom, do you really think this is Minnie's son?"

"Yes, I really do. Oh, Annie, you're being so wonderful about all this. I'm so proud of you. I never thought we had a chance to find him, but through you, I think we have. Emmie was right, Annie, you're the key."

"Mom, I love you. I love how you and Daddy raised me. I am who I am because of you and Daddy; Tony Sabella was my real father, and no amount of DNA can tell me differently. I'm glad they tested my DNA. If it means that we can finally reunite Aunt Minnie with her son, this was all worth it."

Claire rose, pulling her daughter up with her. They stood and held each other in a warm embrace, silently shedding tears of joy. They shared a soft laugh as Claire's cell phone began to chime.

She blinked in surprise when she saw the number displayed. "Colin? Hello, luv. Is everything all right?" She heard the pain in his voice.

"Claire, it's Auntie. She's had a stroke. They've stabilized her for now, but the doctor doesn't hold out much hope."

"Minnie's had a stroke? I'm coming, Colin. Tell Auntie to hang on. I'm coming home. Where is she?"

"Saint Teresa's in Dublin."

"I'll see ye tomorrow. Tell her, Colin. Tell Aunt Minnie to hang on."

"Godspeed, Claire." The connection clicked off.

Immediately getting the gist of his mother-in-law's side of the conversation, Dave quickly hit the last caller ID button on the phone as Claire rushed from the room.

"Susan Brightman."

"Dr. Brightman, hello. This is David Bateman. Ah,

there's been a change in plans. My mother-in-law just received a call from Ireland. Her aunt has suffered a stroke, so she and my wife are leaving for Dublin just as soon as I can get them on a plane. Our meeting with you will have to wait until they get back. I'm sure you understand."

Susan's stomach clenched. "I'm so sorry to hear that. Mr. Bateman, I know this sounds incredibly strange, but please hold off making plane reservations until you hear back from me. I promise I'll call you within thirty minutes." Silence. "Please, Mr. Bateman. I promise I'll call you right back."

Dave shook his head in uncertainty. Claire had just left to go home and pack, and Ann Marie had gone upstairs to gather her things. *I guess thirty minutes won't matter.* "Thirty minutes, Dr. Brightman."

Relief swept through Susan. "Yes, yes. No more than thirty minutes. Thank you."

****

Jim Sheeran was going over business documents when Susan walked into the den and stood behind his chair. She draped her arms over his chest and laid her head on his shoulder.

He turned to kiss her when he tasted salty droplets on her cheek. "Suzie? Honey, what is it? Are the kids okay?" He stood as she straightened and dropped her arms, hanging her head in sadness.

"Suzie, talk to me. What's happened?"

She grasped his hand and squeezed gently. "Jim, come and sit with me. I have to tell you something." She led him to the leather sofa and pulled him down beside her. "This was supposed to be a happy surprise for you, and now it's all gone to hell."

"Well, I guess I'm relieved it was to be a *happy* surprise. Why isn't it happy anymore?"

"Last week, the DNA test results from my freshman class came back."

Jim sighed. "What? You found my father—again?"

"No, honey. I think I found a link to your mother."

****

Dave Bateman answered the phone on the second ring. "That wasn't even fifteen minutes. Now what?"

"Mr. Bateman, my husband and I would like to fly you and your family to Dublin. If you agree, I will have Mark pick all of you up and drive you to the airport. As fate would have it, he's in Manhattan this evening."

"Wait. What? You and your husband are offering to fly us to Dublin?"

"Yes, Mr. Bateman. That's correct. We have our own jet."

Dave nodded in bewilderment and sighed. "Of course, you do. Okay, this is all crazy, but I know how important it is to Ann Marie and Claire to get to Ireland. It will be more convenient for Dr. Gable to pick us up at Claire's in Brooklyn. She lives in Cobble Hill."

"Yes, I have Mrs. Sabella's address. It's in Emma's school file as an emergency contact. Thank you so much for trusting me, Mr. Bateman. Mark will be there by ten."

Dave disconnected the phone and yelled up to his wife. "Honey, where's my suitcase?"

Chapter Fifty-Three

Silence hung heavy in the car on the ride to the airport, everyone alone with their thoughts.

Mark was struggling to conceal his apprehension. For as long as he had known Jim, the guy just wanted a real mother, a motherly mother, to love and be loved by. He spent thousands of dollars searching for her in earnest for twelve years. They were so close; Mark could feel it. They were so damn close.

Claire clutched the prayer beads in her hands. It was the rose crystal rosary that Maria gave her the day she married Tony all those years ago. Her thoughts turned to him, and she smiled. *Minnie is going to meet her son because you loved me enough to marry me. I love you so much, my Antonio.* She sighed as Minnie's delicate face appeared in her thoughts. *Hold on, Auntie. I'm bringing him home. Wait for him.*

Ann Marie clutched her husband's hand. Since her mother's revelation a week ago and then Emma's DNA results, her life had turned upside down. She still had her private moments when she wished Claire had never told her of her true paternity. But in those moments, her dad, Tony Sabella, would come to her. *Princess, you were always mine—and you always will be mine. Like Mom said, sweetheart, none of this would be possible without you.* She felt Dave slide his arm around her shoulders, and she laid her head on his chest.

Dave held his wife close. He was in awe of her strength, her courage. To find out that the man who raised you, loved you, cared for you, wasn't your biological father would devastate most people. But not his Ann Marie. She was made of sterner stuff. He knew she struggled to accept this new reality, but she hid her pain from everyone, especially her mother. Dave knew that her strength and courage came from Claire's example of stoicism, but he also knew that she was able to bear this burden because of her complete faith in Tony Sabella's love for her. Dave would always owe a debt of thanks to the two extraordinary people who raised his extraordinary wife.

Emma sat next to her grandmother, her head on Claire's shoulder. She knew that she had, as her mother put it, opened this can of worms—and she felt immense guilt about it. Emma hated to see the strain on her mother's face since last week. But at the same time, she was excited that she played a part in the search for a lost child. From what she learned in her genetics class and her first-hand experience on the importance of genetic testing, Emma became more and more convinced of her career path.

Mark Gable drove through the private airport security gate and headed toward the last building on the auxiliary road.

****

A tall, slender man stood by the private jet, talking to another man, clipboard in hand. As Mark's car approached, the man handed the clipboard to the pilot and walked toward the car. He waited as the car stopped, opened the rear door, and helped a woman from the vehicle. He was struck by her beauty. Just as

Susan said, the woman appeared to be his age; she was tall and slender, her hair a stunning blend of silver and black, her pale skin like porcelain. He noted a soft Irish lilt in her voice as she thanked him.

A man alighted from the front passenger's side. He extended his hand and helped another woman out. She, too, was lovely. Actually, she was a younger version of the older woman, but her hair was deep russet brown—Ann Marie. A third woman exited the car, the daughter. She was very young, perhaps eighteen or so, petite in stature with the same vibrant hair coloring as her mother.

Unable to contain his excitement any longer, he smiled broadly. "Good evening. I'm so glad I could be of service to you tonight."

Mark joined his friend. "Jim, may I introduce Mrs. Claire Sabella, her daughter and son-in-law, Ann Marie and Dave Bateman and their daughter, Emma Bateman. Folks, this is your host for the flight, and my best friend, Jim Sheeran."

As Mark was making the introductions, Jim smiled warmly and shook each person's hand. "Welcome. Let's get on board and get settled. Susan's already inside. We have almost seven hours to answer the dozens of questions we all have and to get to know each other."

Emma startled as her professor announced the man's name. "Sheeran?"

The man smiled and nodded. "Yes, Emma. I'm Jim Sheeran."

Emma turned to her parents. "The genetics school was established by Mr. Sheeran." She extended her hand. "It's an honor to meet you, sir. Thank you for doing this."

"You're most welcome, but I think I should be thanking you." He looked at Emma's family. "I should be thanking all of you. Please, let's board. I know you're anxious to get going."

They nodded in unison and walked up the stairs of the jet.

****

The interior of the plane was like nothing any of them had seen before. Instead of rows of airplane seats, plush swivel chairs were situated in four rows of four chairs each, two rows on either side of a center aisle, with the rows facing each other. Once airborne, Mark and Jim Sheeran opened a small bar and offered beverages.

Claire and her family sat in one row, Mark Gable, Jim Sheeran, and Susan Brightman sat facing them.

Jim Sheeran softly cleared his throat and began to speak. "I can't tell you how much I appreciate your cooperation in all this. Before Mark shows you the graphics of the DNA test, I'd like to tell you a bit about myself. I know Mark told you how he and I met, so I guess I'll pick it up from there." He took a deep breath and settled back into the plush seat.

"My business career started in banking, as did my father and his father before him. I soon grew tired of the world of finance. I wanted to do something meaningful with my life, so I began the Sheeran Charitable Trust. We fund a variety of charitable endeavors: education, health, family service, children's advocacy."

He reached for his wife's hand. Susan smiled and patted his thigh. "When I married Suzie in 1983, I decided to search for my old nanny, Jacqueline Didier.

As Mark told you, she was the closest thing to a mother I ever had.

"It took us almost fourteen years, but we finally found Zhackie in a nursing home in France. She was dying of some such thing, so Suzie suggested we bring her home, to care for her ourselves. Unfortunately, there wasn't time. When we found her, the doctors told us it would just be a matter of days. We couldn't leave her, so Suzie and I took turns sitting at her bedside for three days until the end. Shortly before she passed, she told me that my parents, Genevieve and James Sheeran, were not my birth parents. I was adopted somewhere in Ireland when I was just days old. Zhackie was Genevieve's personal maid but quickly became my main caregiver. It seems my parents had been traveling in Ireland, and one day, they returned to the hotel with a baby.

"Zhackie couldn't give me any more information about the adoption. She kept their secret all those years. She didn't want to die before telling me the truth about my birth." Jim Sheeran blinked rapidly and took a small sip of his wine.

"I can't explain to you—to anyone—how liberating that revelation was." He placed his hand on his heart. "Somewhere in here, I always knew they weren't my parents.

"Days after Zhackie's death, I confronted my *mother*. With her usual indifference, she told me that neither she nor James ever wanted a child. They had been married for five years and were on a world tour, just gadding about Europe and spending his father's money when they got word that James' grandfather was gravely ill. They then became aware that there was a codicil in the grandfather's will that required James and Genevieve to produce an heir before the grandfather died, or James would lose the family fortune. To ensure their inheritance, they had to act quickly.

"One of Genevieve's friends was a film star. She told Genevieve how easy it was to adopt a child in Ireland. Since they were in Dublin at the time, it was just a matter of picking from one of several convent *orphanages* that cared for the infants of unwed girls." Jim Sheeran shook his head in sadness. "My *mother's* icy nonchalance while telling me the circumstances of my adoption released me from any guilt I was carrying around all my life about my lack of feeling for my *parents*.

"Suzie has her doctorate in molecular biology and explained how DNA could be used to trace lineage. The first thing I did when I got home from burying Zhackie was to contact Mark. I had but one request—find my birth parents. I then established the School of Genetic Studies at Wentworth University. I wanted to help myself, but I also wanted to help the thousands of people like me searching for their families." He smiled then.

"So that brings us here. Please know that I understand how intrusive this has all been for you, Claire...may I call you Claire?"

"Certainly, Jim. I think we can all agree it would be rather strange not to be on a first-name basis considering our close genetic ties."

"Thank you, Claire. As I said, I know all this information must come as a real shock to you, and I apologize for upsetting you and your family. Now might be a good time for Mark and Suzie to show you the test results, so you can better understand the links."

Claire put her hand on Jim's arm. "We can dispense with the graphics, Jim. I think now might be a good time to explain the test results to you, so that you can better understand the connection."

Jim furrowed his brow as he glanced at each one of his guests. He looked at his wife and his friend, who shrugged in shared confusion. "You understand how my father's *and* my mother's DNA is showing up in Ann Marie's and Emma's tests? How?"

Claire's gaze moved around the group, settling on her daughter. Ann Marie smiled, reached for her mother's hand, and nodded in encouragement. "Go ahead, Mom. He needs to know."

Chapter Fifty-Four

Claire looked steadily at Jim Sheeran. "When I was twenty years old and living in Ireland, I was raped. Within a couple of weeks, I decided to leave my home and settle in America; I wanted to put that trauma behind me and start fresh. I was blessed to have found love almost immediately in the guise of Tony Sabella. I soon discovered that I was pregnant as a result of the rape. Tony didn't care that I was carrying another man's child. He loved me and, therefore, he loved the child I was carrying. No one ever knew that Ann Marie wasn't Tony's biological child, that is, until recently. When Emma told me she was having her DNA tested, I knew that my *secret* was about to be revealed. I chose to tell Ann Marie and Emma the truth before the results came back.

"Obviously, this was shocking news to Ann Marie, but she understands that it's not DNA that makes a person who they are, it's what's in their heart. I see that in Ann Marie, and I see that in you, Jim." Claire sipped her wine, inhaled, and exhaled deeply to steady herself.

"Twenty years before my attack, another woman, a child, actually, was raped. This girl—she was fifteen— was not as fortunate as I was in that her parents and her parish priest immediately put her away in a convent for *wayward* young women. They didn't believe she was raped, and even if they did, the parents were too

315

concerned with the perceived shame involved, and the priest seemed focused on the sexual act. It didn't matter that the girl had been forced.

"This young girl suffered horribly in that wretched place. Like most of the girls with her, she was forced to work in the laundry, which was the main source of income for the convent. The girl's hands suffered burns from scalding water and bleach, her fingers broken by getting them stuck in the wringers of the machines. The girl's older sister was the only one who believed the poor child's story. The sister managed to visit the girl only once, and it was then that she discovered the young girl was pregnant. Before the sister could gain the girl's release, she found out that her little sister gave birth to a baby boy and that the child was taken from her when he was only days old."

Claire's voice rasped with unshed tears. "The sister finally did bring the young girl home, but the girl's mind had stopped developing, stopped maturing. Her physical, mental, and emotional pain left her a shell of a human being. The poor girl escaped into the safety of childhood memories, spending her whole life carrying around a doll to replace the baby taken from her.

"The older sister went to her grave feeling enormous guilt for not being able to protect her sister from the sufferings she endured. She promised her that she would find her child. But she died before she could fulfill that promise, and so, that responsibility passed to me."

Susan struggled to find her voice. "How is this now your responsibility? How are your attack and this young girl's related?"

"The young girl was my aunt, and her older sister

was my mother, Arlis O'Brien. I always had my suspicions about our two rapes being related, but it wasn't until Ann Marie's test results came back that those suspicions were confirmed; the man who raped my aunt and the man who raped me were one and the same, twenty years apart."

Jim's eyes grew wide. He leaned forward in his seat and grabbed Claire's hand. "Your aunt? Your aunt is my mother? Your relative in the hospital is my mother?"

Claire smiled as she choked back a sob. "Yes, Jim. I'm taking you home. I promised my mum, and I promised Aunt Minnie. I'm bringing her Brian home."

He gasped as he squeezed her hand. "What did you say?"

"I said I'm bringing her Brian home. That's what she named you—Brian."

"That's my name, Brian James Sheeran. I was named for my grandfather, but my parents didn't like the name, so they called me Jim."

Claire reached across the table and patted his hand. "Well, you've always been Brian to us."

****

After the emotional revelation, Mark proposed a champagne toast amid tears and smiles. Emma settled in a seat with her head on her mother's lap. She quickly fell asleep. Dave and Ann Marie sat across from one another, and Mark joined them as they discussed the wonders of DNA.

Susan and Jim sat holding hands as they faced Claire. Jim wanted to know about Minnie, about Arlis and Jamie. Claire related the story of the day her mother took Minnie home from the convent. She also told them about Liza Brady and the part she played in all of this. Claire related to them that Liza was present when Minnie's child was born. It was she who told Claire about the two wealthy Americans who needed a baby boy immediately and that Minnie's son fit the bill.

Jim was overwhelmed. His stomach roiled in disgust. "So my father was a serial rapist? I can't believe that possibility never entered my mind. As Suzie told you, I've had several DNA hits linking to a common grandfather, so I just thought my father was a major-league philanderer or had married several times. It never dawned on me he could be a rapist. May I ask how Ann Marie reacted to this? I mean one minute, she thinks her father is this great man—a hero, really, giving his life helping others on 9-11—and in a flash, she discovers he's the lowest of the low, an animal preying on young girls."

Claire smiled. "Jim, Tony was Ann Marie's father—in all the ways that truly matter. It was Tony who held her moments after she was born; it was Tony's face Annie saw when she woke up in the morning and when she went to bed at night; it was Tony's arms that held her when she fell off her bicycle; it was Tony's shoulder Annie cried on when she had a broken heart. Tony taught our daughter compassion and trust. Annie might not have a speck of Tony's genetic makeup, but she has his spirit. My husband lives on through our daughter. As I said earlier, Jim, it isn't your DNA that makes you who you are; it's what's in your heart, what's in your soul."

"Thank you for that. I think I prefer to focus on my *mother's side* of my family now.

"I really can't believe this is finally happening. I'm

going to meet my mother. After all these years of searching, I'm finally going to meet my mother. Oh, how I wish I knew her when she was young. Please tell me about her."

"Well, if you'd like to see her face, just look over there." She pointed to her granddaughter, asleep on Ann Marie's lap. "Emma is the picture of Aunt Minnie, only rather than the lifeless look in Min's eyes, Emma's face is full of vibrancy, hope, and joy—all the things that were denied Minnie all those years ago." Tears welled in Claire's eyes. "Minnie was always there for me as a playmate, as a friend. I can still feel Auntie's gnarled and scarred hands every night as she wielded a brush through my hair.

"Minnie would lay awake until I came home at night, and then she would tiptoe in my room and wait until I undressed and was ready for bed. She would sit behind me on the bed and begin to brush my hair. No matter what my mood, I would close my eyes and relax when I felt Minnie's hands in my hair. I never realized how much I needed my aunt's loving touch until I was far away in America."

Claire smiled as memories drifted through her mind. "Once I told Tony about Minnie's nightly routine, and he immediately set about trying to replicate it. I loved Tony's touch, but there was something so incredibly beautiful in the way Minnie handled my long hair. She was an enormous part of my life until I abruptly left for the States. Over the years, I experienced much guilt about leaving her the way I did, but somehow, I knew she understood why I had to."

"And your parents?" Susan asked. "From what I gathered, your mother was a force to be reckoned with."

"To be sure. My mum took all her anger, all her hate, all her frustration after Auntie's attack, and turned them into something positive—a driving need to help people, young girls like Aunt Minnie. She and Liza Brady saved countless girls from the fate Minnie suffered. Yes, indeed, my mum was, as you said, a force to be reckoned with.

"My parents passed away several years ago. Fortunately, Aunt Minnie is being cared for by my brother, Colin. The last time I visited Ireland, it was for my father's funeral eight years ago. Until that time, Minnie lived with my father since my mother died six months earlier. When Da passed on, Colin moved into the family home to care for Auntie. The house has become a rectory of sorts."

"A rectory?"

"Yes, my brother is a priest." Claire chuckled. "It was no surprise to anyone when Colin announced his desire to enter the seminary after graduating from university. He was always a quiet, introspective boy. Perhaps it was because our parents were approaching middle-age when he miraculously appeared twenty-one years after I was born. Perhaps it was because of his close relationship with Auntie, the woman-child with whom he lived throughout his childhood. From Minnie, Colin learned patience and kindness. He learned to find joy in the simple things of life—a butterfly, a flower, the sunshine. He also learned something else from Aunt Minnie; we all did. We learned simple love—and never-ending hope.

"My parents always believed that Colin was God's gift to them because they both chose to forgive the terrible wrongs that were done to Minnie as well as to me. They both chose a life of forgiveness rather than the living death of hatred and anger. They both made a conscious choice to forgive the people responsible for their pain and to help others who were suffering.

"Minnie's mind protected itself from the brutal rape, as well as the added pain and agony of losing her son, by escaping back into the happier days of her childhood. I was much older when I was assaulted, so I guess my mind was stronger than Min's. I didn't flee to the safety of my childhood as she did. My mum taught me the power of forgiveness. Without realizing it, through her love and example, I was able to move on from my assault.

"You see, Jim, I knew in my heart that because I forgave that man, God sent me my salvation—Tony Sabella. I also believed that my purpose in life was clear; I was to help other girls who suffered abuse. That's why I'm a rape counselor. But even more, I believed that, somehow, God would work through me to find Auntie's child—to find you."

Jim watched his newly-found cousin closely. He was in awe of her strength and her unfailing belief in the power of forgiveness, the power of love. "Your parents sound incredible, as does your late husband."

"Yes, I've been blessed my whole life, Jim. Like my mum told me years ago, hating is a waste of time, a waste of precious life. I know we just met, and I have no right to preach to you, but if you're feeling anger for the years spent being apart from your mum, let it go. It's all in the past. What's important is now. Through the miracle of DNA, which I, personally, attribute to the will of the Lord, we've found one another. And very shortly, you're going to meet your mum."

She grasped his hand in hers. "Let's be frank, Jim. Your mum has suffered a stroke. Colin says it doesn't look good. You know you won't have much time with her, so let the time you do have left be filled with love and happiness. Through the Lord's mercy, Auntie has no memory of her attack or the months at that horrid place. The only memory that she holds precious is the memory of you. She's never stopped loving you or hoping she'd find you. Hold those thoughts close to your heart, Jim; her love for you and her hope of finding you."

Jim raised Claire's hand to his lips. She felt his warm tears on her fingers and heard the emotion in his voice. "Thank you. You're like an angel, an Irish angel."

Now it was Claire who choked back tears. "My Tony called me that—his Irish angel. I wish you could have known him. We owe all this to him. If he hadn't accepted my child, she would have been adopted by strangers, and the tangled DNA links would have remained a mystery, or at the very least, the mystery would be solved too late."

Susan refilled their glasses with champagne and raised her glass. "To Tony Sabella, with profound thanks for his part in helping my love find his mother."

The sound of the engines slowing signaled they were about to land.

Claire smiled through her tears. *Please, God. Please let us be in time.*

Chapter Fifty-Five

Father Colin O'Brien sat on the metal chair at the side of the hospital bed. The constant beeping of the heart monitor mingled with his whispered prayers. Colin didn't pray for Minnie's recovery; he didn't pray for a peaceful release. He prayed that God, in His mercy, would allow his aunt the strength to hold on until Claire arrived.

He held his aunt's hand gently in his, occasionally stroking her forehead and her hair. Aunt Minnie. She was as much a part of his life as his parents had been. Her sweet face was one of his first memories.

He cringed as his thoughts took him back to the day his mother told him about Minnie's life. He was sixteen. He had brought some friends home after school. Minnie was sitting on the porch swing, singing to that raggedy doll she always carried with her. He never thought much about the way Minnie acted. She was just Aunt Minnie and her doll. His teenage friends snickered at the gray-haired woman with the gnarled hands sitting there, singing to a raggedy old doll. Colin was embarrassed by Minnie's behavior and complained to his mother.

Colin vividly recalled his mother gently chiding him for his lack of compassion for his aunt. It was then she explained to him what Minnie endured as a young girl and why she always carried the doll with her.

"Darlin, that's all she has left of her little boy. Her soul was too gentle to be abused so horribly, so the good Lord let her escape into a happy place, a simple, peaceful place in her mind. She's suffered enough, Colin, so let her be happy. Let her swing on the porch and talk to her boy."

Colin realized that it was not Minnie's behavior that angered him; no, he was angry with himself for not recognizing the pain of another human being. He massaged his closed eyelids to quell the threatening tears. He was so engrossed in his memories, he didn't hear the muffled footsteps as Claire neared the bed. She placed her hand on his shoulder and squeezed gently. Colin quickly raised his head, then jumped up to greet his sister.

"Claire," he whispered. "Thank God you're here. I can't believe you made it so quickly."

She wrapped her arms around his waist and rested her head on his chest. "Oh, Colin, it's so good to see you." She pulled away and placed a loving hand on his cheek as she smiled up at him. "How's Auntie?" She looked past her brother to the tiny figure in the bed.

Minnie's thin, white hair splayed out on either side of her delicate face. Claire was relieved to see no trace of pain. Other than the tube in her arm and the wires from the heart monitor, Minnie looked like she was sleeping.

The monitor's screen showed a continual flat line with an occasional rise indicating her heartbeat.

Colin spoke quietly. "The doctors see very little brain activity, Claire. It was a massive stroke. As you can see, her heart is barely beating. She hasn't responded at all. Maybe she'll hear you. Come, take my seat."

Claire sat in the chair and took Minnie's hand. "Auntie, it's Claire. I've come home, luv. I'm staying with Colin, and we're going to take care of you together. When you get better, we can go for walks and sit on the swing, like we used to. You'd like that, wouldn't you, Auntie?" Claire waited for some small response, but none came.

"Auntie, if you can hear me, squeeze my hand, just a wee bit. Can you do that for me, Min? Please?" Nothing.

Claire heard the door open. She turned as Jim Sheeran walked into the room. She was astonished when she saw the resemblance between him and Colin as they stood side by side. She hadn't noticed, until now, how much he looked like her brother: same height, same athletic build, even their eyes were the same color.

Colin was confused by the presence of this stranger. He noticed more movement at the door and saw his niece, Ann Marie, beckoning him from the room. He nodded to the stranger and walked toward his niece.

Claire stretched out her hand. She spoke in a whisper. "Jim, come closer. It's all right, come."

Jim approached and stood at the foot of the hospital bed. He peered intently at the woman in the bed. He couldn't take his eyes away from her beloved face, the face he longed to see his whole life. He stared unblinking as imagined memories flooded his mind: a baby being held in this woman's loving arms; a child walking beside her as she holds his tiny hand; a boy kissing her goodbye as he leaves for school; a man just sitting with her, passing the time in conversation; his mother saying his name—Brian.

"Jim? Brian?"

He was roused from his musings at the sound of his name. Reluctantly tearing his gaze away from his mother, he looked at Claire as she stood.

"Sit here. Sit beside your mum."

As if in a trance, he sat carefully in the chair.

Claire leaned over the bed rail and spoke softly in Minnie's ear. "Auntie, I brought ye a visitor."

Jim took his mother's hand in his and gently stroked the back of it with his thumb. He bent his head and reverently kissed the scarred and crooked fingers, tears dropping like rain on parched earth.

As soon as Brian touched his mother's hand, the monitor screen flickered. The slow beeping became a strong beat. The straight line now showed frequent surges. Minnie's eyes fluttered open and looked into the face of the child she had borne so many years ago. Her voice was a breathless whisper. "Brian. I knew ye would come back to me. I knew ye would. I love ye, my son."

Jim's breath caught in his throat. He choked back a sob. "I'm here. I love you, too, Mum. I've always loved you."

Minnie closed her eyes, a peaceful smile radiating from her aged face. "I knew ye would come back to me. Brian, my son."

Chapter Fifty-Six

The caravan of cars wended its way along the winding road, past the now-crumbling walls of the old convent, past rolling green hills, and entered the solemn stillness of the cemetery. The brilliant sun sharpened the verdant landscape as ancient yew trees stood in silhouette against the cloudless sky.

Six men stood ready to carry the coffin from the hearse: Claire's sons, Anthony and Steven Sabella, and Minnie's grandsons, Nicholas, Nathaniel, Alexander, and Joshua Sheeran.

The mourners gathered graveside. Jim Sheeran stood with his head bowed. On either side stood Susan and Claire, each holding one of Jim's hands in theirs. Surrounding them were Ann Marie, Dave, and Emma, along with Claire's two daughters-in-law and their children. Mark Gable stood next to Susan with the rest of the Sheeran family, the wives and children of Jim and Susan's four sons.

Father Colin O'Brien gently swung a censor and blessed the grave. Incense wafted through the air, giving an ethereal beauty to the ceremony. Birds soared high above, like joyful angels heralding a new arrival.

A headstone in the shape of a traditional Celtic cross leaned against a nearby tree, awaiting placement after the interment. The simple inscription on the marker read:

Jayne M. Simon

Minerva O'Shea, Beloved Mother
1931-2009
Love is Forever
Hope is Eternal

A word about the author...

Thrilled with the success of her first book, *Being Strong*, Jayne Simon continues to develop stories based on real-life characters. Having retired from over twenty years in non-profit development, Jayne is excited to pursue her second career: writing novels.

She lives in Erie, PA with her husband, three children, and four grandsons.

CPSIA information can be obtained
at www.ICGtesting.com
Printed in the USA
LVHW081622100221
678835LV00023BB/1140